Lines of Power

Part one of the Eagle's Roost Saga

Daniel Layne

PUBLISHER | City, State

eBook ISBN: 979-8-89795-076-8
Paperback ISBN: 979-8-89795-077-5
Hardcover ISBN: 979-8-89795-078-2

2025 Publisher

Published in the United States by Publisher.

Printed in the United States of America

URL of Publisher

Edited by Lois E. Olena

Cover Design:

Dedication

To my English Literature teachers

Table of Contents

Chapter 1

Flights of Fancy

Fire erupted around her, scorching her arm hair even under her uniform. The automatic extinguishers gushed CO2 into the cabin, immediately dousing the flames. Quickly donning an air mask that dropped from the ceiling and checking the gauges, she saw that everything looked ok. Everything but the nuke. It was far too hot. The nuclear reactor that heated the air for thrust in the massive dirigible aircraft carrier had been hit by an incendiary rocket. They were uncommon in most of the world, but anything could happen in these remote desert locations. The dirigible was going to crash. The core would overheat and meltdown unless the safety measures kicked in. Akira mumbled as she fought the controls to gain altitude, "It'll Probably auto-eject the core at that temp. I need to get a little higher to be safe for us to parachute out." She clicked the button on the control panel that told her pilots not to return to the flying carrier after their low-altitude sortie. The ship's airframe creaked and groaned in protest to her demands on the maneuverability of the enormous airship. The cabin alarm silenced with the fires extinguished. She had no time to look at the gauges. It was hot back there, she knew it., and she heaved against the wheel to get all the altitude she could before the core dropped from the nuclear reactor, and there was no more superheated air, no more thrust, no more expansion gases for lift. There was static on the cabin radio. She could hear the ship's engineer panting and grunting. The wheel bumped against the stops. She could pull no harder and gain no more. "Demetri," She hailed the engineer on the intercom, "Demetri, are you there?" The static from the radio stopped, and the intercom light came on to Demetri's breathless voice, "Yes, Captain. I am here. Are you done throwing me on the floor? I used the condensation tank to blast cool vapor over the core radiator. We're going to be ok." There was silence as Akira sat in stunned silence.

The intercom again announced to her, "We're OK, Captain. Call the pilots back, and let's go home. Let's all go home." Akira nodded, though Demetri could not see her do so. Through choked-back tears of relief, she switched off the pilot warning and switched on the pilot recall signal.

The rigid frame of the airship peacefully creaked and groaned as air pressure and altitude changed. It had been the creaking that had blasted the memory of war into her mind. Below her, the ground retreated further and further away along with civilization and all its noise. The memory of the aircraft carrier drifted away with the ground. Flying allowed her mind to wander when the skies were smooth. The cabin door opened quietly. She could tell that it was the Chief Engineer, Marcus, just by the way he quietly came on deck and began his work without so much as recognition of her presence. He looked at the pressure gauges on the engines and nodded. He looked at the old mechanical needle gauges that tracked the tension of the inner lashings and nodded. He tapped the barometer and smirked as it jumped a point or two. "I need to figure out why that sticks," he mumbled. Akira smiled at him, though he was not looking. The two had worked together for years and she knew that if the gauge worked well enough, he would not fix it. Parts for this antique dirigible would have to be fabricated. That took work that their employer would not fund. Marcus finished his check and leaned back against the flight deck railing. He sighed and spoke quietly," It is a beautiful day for flying, almost no clouds. There's just clear blue as far as the eye can see." He looked around the cabin and then stared out of the port window at the engine air intake. The massive circular intake drew in wisps of condensation. He always imagined they were vacuuming up clouds as they flew. One of the earlier models of rigid framed ships to use nuclear superheaters to expand atmospheric air, the Silver Cloud lacked some of the more sophisticated compressors and shields of later models. His eyes bulged open for a moment as a bird flashed across the window's view and was sucked into the intakes and almost as quickly fried crisp and ejected out the thrust exhaust.

"I guess there's something to be said for simplicity," he mused silently," That could have damaged any newer engine." He loved the Silver Cloud as much as Akira. Blue hues reflected on the stainless steel inside and turned golden over polished brass accents of the ornate cabin, with the reflection of the clouds drifting around the knobs and bars like brightly colored, yellow cotton balls. They had only now truly settled into level flight. Akira stared through the window, relaxed back into her seat, and drew a deep breath. "Yes indeed, Marcus. It's hard to get a much better sky. I wonder if our passengers will let us fly it or if we will be making another stop in the middle of a cow pasture to watch cows be milked." The dirigible cruise had taken longer than usual due to the frequent stops the passengers had scheduled. This had been one of those numerous stops, a small airfield for crop duster planes in the middle of farmland. Marcus again grunted as he pushed off from the railing to stand. Walking back to the cabin door he intoned," Still, you have to admit it beats the rushed pace of commercial jetliners." Akira nodded agreement, "...or military. You're dismissed, Chief. Thank you." Marcus half saluted in the open doorway and let it swing closed as he left.

Memories of her time in the Air Force occasionally intruded upon her otherwise restful thoughts. Briefly, even after a few years, a creak of riggings or hiss of steam from the engines would take her back to the flying aircraft carrier she had piloted back then. She wished she hadn't mentioned the military to Marcus. Now she found herself in the quiet and peace of the cabin with her memories. She could hear the fighter engines roar to life and fondly remember the pilots she had carried. All of them were young. Most of them had dreams of families and jobs. There were brief love affairs between the male and female pilots; sometimes she could remember the joy and drama, making her laugh. The Silver Cloud hummed along with a sound sort of like a gargantuan vacuum cleaner, just like that aircraft carrier. Heavily laden, the two dirigibles even bobbed along in the wind the same way. Those were the good memories.

Then the other memories came. Her work before piloting the carrier. If not kept in check, they would inevitably drag her back to when she served on the ground, with the Air Force's Special Operations Wing clearing buildings and hideouts. She hated remembering the person she was back then. Alone in the cockpit of the huge dirigible she talked through her memories. "I was different then," she began. "I believed that all of that killing was necessary; maybe it was." The face of a local soldier, a boy of only 16 years old or so flashed into her mind. "He may have been a kid, but so was I. I was only nineteen. He had a bomb, a rifle, and a knife and would have killed me and my whole team," she mumbled. "Why can't I be proud of how good I was at doing my job either? My gosh I was efficient," She breathed out heavily and continued," Or why can't I be ashamed? It seems I should be one or the other, not both," her voice was little more than a whisper.

The cabin door opened again. This time her copilot, Captain Davyn Morris. "Permission to board?" Davyn posed the formal request to board the ship in jest. Though this was only Captain Morris' third flight with her, she had requested him. He was a good pilot and even if he annoyed her at times, he had a good heart. Akira looked back at him from her seat. "Permission granted," She responded sarcastically with an eye roll. "The passengers are all telling stories. Some of them are pretty entertaining in the 'there is no possible way that happened' sort of way. I know you sometimes like that stuff," he said cheerfully. Akira just sat staring out through the miles of endless sky before replying,

"No, Captain, I think I like my company up here for now." Davyn grinned and plopped down into the copilot chair next to her," Go on, tell me what's on your mind, then, "he encouraged. Akira looked at him confused. Realizing what he had misunderstood, she clarified," No, I meant the quiet, alone. You're a fine copilot, Davyn, but most of the time I just like it up here in the quiet. Besides, if you're bored, why don't you call your wife or kids? The cell reception is better here than down around all the teslator interference. You talk about them often enough. I know you're missing them." Davyn looked thoughtful as he responded," You know, Captain Logan, I think that's a good idea. I am still not used to civilian work where I am free to do that whenever I please. You know how it is, or I guess it was the same in the Air Force as the Navy. I see you on the phone up here quite a bit. Do you have a family you call?" Akira continued staring out and down at flat fields far below and tiny whisps of clouds, insignificant in a blue ocean of sky. She turned her head slowly to look at Davyn,

"No, Captain. If there is nothing further, you are dismissed." "Aye Captain," Davyn replied downcast. Marcus met him in the common area and called him over for a drink," Captain Logan is just a private person, Captain Morris. Don't take it personally. I've only seen her light up once and that was when some friends of hers met her at the landing tower once. I honestly didn't recognize her. Giddy? Giggling and joking, she was a totally different person. One of them is who she calls and she won't even tell me who it is," he explained. Davyn took a drink of his tea," Giddy and giggly, you say. Yeah, I would not recognize her like that. My wife won't ever stop talking and my only close female coworker won't start, if I could find a way to blend the two..." He winked and laughed a little. Marcus only shook his head at his new coworker's jest.

The two sat for perhaps twenty minutes, waiting on a snack tray, when Akira emerged from the cockpit, rubbing her temples. "I forgot I hadn't eaten today," she answered. Marcus and Davyn both stifled a look of surprise.

"Do you guys have anything ordered?" She asked.

"Just a small cheese tray snack box thing," Davyn answered. "Autopilot?" he asked. "Only while I grab a bag of peanuts," Akira began, "I have some calls to make but realized I was foggy headed from not eating." The passengers were arguing about how a dirigible this size could be this fast and stay in the air while also being quiet enough to enjoy. 'Please hurry' she tried to will the barista into quick action. Her arrival at the bar was not unnoticed. In a matter of seconds, one of the arguing passengers addressed her," Captain, you know more about this big old ship than anyone, how does it stay fueled? Jenny says it burns water like a steam train and I say it shoots nuclear power out of those engines!"

Akira put on her public service face and turned to them," It's sort of a little of both, actually. You see, since the revival of steam power in the Second World War. Nuclear reactors have been used for cheap steam. Wherever there was water, there was fuel. Supply chains for the battlefield were no longer as costly or as complex with no diesel or gasoline to deliver. Steam runs airplanes, automobiles, generators, and even rockets. Even firearms use superheated air, now. Science changed society forever. That's why the Nazis gave up, no more supply lines and endless range on our planes. They still used petrol. Now you can barely find an old antique petrol engine. This ship was among the first to use nuclear reactors to heat up the air that comes into the engines, expand it, and shoot it out the back for thrust," she explained. The arguing passengers were quiet, which was her goal for such a long exposition then the one she figured was Jenny spoke up, "So was Brian right or was I?" Akira groaned inside. Then, rising with her pack of peanuts in hand replied, "Really, neither of you were," and strolled to the flight room again.

A small green light illuminated the ship's system board: snacks were being served to the passengers now. "Good," She thought," Maybe that will calm them down a bit." She seldom had much in common with the pampered and wealthy types she transported on longer tours. She loved flying but was ready to be back in Eagle's Roost. "I guess I am still just a small-town girl," she laughed to herself, homesick. She missed her dog and missed her old friends that she spent time around. Frank and Josh were the two she saw the most often. She mostly saw Josh because he was usually with Franklin Greene, who they called "Frank." He was generally at Frank's shop, helping him complete mechanic work on the steam-powered vehicles and equipment that came in for repairs. Frank was something special to her. She could barely admit it to herself, but she was in love with him and had been since they were acne-afflicted teens. Cellular phones didn't often work on the outskirts of town due to the teslators creating too much interference. She knew Frank was busy, but even if he couldn't take the time to talk very much, she was thinking of him and home. "I hope he can talk a little today. Military memories and arguing passengers and Davyn....at least he has a family to call. I guess Frank and those guys are my family, at least for now," she thought as she picked up the vintage phone receiver.

"Gramps Garage," Frank answered.

"Hey grease monkey!"

"Akira! How are you?" Frank answered excitedly.

"Oh, just flying," She tried to act bored despite her heart fluttering from hearing his voice.

"Yeah? Crazy passengers?" Frank questioned as he loudly grunted.

"Always. What are you doing?" She asked.

"Just turning wrenches like always," He answered.

"There's some political rally coming up and I'm supposed to speak at it. It's got me distracted so I tightened this bolt instead of loosening it for about ten minutes and now I'm having trouble getting it to come off without twisting in two," He stated in frustration.

"Political rally? When did you become a politician?" She asked.

"You know that electrification thing that Melody is working on and I hate? Well, I got interviewed and now I guess it's blown up on tv here local. They think I'm some sort of somebody and want me to speak. The thing is, the bill is growing and other places are looking to adopt it if it passes here. I'm just a mechanic. I'll speak out but I don't know what difference it will make. Who listens to a mechanic about politics anyway?" Frank answered while grunting and panting underneath the car.

"Well of course Melody is still beating that drum. She hopes it will be her 'cause' to ride to Federal office," Akira grumbled sarcastically.

"Now Kira, I know you two are at each other's throats sometimes, but she has a good heart in this. I don't even disagree with her wanting poor folks to have electricity, hey I got another call on the repair line," Frank said.

Akira could hear Frank talking in the background to someone whose generator had burst into flames and something about a factory. The phone rattled on the table and Frank spoke again,

"Hey Kira, I have to go save the world. Do you want to talk to Josh?" He asked. Akira understood the situation.

"Yeah, put him on," She answered, trying to hide her disappointment.

"Hey Kira!" Josh joyfully intoned.

Akira smiled in spite of herself. It was difficult not to like Josh even if she was unhappy Frank had to leave.

"Hey, Josh. Tell me about this political rally. Who's going?" She asked.

Josh filled her in on the details as Marcus came in for a look at a gauge, saluted, and left silently. Marcus figured he knew who she was talking to and it was none of his business. Akira blushed when he saluted, returned the salute and felt a deep gratitude for his understanding.

Braegan, also in the shop this time, grabbed the phone from Josh and shooed him away. He cheerfully began,

"I see you're still only calling one person. They need to pay you better so you can afford to call your other friends! I mean, I'd love to hear from you more, and so would Josh, Penny, too ... actually," he paused for emphasis, playfully teasing her quietly in a singsong voice, he continued.

"It makes one wonder if you're in love." Braegan was closer to her than any of her friends, save Frank.

Nevertheless, she did not feel like discussing these long-standing emotions over the phone when he felt like teasing. Braegan was one of the few people intuitive enough to know already how she felt without being told. The five of them: Frank, Josh, Braegan, Penny, and Akira, were the closest of their friend group, and the only people who knew Akira's more talkative and funny side. If the passengers, or even her coworkers from the airline, saw her talking, let alone joking and laughing, with her friends, as Marcus had said, they would not have recognized the stunningly beautiful, charming, even jovial, Japanese American that they saw.

Penny would meet them at the rally as she was ordinarily available after work. Melody would be there as well. Akira, Josh, Braegan, Penny, and a seventh named Emmett were the ones who stayed in touch. Akira and Melody had always been competitors, and time had not changed that. She shook her head mildly disgusted as she thought about Melody and how important she seemed to be, at least to herself. Emmett was busy with business and trade deals of his own, but he still made time when he could, sending cards and letters and also regularly called Josh and Frank. She was proud of Frank. He had only ever really wanted to build things, and it had been an enormous challenge for him to speak out publicly about the government's plan to take control of the electrical system. She didn't necessarily agree or disagree with him, but she was proud of him for standing up for the people. He believed that the government was already too powerful, and this bill made it more so. He was a folksy, charming man, intelligent but of a simple, down-to-earth manner. He was large and tall with an intense expression that would break into a warm smile. He had quickly become the face, locally at least, of the opponents to the energy bill. He had tried to shy away from the spotlight, but when he could not, he had filled that spotlight well. Frank spoke convincingly, swaying many who were previously indecisive about the energy bill. Her heart swelled with pride for her friend. She was excited to watch him speak or merely associate with the people in the crowd. She was most excited about getting to see him and talk to him herself.

"Braegan, get me the rest of the details from Josh and I'll meet you guys at the rally," She concluded with goodbyes to each. She then sat back in her captain's chair for a moment and allowed herself a touch of schoolgirl crush on her friend.

Her chief engineer and her co-pilot were both in their quarters, so she took in the quietness, drinking it in, and stared out into the open sky.

"Three days and home. These months-long cruises always make me miss it. I wonder what's been going on while I was away," she sighed and smiled, "Three more days, sir, and I have something to tell you, Oh my...., that I've waited years to say."

Frank went on his call in the Ozark city of Eagle's Roost. Josh and Braegan finished up the repair at his shop: life seemed to progress much like always. While Akira flew her cruises, her friends: Frank, Josh, Braegan, Penny, Melody, and all the rest, similarly went to work and kept to the daily grind. Emmett was working on big business deals to make the area an even greater financial and political hub. Frank repaired automobiles and other steam-powered things while trying to help those in need. Penny helped the neighborhood, babysitting after she was off work from work at the steel mill, and so on. Out of all of Akira's old schoolmates, only Melody was trying to change the world and put her stamp on it.

Chapter 2

Mists of Morning

Melody passed through the old railway station's ticket booth that stretched across the City Centre and ran her finger over the smooth walnut railing. The mist emerging from the river valley and drifting through the city mingled with the steam from the engines, making everything damp but luminous with an ethereal shimmer in the rising sun. This station had once marked the city's outskirts. However, decades ago, it had become the central hub of the new city. Over the years, it had been remodeled and expanded to accommodate increased traffic, always maintaining its turn-of-the-century styling by salvaging closed stations from the same era. She relished the warmth of the old wood and the retrofitted gas lamps. Her Victorian-era replica white dress, reminiscent of a corset, was perfect for these mornings. She knew the tabloid media cameras would be there, as well as reporters from all the political magazines. The fabric was water-resistant, preventing it from becoming see-through in this atmosphere, instead, it retained moisture on the surface and sparkled and shimmered in the growing daylight. She wore a similarly purposeful Victorian hat, but this vintage piece was worth a fortune in the retro chic market of the day. Its flat brim swayed as she moved through the VIP boarding line.

She carried a laptop computer in a retro-styled case designed to resemble a small traveling bag that complemented her dress and hat.

As always, she was accompanied by a small group of assistants who were responsible for checking schedules and marking down checklists. They, too, were dressed in Victorian-inspired attire, which would have seemed almost comical if it hadn't been the height of fashion at the time. Even the train was perfect today, in her estimation. It had been retrofitted from an old steam engine. The coal box had been removed, and a nuclear heater had been installed to make it efficient and powerful. It greeted the morning passengers on their way to work in The Centre with a cheerful "hello." It was an old, streamlined model that glistened in the dewy summer morning light, casting red and pink reflections of the sky on its smooth black metal. The brass accents sparkled and glowed gold in the sunlight, and Melody couldn't help but think that maybe, unlike what Robert Frost said about gold, things made of brass could stay. All the passengers had boarded, and the engineer was now calling, "All aboard!"

Melody smiled broadly at this old-fashioned, nostalgic touch. She thought to herself, "How nice. He didn't have to do that. They check tickets before they close the gates now," and settled into her seat. The engine emitted a long, growing, rushing hiss as the air valves purged and the engines began to push. She wondered if Frank had worked on this old engine, then laughed inwardly with an eye roll. "Of course he has," she thought silently. "He's worked on every important steam engine in the city.

He probably retrofitted this whole train," she added with a touch of sarcasm, "that's why it's still running." She opened her laptop case and began to work. Today was an important debate on a bill she was sponsoring locally with the state to unite electrical companies under state government control. It would bring state-sponsored power to places where local governments couldn't afford to guarantee electricity.

The porter entered her private berth with a quiet knock, offering some wine, snack packages of cashews, and cheeses. She shook her head politely, saying, "No," and smiled at him, then touched his arm to stop him as he turned to leave. She smiled up at him and said, "Porter, would you please serve the coffee and drinks in business class, then let them know that Miss Maine has paid for them? It's such a lovely morning. I'd be so pleased if everyone got a happy start to their workday."

He nodded and replied, "Yes, Ma'am, er... Miss," before continuing on his way. Many of the passengers in the business and coach cars were government employees or contractors who received their pay on a debit card. Their payments were loaded onto the card, and any public service expenses, such as rail or bus travel, were deducted from it. The morning news played on the small, seatback-mounted screen in front of her. She watched it distractedly as she typed her speech.

"I come to you today to speak of justice..." she wrote.

The subtitles on the screen answered her, "Political rallies all over the state, both in support and opposition to the electrification bill..."

"That no person in our wealthy nation..."

"One of the more outspoken opponents in the same city where Melody Maine, co-sponsoring this bill..."

"... must do without..."

"Franklin Greene," said the anchorman.

The female anchor interjected, "It amazes me how much traction he has gotten in this debate. I get it that he has been in the business for a long time and has helped some people, but what do you think has made his voice so important in this debate?"

Melody stopped writing for a moment and listened. Frank was a longtime friend. He had even donated what he could to her campaign fund years ago. She sighed as the newscasters searched for why a humble mechanic had become a folk hero to many. "I get it," she nodded and whispered to herself. "He's the everyman. I just wish he could understand how this would help every man. I also wish there was not so much pressure to get him to stop talking about it! He's in my own backyard and ..." She sighed deeply, "we were a couple ..." She silently finished her thought. Their personal history made the political aspects of it all even more emotional and difficult for her. She reached up and turned off the television screen. She pulled out her planner to check the date. There was, in fact, a rally very soon by a senator she despised. He was pompous and rude but good at energizing his voters. She wondered whether he had cajoled Frank into speaking. She scowled as she imagined Frank speaking on the government's evils and the need for greater personal liberty.

She mumbled to herself. "He has no idea how much influence he has gained. He still thinks it's only the gearheads at his garage that listen to him."

The train was easing down the track with the drive pistons' pulsing rhythm, creating the slight but noticeable forward and backward rocking motion familiar with antique steam engines. The smell of cappuccino filled her private berth, flowing in around the seams in the door from the morning service cart working its way down the car with careful attention from the stewards. The dark plum curtains cast the tiny room in a purple light, even with them open and catching only a portion of the morning light pouring in the windows now. Melody sipped her juice and chewed on granola, careful not to get any crumbs on her dress. The *click-clack*, *click-clack* of the locomotive wheels passing over the tracks soothed her nerves. She leaned back from her speech when there was a knock on the door. She took a sip of her drink and took a breath before answering. "Come in," she intoned.

One of her assistants stood in the doorway with a note in hand. "Miss Maine, apparently, there was a message left at the office and forwarded to the engineer," he announced.

Melody waited a moment, then made an incredulous look as she answered, "Well, what is it?"

Her assistant cleared his throat, then read it in a businesslike voice, "'Mel,' pardon me, Miss. That's the note, not me." Melody nodded, looking bored. "'Braegan, Akira, and I are looking to meet Frank at rally. Would like to see you there as well.' It was left for you by a fellow going by the name of Josh," the assistant said, then stood stiffly waiting.

Melody nodded, then waved him off. She thought for a moment, "It might be good to be seen with perceived political opponents. I mean, they've been my friends since grade school," she thought. Suddenly, her thoughts were interrupted by a muffled crash and the rattling of wood and debris. The emergency lights clicked on in the walkways and overhead. Melody looked out of her window to see boards from homemade wooden barricades scattered over the ground alongside the tracks. The train hadn't slowed. They were not far from the station in the City Centre. All of the more affluent passengers would debark. Shouting came from the coach section cars. Heavily booted feet ran past her berth. She quickly shut down her computer to protect sensitive information and began locking things away in her briefcase. Startled, she jumped as her assistant pounded on the door and yelled to her through it: "Miss Maine, we are being instructed that you must stay in your cabin! Some protesters had set a barricade and had intended to force their way to speak to you, but the engineer ran the barricade, and they are being arrested as we, Ahhh!" There was a loud thump as the assistant fell to the floor.

"Stay down!" A female voice yelled. The door to Melody's berth rattled but stayed locked. More shouting.

"Give me the key!" "There is no key, but the one she and the conductor have!" the dazed voice of her assistant mumbled. "Give me the key! Miss Maine, we only want to talk to you! The electric wires and stations will hurt our communities! Please let me in!" The door to the first-class car opened with a whoosh. The sound of the train car wheels and the outside wind roared for a moment, then were quiet. There was the sound of pounding on it from both sides. The protester screeched, "NO! Stay out! Let me go! I just," "Get on the ground!" "Put your hands behind your head!" "Do it now!" "to..." There was a loud thud as the combatants tumbled to the floor, followed by grunts and banging against the walls as they rolled around the hallway. Melody noticed the sounds from the two other first-class passengers for the first time. Muffled and indistinguishable through their own locked, thick doors, she could hear them scream and talk on their phones but could not tell what they were saying. It was surreal. She felt confused and afraid, angry. For a few tense moments, all she could hear was the sound of heavy breathing from the hallway, then her assistant speaking with someone. "Rail medic is on his way from coach, sir. Are you OK?" the man's voice asked Melody's assistant. The assistant answered deliberately while feeling his forehead. "I will have a headache, but I'm fine." "I am Rail Enforcement Officer, Roy Waters; I need to speak with Miss Maine. Will you let me in?"

"I'll ask her. Will you help me up, please? I'm still a little shaken." Melody announced through the door, "Let him in!" "Very well, Miss!" The assistant called back through a groan as he stood. The assistant stood at the door as it opened. He had a large red mark just above his eyebrows all across his forehead, where he was struck with a blunt object. Melody looked at him and put her hand on his arm. She paused as she began to speak, unsure what to say. "Thank you, Brian. I wouldn't have expected ... Thank you," she spoke quietly, sincerely. Brian straightened himself a little, with pride in his eyes. Melody very rarely addressed him directly and even more seldom by name. She would call him Page or Assistant or simply motion for him. She never meant disrespect; it was just business. He was her helper, not her friend. "Miss Maine," Officer Roy interrupted, "the protesters have been apprehended. This one got past us while the others were brawling in the cars farther back. I'm very sorry. Hope you're OK." Melody smiled her "ready-for-the-camera" smile and replied, "Yes, officer, I am well. You have taken care of us very well, thank you." Officer Roy nodded," Then I'll file the reports and take care of things at the next stop. Good day to you, Miss." The officer nodded a slight bow as he turned and left. "You may go and rest, as well, Brian," Melody told her assistant as she patted his arm. The train whistle tooted its whistle as it approached the City Centre Station. Brian straightened his tie and replied, "Thank you, miss, but I will prepare for debarkment and have your itinerary for you." Melody smiled and dismissed him as she went to gather up her things from her private berth. She needed to compose herself for the cameras. Steam energy terrorists cannot be allowed to make her appear in disarray. "I am the powerhouse here," she whispered to herself as she picked up her computer case. Out of the berth and to the exit door, she purposefully strode. The train eased to a stop with a whistle blow, a fog of steam, and hisses of pressure releasing. The cameras flashed, and she was pictured in the clouds of steam, glistening and poised after a Nuko-Steam terrorist attack. "The powerhouse pushing the electrical power bill," the article called her. She was unstoppable.

18

Chapter 3

Water Vapor is a Greenhouse Gas

The political rally was going remarkably well, by all accounts, with all the typical fanfare for overblown and pompous politicians. Jets screamed past in formation overhead, weaving colored trails around and between military dirigibles lazily floating like a bank of clouds while drawing huge banners flapping behind them. The trails of steam and vapor from the airships made real clouds of their own that seemed oddly surreal as they floated nearly still. The retro-chic fashion revival was full blush and on full display with its Victorian-era vintage and reproduction clothing. Men checked their brass pocket watches and wore monocles, stove-pipe hats, and blouse-sleeve shirts with arm garters. The ladies wore vintage dresses and hats if they had the financial clout to purchase the old clothes that were suddenly worth a small mint. If they did not, they bought modern re-imaginings. It was early summer, and the sky was a bright blue. The temperature was only slightly cooler than it would be in the heat of summer, just a month or so in the future. The men wiped at their foreheads with decorative handkerchiefs, and the women cooled themselves with delicate fans as the noon-day sun beat on them, unmoved by their discomfort. The cellular phones, which worked best in the cities, were restyled to have Victorian-themed covers and cases. Several more backward attendees, transfixed by the sight of all the stylish phones, accidentally bumped into things as they gawked. The teslator generators interfered with the signal so much that few owned phones outside the city's center, where electrical wires might not exist. Frank laughed out loud, now and then, at how foolish these people were, slaves to fashion and dying of heat exposure.

It was surprising to Frank that so many turned out for what he thought most would see as an antique car preservation event. Frank knew much more was at stake. The news media had been persuasive in rebranding the energy bill and its opposition as nothing to worry about. Unless a person was a nostalgic old-timer with an antique car, this bill was of no concern. If this was not the angle taken on the newscast, the bill was the most critical law ever that would save lives taken from us far too soon. The news stations dutifully repeated that people without government-regulated electricity could freeze to death or not have hot showers. A few even more ambitious reporters also pointed out that steam power flooded the atmosphere with water vapor, the number one greenhouse gas in the world!

"This legislation, if passed, will effectively turn all these historical and classic steamers into museum pieces and nothing more!" intoned a senator from the state capital.

"Not only will the antiques be forced off the road, but the cars and cycles that many of you use to get to and from your jobs will no longer be legal without expensive upgrades!" he continued.

Frank had been asked to speak and had turned down the opportunity. He had asked the senator's staff why a mechanic would be convincing to anyone, anyway. Frank had advertised his attendance at his automotive steam and generator repair shop just for his customers to generate greater awareness and interest. He was unaware of how well-known he had become, and many people from across the region hoped he would speak at the rally. It was only a few miles from his shop, after all. He was passionate about older generators and vehicles. The personal-sized generators were all that many in the parts of town known as Truitt and "The Run" had to keep their lights going. Their old, worn mechanisms still ran inexpensively and kept security lights, heat, cooking, and washing available for many. It wasn't just that he thought the old cars and quirky old generators were unique or beautiful; there was simply no reason to do away with them. In his mind, they kept the people most in need supplied with power for almost no expense.

The news had taken a few isolated incidents over a few years and inflated the sense of danger. By the time of the rally, it had reached a point where many in the general populace felt the nuclear-heated steam engines' risk outweighed their benefits. Frank had repeatedly asserted that there had never been a reactor meltdown or any explosions. For months leading up to this event, as he lay under vehicles or leaned over a machine, he had talked at length with anyone who asked questions. A dozen or so reporters had interviewed him. Afterward, they all misquoted him, some to the point that he had threatened suit if there was no retraction.

"No one harmed any spotted owls in the generation of power, and the great, scary steam engine ate no handicapped children," he sarcastically told one reporter.

The news report read,

"Local Energy Opponent Mocks Special Needs Children."

As a result of his vociferousness, he now found himself a secondary rally attraction for all to whom he had spoken. Whether they had approved or disapproved of his message, they now sought him out and shook his hand while taking pictures. His business suffered, at first, from what many saw as anti-government rhetoric. Now, he felt a faint perplexity at his sudden popularity. Frank was hard to miss in this crowd of what he considered posers. Not only was he a head taller than most at the rally, but he was broad and powerfully built. His only saving grace from being a total misfit in the assembly was that, although he didn't realize it, he was wearing retro-chic clothing, at least almost. His deep-pocketed, Big Smith bib overalls paired with a short-sleeved, cotton, summer weave shirt, topped off with his grandfather's conductor hat and riding goggles that garnered praise the entire day. He replied sincerely, as only he could:

"I was at work, then I rode my bike here."

He wandered through the crowd, shaking hands, smiling, and joking. "Hallo, heir fraulein," he said, in a terrible German accent, to a young lady he knew was from Germany. He then shouted,

"Pete! What are you doing out of the house? Does your wife know you escaped the six children without her? Oh, she's here? You had best watch your language in that case! Haha!" Frank was a great people person; it just drained him physically and emotionally to do it for very long. He was in his early thirties, and his years of large parties and wild times were far behind him, even though he never really had any of those. Now, he preferred small groups of friends, but he feared people would perceive him as rude, or even hypocritical, not to come to the rally against the energy legislation after he had spoken so much about it.

All Frank wanted was for people to be free to make their own choices about where and how they generated power for their homes or in their cars. The city government and, more broadly, the entire country's government was against his position. People like him were being called domestic terrorists for the ideology that everyone could be autonomous and make their own choices. The population, as a whole, seemed in favor of a centralized, tax-funded, electrical grid. They did not care so much about whether people kept their old generators for backup.

Consequently, if the government said the old generators had to go to get this beautiful, reliable, and safer energy, then most would say,

"So be it." Frank always rolled his eyes with disdain at the claims of safety:

"Oh, they always brag about people's safety being their main concern," he often related.

More liberty-minded folks wondered why the government was so adamant about seeing personal generators destroyed. Frank did not consider himself an activist; he just loved old cars and didn't much trust any government. He also recognized that hundreds of more impoverished people would be out of power if their radiated steam-driven generators, radiating electricity to them, were banned, confiscated, or outlawed. Sure, no one was saying they would seize them, but to suddenly need registration after more than sixty years of their use was needless. Regulations heavily restricting replacement parts also seemed excessive and would not make anyone safer, as the bureaucrats claimed. Modern automobile production was cheap. Once the nuke went dead or the boiler cracked, it was best to throw them away as worthless. As more and more 'techs-mechs,' a nickname given to technicians/mechanics for steam engines had gone under financially, the government started passing regulations on generators and automotive safety. The latest legal mess threatened to outlaw repairing the equipment altogether. The claim from bureaucrats was that repair shops would not be outlawed entirely. Instead, they would phase the dangerous older machines out of use. In practice, steam repair would be so over-regulated that no one could afford to stay in business fixing anything.

The fever pitch on the stage had risen to a crescendo as a heckler mocked the senator. A mockingbird in a nearby field imitated a cellphone ringtone. Frank wasn't much for the name-calling that was beginning and decided it was time to leave when suddenly he heard, "Frank's done it! He has some generators out there that are over fifty years old and still just as reliable as day one!" With his eyes closed Frank let a small groan escape his throat. He did not know this senator, though he was undoubtedly the one who had asked him to speak, and could only assume the television interviews were how the senator had recognized him. On the spot, however, it would be impossible to refuse without damaging his cause. Turning around, he could see now that he was the focus of the entire crowd.

A pair of bluebirds flitted by and sat in a nearby tree. The mockingbird 'rang' again, and Frank half smiled as a man checked his phone. Averting his eyes from the finger pointed at him from the stage, he began to approach, then caught the microphone the senator tossed at him.

The heckler now turned to him and spewed angrily,

"Anyone who keeps a nuclear reactor on the road wants to kill kids, just like in that bus wreck last month!" Frank was familiar with the story.

An industrial truck had struck a bus. The high-pressure water line on the bus had ruptured, injuring several. There were no deaths. An overcrowded, inner-city school used the bus, and though it was not over ten years old, a low bidder maintained it with used and low-grade parts to cut costs. The flash boiler one-way valve malfunctioned, allowing boiling water back into the main tank. The built-up backpressure had been released, ripping through the bus's engine bay with a boom that scared the children. When they were scared, and the broken glass hurt the driver, they tried to force their way out of the rear of the bus in panic and trampled several of the students. Because of the spraying water pelting them and the panic and fear pervading the scene, it appeared to be a massacre.

Of course, the news had reported it as an explosion from a nuclear-driven steam generator.

"But we have been assured that no one outside the accident site was exposed to radiation, though no one has taken readings," the news had said, sounding ominous.

Frank spoke slowly, calmly,

"The nuclear containment was never damaged, only a pressure line. The accident didn't even crack the steam generator coils. There was no radiation leak whatsoever. Any poorly maintained machine can be dangerous. That is why keeping this bill from passing is even more important. Yes, over several years, it will take all the older vehicles that need repair off the road." There was a mixture of boos and cheers.

"But until then, they will still be operated by the poorest people, those most in need of transportation, without any safeguards to protect themselves or others. Experienced mechanics will be driven out of business by regulations, but the same number of mechanics will be needed to maintain new machines."

"Just what kind of person do you think is going to keep all those old junkers going for poor folks? Them folks can't afford to pay!" the heckler countered.

Frank just set his jaw and stared out over the crowd, looking back to the bluebirds. Past them, far in the distance, was his shop. He thought for a moment how best to answer this belligerent buffoon. He wanted to ask if the heckler had heard anything he had said.

No one could afford to pay if the bill passed, and the people who couldn't pay would also be out of power, not just transportation! He bit his tongue and waited for a proper response. Before he realized it, the crowd had misinterpreted his gesture and was chanting,

"Frank! Frank! Frank!"

He laughed a little, then put the microphone back in his mouth,

"No, no," he chuckled,

"No, I can't do it all. But, if this bill is defeated and a law passes that preserves the right of classic auto owners to drive their rides on the streets, maybe more truly great mechanics can stay in business."

There was an explosion of applause, and after grudgingly shaking the senator's hand for the camera, he left the stage and quietly walked out of the rally through the back so no one would follow him. He did not feel like backslapping or shaking hands and couldn't help but feel sad despite the crowd's applause. He felt like David facing another Goliath, and this time without so much as a sling. However, he was not entirely successful at avoiding all of the crowd, and a few were trying to pat his shoulder and shake his hand as he went. It was a somewhat heady feeling; everyone enjoys praise. However, he did not like feeling that the crowd's affection was because they happened to side with him for the moment.

"Hey, grumps!" Josh interrupted.

Frank recognized the voice but did not expect his friend Josh to be there. Frank paused and slowly, with a puzzled look, turned to look at Josh. He was there with Frank's friends Melody, Braegan, and Akira. Frank looked up and raised his eyebrows in surprise at the group as they smiled knowingly and amusedly at his discomfort. Melody laughed openly, a lilting and musical laugh that would have seemed suitable with her hand held daintily over her mouth,

"Franklin Greene!" Her slightly southern accent rolled with the Victorian slang,

"You look like you have positively gotten the morbs!"

Akira smirked as well.

"Come on, Frank, it's not that bad. Just think of all the business that senator will throw your way for getting him re-elected!" she goaded.

Frank snorted cynically, then sighed, and grinned his well-known little half-smile. He raised an eyebrow and said to the group of friends,

"I'm a little surprised you are all here together. Such a band of miscreants and malcontents and ..." he nodded toward Melody,

"One politician showing up to meet with a dangerous activist behind the scenes? For shame, all of you, for shame ... tsk tsk." Frank was now smiling and no longer in dark introspection, and all five laughed comfortably.

"Akira," Frank said, turning to her,

"You're not usually able to get free from the blimp tours in the summer. It's a surprise to see you!"

Melody batted her eyelashes and replied as Akira grumbled the words, "dirigible."

"I see," Melody exclaimed,

"So you're not so pleased to see me because we often see one another?"

Melody feigned offense as Akira rolled her eyes at her and answered Frank,

"The flight got back in time, and the next one isn't leaving until next week. It's a trip into one of those politically unstable spots that have a pretty jungle, anyway. They are always canceling and rescheduling, so who knows if it will happen or if another will take its place? To use the en vogue slang that Mel uses it would make a stuck bird laugh."

"Stuffed bird. It would make a stuffed bird laugh, Akira," Melody corrected her.

Frank smiled. There had always been a rivalry between the two of them. Braegan decided it was time to stop hanging out behind the cars and go somewhere out of the heat and pointed at a small restaurant he knew served beverages.

"There!" he exclaimed,

"There lies the great and beautiful bounty for the day and drinks!" he added with a wink.

The restaurant turned out to be an old corner diner and gas station remodeled into a bar and grill. It had all the 'retro chic' trappings just by being a formerly abandoned business, now gentrified. From the ornately carved faux wood bar to the laced curtains, it was evident that this was not a bar in the sense that Braegan had hoped.

This bar was a watering hole for the wealthy and trendy. At a small round pedestal table in the front corner, easy to see, was a man in a suit waving his hand at about chest level, not to be obvious enough to seem to want attention yet wishing to gain the attention of the five friends. Frank smiled amicably.

"Meri's here," he said and looked at Melody.

She looked at the man, now looking around slightly to see if anyone had noticed his moment of friendliness, and stated flatly,

"Of course he is. This place is just the sort of venue where a person goes to be seen, and he loves being seen."

Akira scoffed under her breath,

"Sounds familiar."

Frank walked over to Meriwether, who stood and shook his hand warmly. Melody came over and tolerated an embrace while the others accepted invitations to sit. Meriwether was not a part of this close-knit group, nor yet one of the friends from school whom Frank sometimes met. Meriwether was, however, a frequent customer of Frank's and a member of the City Centre's high society. Frank had to stifle his laugh as he observed Meriwether piecing together connections in his mind. One of the city's political elites, two working-class men, another woman he thought he recognized from the news many years ago, more exotic and shapelier, but not as polished as Melody, certainly not a celebrity apparently close friends, but he had never met any but Frank and Melody.

"Poor Meri," Frank thought silently.

"He doesn't know whether to be snooty, generous, pompous, or humble!"

Melody could see him twisting in social anguish as well and letting it go just a moment in sadistic pleasure before making introductions,

"Meriwether, thank you for the seats. These are friends I graduated with from high school." Meri sighed a little more audibly in relaxation than he intended but mainly remained composed.

"You know Frank," Melody pointed with her palm up as though presenting a banner.

"This is Josh, and to his left is our honored Air Force Veteran, Akira." Akira smiled and nodded wryly. Melody continued,

"Braegan is the gentleman already halfway through his first drink. Friends, this is Meriwether Lewis. He is, well, he is into about everything in Eagle's Roost."

Meriwether explained eagerly,

"I operate primarily in an advisory role on several political committees and for several multinational corporations. To speak in simple terms, I am a geographer who studies resource allocation and movement. Now that I have heard the young lady's name, I believe I have quite frequently flown on your airship and used its capacity to haul my freight, as well."

It seemed strange to Akira for him to call her a young lady as he was only slightly her senior. Meriwether looked at her more closely and continued,

"You are the Air Force veteran honored in our local parade only a few years ago, are you not? Thank you for your service, miss," he concluded with a raise of his wine glass. Akira nodded her head. She hated that her name was so uncommon that it didn't take very long for people to remember it if they had ever heard it.

"Are you, then, the same pilot that was at our city's Veteran's Day memorial service with all the ribbons and honors several years back? I had no idea you were the same pilot and a decorated veteran! How exciting the way paths cross, crisscross, and come back! How small our world is!

Whatever are all of you doing at such a steamy park in the city in the summer heat? Aside from the heat, you have all this mafficking of the crowd all worked up about this or that thing, whatever it is," Meriwether waved his hand as if shooing a fly.

Akira laughed, and Frank only barely lowered one eyebrow as he shot her a glance. Melody smiled and intoned,

"That was partly from our friend, Franklin Greene. He appears to be trying to fan a grass fire against the energy bill I have been supporting." She cocked her head slightly and winked at Frank as she sipped her chai tea.

Meriwether stammered a little and muttered a simple,

"Oh, Um … Oh."

Melody laughed and patted his arm.

"Meri, Frank, and I have been close for a very long time and often at odds. Neither he nor I will be letting a disagreement on politics come between us. Did you know he was my boyfriend once?"

Akira leaned back and ordered a double shot of booze. Braegan's head turned slowly, just enough that he could make eye contact with Akira and roll his eyes.

Melody continued in a falsely conspiratorial whisper,

"I thought to marry that gent at one time." Braegan and Josh both stuck their faces deep into their drinks, and Frank began lifting his hand to interject, but Melody went on,

"We were just out of school, although we had also dated in school. He had decided to work at his grandfather's shop and take it over. I had decided to become an actress as a stepping stone to political office."

Frank managed to step into the conversation,

"I didn't see you for three months, Mel. I didn't think you were interested any longer."

Akira scowled darkly into her double shot, Frank noticed, and sweat beaded on his forehead. Melody had the look of a cat playing with a mouse for a fleeting moment.

"So, you see? If we can be friends after all these years despite such things as usually tear people apart, electrical wires aren't such an issue for us," she proclaimed as she sipped her drink.

Akira was obviously uncomfortable, more than any of the others, as she stared into her drink with a look of deep disdain. Braegan put his drink, a fruit drink with Hawaiian Punch in it, loudly down onto the table and proclaimed,

"And here I was, while all you other folks were dating, and marrying, and flying planes, and all I did was get a dog!"

The group laughed, but Josh shook his head and retorted,

"You did not! You are the only one that has children, and you married twice!"

Melody laughed abnormally loudly,

"I have you bested, B. I have three marriages behind me now! If you need to know the wrong way to be married, I'm the one to talk to!" She laughed as she slid smoothly back into her typical, more political demeanor.

Frank smiled wide; seeing her act like the Melody he had known in school was good. He looked at Akira as she listened to Braegan and Josh telling jokes. The scowl had eased from her brow, and he could not take his eyes from her. Her eyes were dark brown, and they sparkled. Her straight black hair ran down over her shoulders and onto her breast. She was curvier than the stereotype of Japanese women, but weren't stereotypes stereotypically oversimplified? Her skin glowed with warmth from the time she regularly spent outside while landing. It wasn't the right time to tell her how much he missed her every day, so he found himself lost in the shape of her earlobe today. How dainty and cute and perfect, not like his own at all, he thought.

"Frank!" Josh interrupted his thoughts, causing him to jump,

"Meriwether said you have been keeping his Rolls Royce going for him for years? Why have you not asked me to come help you with that? You let me come work on service trucks and old lady station wagons, but don't even tell me you have a Roll's customer?"

Frank's eyebrows raised, and he breathed in deeply,

"Easy, Josh. Do you see how excited you are? That's why. What if you couldn't take the excitement and you broke something?" Frank teased.

"Oh! My phone buzzed. It looks like I have a message from work that's been trying to get through for a couple of hours," Akira stated.

Cell phones worked poorly outside the City Centre due to interference from generators and static electricity. It was unusual for a significant event in the Centre to disrupt reception, and Akira was surprised by the wait time. As a commercial pilot always on call to book high-end, dirigible cruises, Akira needed to carry her phone as she could be called for an extra flight even when there were none scheduled. She had to handle her own scheduling in such cases.

Josh stood up also and agreed,

"Yeah, I should get home too." The mood had, apparently, shifted, and so each of the six excused themselves and shook hands in parting.

Melody turned to Frank as they walked out the door. She smiled up at the big man and said,

"I had no idea, all those years ago when we were children, how powerful a speaker you would become. If I had known you could do with crowds what I saw today, I might have just coerced you into coming with me into politics, as well as other plans I had held for you."

Frank just laughed and shook his head. He looked straight into her eyes, the eyes of an old friend. They were bright and green.

She was truly stunning, even to him, though he had no interest in her. He smirked and said,

"Mel, I wouldn't have made it in politics. Someone would have had me killed because I can't keep my opinions quiet."

Melody laughed and shook her head in reply,

"You underestimate yourself." She gave him a tight hug and strode her politically trained strut down the sidewalk, under the flashes of cameras, to a car that she had called from the phone inside.

Franklin Greene was alone on the sidewalk, contemplating his motives and the politics involved. He looked into the park trees for the bluebirds or the mockingbird he had seen and heard earlier. Frank listened to the birds' early evening singing juxtaposed against the psssht puff, puff, puff rhythm as Meriwether's Rolls Royce rounded the corner and puffed away behind Melody's limousine. He smiled a little half-smile at the irony in his life and walked to his service truck.

34

Chapter 4

You're a Good Man, Franklin Greene

Frank regularly spent several hours helping some of his older customers with their generators, then not charging them for the work. He stood thinking about that cursed electrification bill and all this mess. At one time, there had been hundreds of repairmen like him. They could be seen all hours of the day in a variety of service trucks, running up and down the road. This was the world in which Franklin Greene had grown, a world of steam and repair. He had seen his industry shrink due to over-regulation and taxation. The nuclear power required respect, but the government's involvement had not created it, only barriers to tradespeople. He knew very well what laws like this would do. His shop was well-known in the area for being one of the best. Frank was inventive and creative, skills that made his custom work awe-inspiring and his repairs long-lasting and high quality. His grandfather had made the shop a landmark long before Frank had taken the reins and focused on the steam engines that his Grandpa had not particularly liked.

Grandpa Greene had been one of the few old-timers who kept working on gasoline and diesel, called petrol engines now, long after the demand for nuclear-heated steam had driven them from production. As a result of his skills and unique personality, all the old hot rodders and classic car fanatics came to Gramp's Garage to talk, work, and repair. Over the years, the petrol burners stopped coming, and Grandpa retired. Frank inherited a debt-free shop but with an uncertain future. Gramps had kept his clientele limited to the old "Gas Heads." They stayed with him to the end, even though most of them knew how to fix their own vehicles by then. Frank remembered their chatter and laughter. There was one small group of friends who always showed up together. They and Grandpa would retire to the back to play pinochle, and Frank would be left to fend for himself.

When Gramps passed, he left Frank armed with his Grandpa's training and advice, a trade school education, and a love for learning and experimentation. His legacy lived on in Frank, and he became the best steam mechanic around. He was a talented antique petrol mechanic, too, but there had not been any demand since he was a child. It had been many years since any petrol had come in. People came to Frank for steam repair even as the business that Gramps ran for petrol engines had faded. Frank had a particular love for post-WW2 era steamers and Teslator generators. He loved their simplicity, even though no one mass-produced parts for those old autos anymore. As a result, he sought after the machines to build those parts himself.

An old factory that used to build Edsel-Fordson steam tractors and Edsel steamer cars came up for auction. It was near enough to Gramp's old shop and his house, and Frank saw his chance to buy the machinery to produce all the parts needed. He placed his shop in the front office of the warehouse and moved "Gramp's Gearhead Shop." He drove past the old warehouse for years on his way home from the shop's original location and had always wondered what, if anything, was still in it. Franklin was thrilled to find most of the lathes, mills, and other machinery needed to build every part he would ever need for the steamers he loved. There, he worked quietly or read through the mountains of technical magazines left in the warehouse of the factory, not listening to the politics roar around him and not realizing he had been swept up in the storm.

Frank blew the metal shavings from a newly crafted part with an air hose. It was a restrictor valve for an old teslator. He wrapped the valve in a clean rag and put it into the toolbox of his old service truck. It was antique, like most of his things, but it was reliable, and the bed had toolboxes down the sides that locked. It silently heated for a few seconds as he hit the key, and then the dash light that said

"Cold" flickered and went off, letting him know the steam generator coils were heated enough to begin. He idled out of the drive and opened the throttle to cruise into town. "It wasn't that long ago." Frank thought to himself as he passed burned-out or abandoned buildings at the edge of the city limits.

The rally had faded into the past. Frank was feeling less an activist lately and more a mechanic once more, despite video clips from the rally regularly featured on the news. Frank was tired of being on the road today, but there had been promises made. "A promise made is a promise kept," he always recalled his grandpa saying. Frank maintained boilers, heaters, copper, and every aspect of steam generation for the industrial buildings scattered across Eagle's Roost. He was very familiar with the route to and from the city to do maintenance.

Now, most industry was hard-wired into a public gridwork of wires and meters, no longer generating their own power. At a road sign marked "Locust Grove," he turned right and began spiraling through the poorer communities in the pattern that the truck route wound through to avoid low bridges and sharp corners. He used to make this drive more frequently. His service truck was not a tractor-trailer, but he pulled a trailer with supplies quite often, and the habit of taking the truck route was muscle memory at this point.

Today, he was on business, just like all those trips he was thinking of that had taken place not so long ago. He would not be walking in as the blue-collar savior of a multi-million or multi-billion-dollar plant that was temporarily inoperable, like so many other times in the past. No, today, he would be turning on the heat and air for Mrs. Reynolds. Her generator was broken, and she couldn't pay the electric company to get her service turned back on. How many times had he soldered a copper fitting back into place, resulting in hundreds of workers returning to work? More times than he could count. "It wasn't as long ago as it seems, leastwise. I used to do this route a lot," he whispered as he thought out loud. They charged Mrs.

Reynolds a small fee for having the old generator while also being on the electrical grid. She may as well get the full benefit of both working.

The city lay in an odd, deformed maze pattern with all the poorer communities in the outskirts of the city, instead of the more impoverished communities in the center, as is typical. This layout was not an accident. Eagle's Roost had grown up like nearly every other midwestern town, with the earliest instances of infrastructure based on horse and buggy or access to water. The streets were narrow, and the buildings had porches, allowing patrons and residents to stand in the shade of their favorite stores where they would visit with one another. Eventually, the streets became paved, the buildings expanded, financial success moved to another part of town, and structures were destroyed as new ones were raised. More time passed, and the block and grid system of city planning restructured the city. More time passed, and the new became old. Jobs moved and changed, people moved, and slums developed. The unskilled factory workers found themselves unable to compete in the job market.

The story was very much like any other city's tale of growth, decline, growth, and fluctuation based on economics. However, what Eagle's Roost had done that was unique and ethically questionable was that when the latest economic boom came along, they fought urban sprawl, inner-city poverty, and crime and moved the inner city to the outskirts. The city planners rezoned everything. No new businesses were built atop the old. No new highways were constructed on the bases of the old roadways. The city could have just as easily grown back up around the stalwarts that lived in the outskirts now. The mayor and the council members ran the numbers and decided it was cheaper to start over from scratch. They would build a new city next to the foundation of the old. In response to a class-action lawsuit from the citizens of these communities, the town of Eagle's Rest, the name the city was originally chartered under, was declared bankrupt. Eagle's Roost was born.

The center of the city, now nowhere near the original center, was made the financial headquarters with fancy offices erected. The wealth spread outward from what was considered the center of town but was to the west. In the innermost sanctum of Eagle's Roost, the government and high financial district commanded its infrastructure and economy. Next in line on the six-lane highway from "The Centre" was manufacturing and skilled labor. From there, one passed service industries and unskilled employment. The housing was optimized and limited along the thoroughfares to minimize traffic in each zone.

On the way out of the pulsing heart of the city, one passed the high renters in their look-alike mini-mansions. This marked the beginning of the residential areas approved by the mayor and city council to have rental properties. Here, the people tried to appear and act as affluent as those farther inside the center, even though they could not afford it. Beautiful and luxurious public transportation, the likes of which were not to be found in the rest of Eagle's Roost, serviced these homes so they could ride in comfort and style while satisfying the common incentive of being "green" for the planet's sake. Next came the skilled blue-collar workers, whose transportation was either personal or not quite so luxurious, buses and subways. The condition and location of these subways and buses made clear in the working-class minds using them that the wealthy and powerful did not wish to be reminded that affluence was fleeting and hard to come by for some. Indeed, in many places where the wealthy drove and the public buses ran adjacent, there was a high dividing wall, painted and decorated on the side of wealth and bare and stark on the other, to separate the two classes of commuters.

Eventually came the part of town where Franklin Greene kept his shop. The rent was low. It was so little that Frank had bought his shop at an auction when the owner had failed to pay property taxes. No one else bid on the property. Frank liked it out there. The people were friendly and lived a simpler life—partly because they could afford no other and partly because they felt it better. The city had moved and abandoned their communities. Police and public services rarely came out this far. These were the outermost rings of the city, the slums. Formerly the center of Eagle's Rest, they were now its outskirts. The Bull's Run, often called "The Run," was the oldest part of the city and the poorest. Essentially a shanty town, it lay to the east of the City Centre. As a result, it never saw the sunset except as an orange glow on the cityscape horizon.

Night came early as the skyscrapers and high-stacked residences blocked out the sun like a man-made mountain for the people of The Run. This was compounded by the actual mountain to the Northwest of Eagle's Roost, where its low peak poked slightly above the morning's clouds and the fog rolling out of the hydroelectric dam halfway up its slope created a picturesque backdrop to the city. The Run's buildings were decrepit, and most lay condemned or abandoned. Many residents moved into tents or recreational vehicles parked in the same lot as the homes they owned. Crime was rampant as the police felt they had no good reason to be present in the area. Most of the streetlights hung broken, with rocks thrown through the globes or the glass shot out.

When driving through Bull's Run to leave town headed northeast, people would joke about ghosts to ease their fears of what did live there—people. These were the people who everyone wanted to forget because they lived in such poverty. Sure, the poor of Eagle's Roost were still rich by world standards, but with some of the wealthiest of a wealthy nation only miles away in the City Centre, these were a stark reminder of how easily life could leave one behind. The roofs were mostly rotting or caved in, and eyes peered out from dark windows because the owners could not afford electricity. Frank was a well-known figure in The Bull's Run; many of the homes here that did have lights only had them because Frank had repaired their teslator. They carried buckets of water to the generators so they could generate enough power for the family to cook or bathe. Afterward, they gathered the water that had drained into the condensation bowl jury-rigged to the machine and drank it. The water lines to The Run were so antiquated that often, this was the only good water they could afford, distilled by their nuclear generator.

Just to the south of The Run was the part of the city called Truitt. The inhabitants here were slightly closer to the main road in and out of town and had, in general, somewhat more marketable skills. Here, the homes were marginally more modern than in The Run. Though still many, there were fewer abandoned homes than The Run. Streetlights flickered on and off when headlights hit them, and sidewalks crumbled, threatening to turn an ankle, as people walked by on them. The buildings were mostly still standing and if the winds of change were to blow correctly, Truitt could once again be a thriving community. There was a growing movement gentrifying old Truitt, and it seemed that a wild dream of Truitt shining and clean might come true yet! While still well below the poverty line, Truitt was an obvious step above The Bull's Run.

The city's outskirts comprised three other communities. These were new developments built intentionally for the poorest of workers or recipients of benefits. The city seemed to accept them as part of itself and called them "The incorporated housing zones." The residents of these communities gave them other names from block to block that matched their purpose. Though the actual names might change depending on the owner or the year, the nicknames given by the more affluent tended to stay. The taxpayer-sponsored housing was often called a "Green Wall" district. The name was due to the prolific use of the city's official "Go Ahead Green" paint (crafted with pride by Demaris chemicals here in Eagle's Roost so you can be proud!). These were multi-story buildings made from brick and meant to be durable but not aesthetically pleasing. Most of the housing in these areas is rented on a sliding scale based on income. The government then used tax money to make up the rest of the rental cost. It was arguable whether life was, in fact, better in some of these places than in Truitt. These government slums and tenements were only better than living in the Truitt version of the slums in that no buildings were vacant next door, and amenities were nearer. Everywhere you looked, there was "Go Ahead Green," meant to encourage people to go ahead and work their way up from the bottom! The low-rent districts that were not sliding scale rentals were the next closer areas to the Centre. These were often called Jack in the Boxes because of the way the housing would 'pop up' overnight and then be demolished and renewed once they were no longer economically viable.

The lower-middle-class single-family residences in the incorporated areas were called "The Smiths" by those of greater means. No one could say precisely why, but it was suspected that it was because Smith was such a common name, and there were so very many of these houses and housing areas. The incorporated housing and the connected businesses within them were not fancy. Utilitarian might be the most accurate word to describe the appearance and atmosphere within them. With public support from the city, however, they were head and shoulders above Truitt and particularly The Run, which were unincorporated areas. Here, the citizens were not all but forgotten as in those two areas farther out.

Through the long and winding roadways of The Bull's Run, Frank continued, stopping at traffic lights that worked today, but maybe not tomorrow until he got to Mrs. Reynold's house. He sighed a raspy, exasperated sigh. The house was about to fall down on her. It looked even worse than the last time he had been out. The porch roof was rotting, and the yard was overgrown with brushy weeds. He knew the inside would be as clean as she could make it, but at her advanced age, she could not keep a house in a condition suitable for living as it rotted and fell around her. Mrs. Reynolds was the widow of a machinist. Although she qualified to relocate to one of the 'green wall' districts and live in a residential facility, she would never move. The other residents had also never taken an interest in helping her as they expected the city government to do so, and she vehemently denied needing help. Greta Reynolds would accept no help from any government and no handouts from anyone. Frank admired that.

He walked to the door and knocked on it just hard enough to be heard. He was careful, but even this cautious approach dislodged crumbling siding and stirred up the roaches in the wall. Greta answered the door in a faded pink, flowery dress. It was summer, and even the mornings were warm. Around the back of the house, they went, and Frank began to work as Greta told stories of life and having lived in The Bull's Run before its abandonment, before WW2, before teslators. She spoke with shining eyes of the songs on the air during summer concerts and block parties this time of year. She recounted her husband's strong arms and hands as the two of them danced in the streets under the moonlight and streetlights just after the war, a couple of teens in love. She began to sing as she hung up laundry just behind Frank as he worked. The clothes were faded and old. Some of the dresses had patches from conspicuously unmatched fabric. They were never clothes anyone would have called fancy, but now they were barely nice enough to remain useful. Frank stopped for a moment and listened as she hummed and sang. She noticed that he had stopped and turned around, giving him a warm smile. Before he could tell her not to stop, she had scurried inside. Frank warmly smiled while he returned to work but didn't have the time to get anything done before she had reemerged with a glass of lemonade for them each and a fold-out stool for him. She handed him the stool and lemonade. The glass was spotted and had a film of unrinsed detergent on the rim. Frank quietly wiped the lip of the glass and sipped. She sat in an old lounge chair that had been propped up with blocks in the back so she could get up and down from its low position.

"Thank you, Mrs. Reynolds. I was getting a little thirsty," he fibbed.

She smiled at the kindness in his voice even though she knew he was merely being pleasant. "I wish I could have you into my sitting room and play the old Victrola for you, Franklin. Have you ever heard one? They are crackly and probably not that great to listen to compared to your newer music boxes. But, oh … the warmth. They just sound like happiness and warmth." Her eyes glittered. "I remember playing the music with the horn pointed out the window, and I would dance with Neville in the front yard on the walk," she laughed at the memory. "We were a silly pair. Hahaha!"

Frank smiled with her.

"But, now, Franklin, don't you think it was just us? Oh no! All of us here on this block would dance! We had street dances, oh my, such dancing and music! It wasn't always just the Victrola, either! Why old Littrell Walthorn played the jazziest saxophone and had a band that would come over, and they'd play 'til they would bring down the house!" Greta became more animated, and Frank sat sipping the lemonade as he listened. "Boogie Woogie Bugle Boy of Company B, and on and on. We'd dance the Lindy, and we'd waltz. Their singer was handsome and had a voice, oh my heavens, Franklin, his voice could melt butter!" She was holding her hands together up under her chin, and her eyes were far away. "This was such a beautiful little borough back then. Each house had a little picket fence and a flower garden. The kids would play on the sidewalk. The women stayed home mostly, but a few of us worked in the factories. I worked right along with Neville for a while 'til we had children. My Neville, what a wonderful man he was," she sighed. "He would be running the mill and need some more steel and just picks it up by himself and chuck it in the machine on his own, nigh on one hundred pounds. Let's see you do that all day, big as you are!" she considered, looking at Frank up and down. "Well, you probably could," she conceded with a snort. "But most couldn't."

Frank just smirked his half-smile and nodded. He wanted to hear her stories before all of them disappeared with her.

"Neville couldn't sing a lick, couldn't carry a tune in a bucket. Up until the day he got sick, though, he sure did try. The football team still jogged by in the evenings back then. Did you know that was why they called it the Bull's Run, this street? It was only this street, not the whole area," she rolled her eyes. "They said those boys were all big as bulls and thundered like them when they ran past! It had nothing to do with the farms all around the city and their cows getting out into our part of town because of rotted fences and unmowed grass as those snooty people in The Centre say. I remember the day Neville got sick; the Eagle's football team ran past."

Frank looked slightly confused. He hadn't heard of that team before.

Greta patted his shoulder. "They aren't around anymore, sweetie. When this was Eagle's Rest, the team had the same name. They were from the city that was mine, and Neville's, before they moved to the new city. But they ran past, and they all waved at Neville sitting on that front porch. He waved and said, 'Such good boys in that college, Greta. I'm really proud our boys went there.' Then he looked at me. He was still strong, mind you; he just had a rattle in his breathing. We didn't think anything of it. Nobody knew …" She started to choke up a little, and Frank just waited. Greta laughed again, "He couldn't sing a lick, but he could see I was scared, and he started to sing. A kiss is just a kiss; a smile is just a smile … he always got the words wrong."

She laughed, and Frank could hear the tears in her voice. He waited a moment until her sniffling had stopped, and she had finished wiping her eyes. Still looking at the ground, he said quietly, "So, did you two waltz to that song?"

She softly, tearfully, replied, "I was too tired that night from doing all the housework. I never got another chance. He didn't pass right away, but with the doctor visits and all the treatment … we just missed our chance." The tears ran silently down her cheeks. The regret was thick in the aged woman's voice.

Frank cleared his throat; he knew the song. "This day and age we're living in," he began and looked up at her face. Her smile was too large to describe as another tear ran down her face. "Gives us apprehension …"

"The chorus, Franklin. It's all my Neville knew, and he always got it wrong." She choked out in a whisper. "A kiss is just a kiss; a smile is just a smile."

Frank continued substituting Neville's words in place of the correct ones. Greta laughed a full and joyful laugh and swatted Frank's arm as they stood up, and he motioned to her until they moved in a simple back-and-forth slow dance.

"As time goes by …" Greta hugged Frank and told him, "You're a slightly better singer than he was, but it's best you keep turning wrenches." Then, as they both laughed, she returned inside humming, and Frank could hear her washing her face.

Frank finished the generator quickly; it was a minor repair once he removed the fragile housings. He stayed a little longer as she told the story of how a pet pig had gotten loose and terrorized the neighborhood for a month, rooting up flower beds and vegetable gardens and hiding under cars. Finally, he got up and gave her the charge.

She read it, and her eyes again filled with tears. "Mr. Franklin Greene, you can't do this." She managed to say through her emotion. He just smiled and put his hand on her shoulder.

"Yes, Ma'am, I can. And, if you try to shove money in my lunch box or my truck door, like last time, I will come back with someone to fix your roof while you are away, and you won't know who to pay!" He laughed.

She hugged him tight. The service call-out minimum was on the ticket because it was stamped on all of them. Under the 'Time at Site' and 'Hourly Rate' headings, however, there was nothing. In the payment section, there was only the message written, "Stories of a life well-lived: Paid in full." There was money in his pocket when Frank got to the shop. How had she sneaked that in there so slickly? Frank walked over to the rotary phone on his desk and picked up the mismatched receiver, brown on a black base. He ran his finger in the circles to dial up a friend and laughed when Josh picked up the phone, saying simply, "Hey there, it's me! Whatcha need?!" without knowing it was Frank. That's how Josh always was with everyone, Frank thought to himself.

"Hey Josh, it's Frank. I've got a roof job needing done. I'll pay you for some shop work later this week, but I can't pay for the roofing this time."

"Hey, Frank, no problem! You know I love to help. Is this on the sly, or can I just show up normal?"

"Keep it quiet, but I think I can get someone to get the owner out of the house for the day," Frank replied. There was a new roof on Greta's house the next weekend, replaced while she was visiting her great-granddaughter and getting her hair styled, which had also been paid for by a stranger no one would name. Everyone knew it was Franklin Greene and his usual shop hand because those are the sorts of things they did—as time went by.

Only days after the Reynolds' roof job, Frank was back to a work-a-day routine. It was a cooler-than-average summer morning but beautiful outside, nonetheless. The coffee percolated in the art deco antique coffee maker, filling the shop with its aroma. Birds sang in the trees near the shop's parking spaces. A light fog melted away as he drove in to work. Melody came by Frank's shop this particular morning. It was uncommon anymore for her to venture out this near to Truitt or The Run without a large security detail. She was well known, a celebrity of sorts, and turned politician at a young age. At one time, it was more the norm for her to swing by on her way to a meeting and show off a little for Frank with how well she was doing and how nice she looked.

"The City Centre is the place to be, Frank!" she'd typically say as she swayed her hips out the door. This time, however, was a little different. She sat in a retro-styled jumpsuit with a pinup girl emblazoned on the sleeves and talked to Frank about the rally. "You really underestimate how loud your voice has become," she told him. Frank was working on an old green wagon for a man who would likely not be able to pay. Frank was checking out the old wagon as he worked on it. It was in good shape. The man did not need it.

"Shoot, I may just buy it from him once I'm done. It'll use less water than my truck getting around when I am not working," he mumbled as he was tightening a fitting.

Melody bent her slender figure down on the seat in the shop so she could see up under the car. "What's that dear?"

"Just thinking out loud, Mel," he answered.

Melody smiled and returned to looking through the old automotive magazines lying around while talking to Frank. "It really took me back, seeing you, Josh, Braegan, and ..." she paused with a slight eye roll, "Akira. Are you sure you won't switch sides and help me sell this bill to the people? We actually want the same things, you know. I only want to help everyone have safe electricity, Frank."

Frank kept working, focused on the fitting and the holder that was also loose. He replied after a grunt and a pull on the wrench. "No, Mel. I know you have the best of intentions, but the bill opens the floodgates for regulation where it would be the least effective and most damaging. We've already talked about it. I know you think the government can ensure that the poor are taken care of. I think it won't, even if it can. Look at the way it abandoned the poor when it moved the city."

"Maybe you could help tweak it a little, like one of your steamers. Having you helping us instead of being the voice of resistance would soften the hardliners, and maybe the feds would back off of me a little," she tried a little laugh.

Frank shook his head, "You know they won't change it enough."

"No, I suppose not. How much does it need to change?" she asked.

He stopped for just a moment with his hands resting on his chest, looking like he was lying in a coffin instead of under the car. He turned his head to see her peering at him, still seated but bent over at the waist with one eyebrow raised above her sunglasses and her jumpsuit unzipped a little farther than he felt it should be. "It needs to be completely reworked," he said, looking into her glasses.

Her expression changed to pouting. "It really is my best work so far, Frank. I was put in charge of this because of all the humanitarian work I did while I was modeling. I want you to help me make it right for those who need it. You're sure just a little here, and there wouldn't be enough to bring you onboard?"

Again, he shook his head. "No, Mel, I'm sorry. I just cannot support the framework it sets up for the government, the federal government at that, to swoop in and dictate everything pertaining to any form of energy. It needs to be taken back to concept," he stated.

Melody straightened up in the seat and flipped the magazine pages a few more times. Finally, she closed the covers and sighed, "Franklin, dear, I suppose my free time has expired. I just had to give it one more chance to woo you to my side in political theater!" She laughed and waved her hand around as though waving at the crowd. I think some friends are planning to get all our crowd together to bowl in a month or so. I do hope you'll be there! I rather miss us having time together!" she said as she strolled over to the magazine rack and returned her material.

"Yeah, they …" The phone rang, interrupting him.

Melody cheerily chimed, "I'll get it!"

"Hello? Oh, hi 'Kira," she said flatly. "Yes, he's here," she answered.

Frank slid out from under the car and quickly took the phone receiver, "Hey Akira, how are you?"

Melody strolled to the door. "Goodbye, Mel! Stop in more often and catch me when I am not committed to a repair!" He called behind her as she left.

Frank was unaware as he had taken a drink of coffee and slid back under the car with the phone pinched against his shoulder, but Melody stopped at the door to see if he was watching her. The glance back over her shoulder had been self-assured, then disappointed. She had truly hoped to be able to bring him onto her team with the electrification bill. She hadn't said as much, but it seemed that she may have wanted to bring him along in some personal pursuits, as well. His speech and power with the crowd at the rally replayed in her mind day by day. It made her wonder whether she shouldn't seek him out as more than just a partner in politics. As Melody got into her electric sports car, she had to begrudgingly admit that she had been impressed with him and was having trouble forgetting him, his words, and the past the two of them shared. She sighed a little, turned the key, and headed for more suitable parts of town. She took the most direct route, trying to avoid as much of The Run as possible and bypassing the housing entirely by getting up on the elevated highway. She sped along, thinking about her report to her political sponsors and how Frank was still going to be a thorn in their side. "How do I tell them in such a way that they can see his side of things?" she thought to herself as pop music played on the radio. She flicked a cigarette out of the car window as she watched the planes landing near The Centre. Shaking her head with a sigh, she accidentally said out loud what she had thought many times: "He just won't be coming my way, no matter what kind of man he is or how much time passes by."

Chapter 5

Cool Breezes and Hot Coffee

Josh beamed as he came through the shop door. There wouldn't be any charity work today. Today was pure mechanical repair. The glass door swung closed quietly behind him, and Frank looked at him with a quiet chuckle. Josh was a good mechanic, for the most part. With some experience and training, he could be excellent. Today, however, Frank looked at the old classmate and realized it was much more fun to wrench on machines when it was a hobby than when it was your living, and there was no way he would offer Josh a full-time job and ruin that fun for him. Frank was back to business as normal after the rally, and Mrs. Reynolds' home repair, but no one else seemed to be. As he worked on their equipment, they would talk about the school bus accident and whether he had made up the facts he quoted at the rally. There were questions about why the city would want to force this energy bill if the generators were safe. Few seemed to like Frank's response that it was all about power and money. Thankfully, a few long-time customers still came in and knew that what he enjoyed most was not politics or arguments but his machines. Those faithful few—an eclectic collection of drivers, builders, and connoisseurs who would come and not ask about power lines but about pressure hoses and gear ratios—those were the people who made Frank's days go by smoothly, no matter what else was happening. They weren't bringing in as much work currently, however, as conversation.

Josh was finished putting on his coveralls and gloves and was looking the part of a mechanic now. "So, what today, Mr. Greene?" he queried.

Frank looked around. He had one secret project of his over in the corner from which Josh was trying hard to avert his gaze. Frank pointed at a small pickup truck that had been brought in for tire rotation and balancing. "There ya go. Just rotate the rubber and balance the wheels. Make sure you check all the coolant in the gear reduction and the transmission and then check to be sure the high-pressure recycling injector is seating. That's a common problem on those compact Mercedes trucks."

Josh tried not to act disappointed that he didn't get to lift the cover on the top-secret project but went about the tasks with smiles. Frank had to smile, as well. He enjoyed Josh being there, not just because he could tease him with things that he wasn't allowed to work on, but for the company. Josh was a genuinely good person, and it was nice to have an old friend hanging out.

"Hey, boys!" came a cheerful female voice. It was Penny, another old friend who worked at a steel mill in the city. Frank looked surprised, and Josh slid out from beside the pickup. Penny responded to their expressions before they spoke. "Yeah, I know. I never get off work," she began while smiling widely. "But today I did! There was a big scare at the hydroelectric dam upriver. The alarms went out before anyone knew what was up, so we didn't receive any steel shipments today. You can't make consumer steel with no raw materials!"

Frank gave a big thumbs up and told her he was happy she got the day off. Josh was more curious and asked, "What kind of scare? It's a dam; how much scary stuff could happen?"

Penny shrugged, "I don't know. There was something about a power surge, and some substation blew up not too far from the dam. It didn't amount to anything. The news said it was simply a wire that got crossed, and the state maintenance got it all cleared up before anything happened, other than The Run was out of power for about an hour. That's nothing new, though. Is it Frank? Only real interesting thing about it is that there's 'sposed to be some kinda deal in the works to sell the dam to a private investor."

Frank shook his head, and Penny could see a huge smudge of black over his cheekbone and into his eyebrows, effectively giving him one giant black eyebrow and 'war paint.' She laughed to herself as he worked, removing a grease seal from a steam turbine. "No, not unusual at all. That's why so many in The Run use those teslators. It's not optimal, for sure, but that option is better than eating cold food, bathing in cold water—or not having water, and living in the dark most of the time. That's odd that there was a power surge up there. The only buildings are the old construction camp village, whatever they call it. More or less, it's a ghost town now. I wonder if some squatters were up there."

"Or bandits," Josh interjected with just a hint of excitement while taking a lug nut off.

Penny grabbed a roll-away jack and started lifting the pickup for him. "Probably bandits. I hear there are a lot of them out there in the wastes between the city and the mountain."

"Why do they call it 'The Wastes,' anyway?" Frank asked rhetorically.

"It's a forest. There are thousands of trees; the river comes up to the dam, then runs down the side of the mountain, which is not very tall, more of a steep hill. Then, it runs down right through the edge of the city's western side. From the river to the mountain and then back to The Run is all forest and trees with a few old abandoned houses. If anything, they should call it what it is on the map: Truman Forest."

Josh and Penny both laughed at him. Josh snarked at him, "Maybe you can start some protests for that too, Frank! Call the forest what it is, by Frank Greene!"

Frank rolled his eyes. "No, I think I have had enough of protests and politics. I only want to fix my junky cars and drink coffee."

Josh had dropped the wheel and tire of the pickup, and Penny quickly grabbed it and lifted it, carrying it to the front of the pickup. She was strong, especially for a woman slightly smaller than average. She set the wheel down and looked around. "Junky? It may be old, but most of your equipment in here is as nice as what's in the mill."

Frank smiled a thank you. "Speaking of coffee, I need to put on another pot. Josh has, apparently, enjoyed the last one more than I expected."

"Oh no," Josh retorted, "You did that one all by yourself, you coffeeholic!"

Frank's eyes glittered when he was sharing jests. He asked Penny, "Penny, would you like some?"

Penny shook her head and replied, "No, my husband drinks coffee on occasion, but I don't. I get arm cramps if I drink it and go to work. He sits in an office in the Brookes building all day, so it don't matter if he gets dehydrated."

All three of them laughed a little at her poking fun at her husband. Frank had worked on the backup generators at The Brookes building, just as he had at many buildings in the City Centre. "Isn't that all a data center for government processing?" he asked.

She looked thoughtful for a moment, then replied, "I think so? Honestly, we never talk about his work. He says it's so boring at work that my work sounds full of intrigue and mystery. I think you both know that running a blast furnace to make hot rolled steel ain't like that!" she chuckled.

Frank winked at Penny and began to rib Josh, "Josh needs to have someone he can joke with like that. Don't you know some good ladies from work?"

Penny eagerly dove in to pick on Josh, "I have a friend from the mill I can set you up with! You and Frank and Akira are the only ones that haven't married at least once! How many marriages has B had now?"

Josh held up two fingers and said, "No, no, I wouldn't impose for dinner, and I'll meet a lady on my own someday. Braegan has had the two, so he has married enough for us both, for now."

Frank turned and pointed to Penny, "And you leave me out of your matchmaking; if I ever get a chance, I'll take care of it myself."

Penny's eyes widened in excitement. "Who, Frank? Is it 'Kira? It's her, isn't it? It's about time! She's been in love with you since grade school!"

Frank shook his head, "No, she hasn't, and I am not going to tell until something comes of it. Josh only thinks he knows."

"Mel," Josh whispered loudly, "I think he's going to reignite the old flame. She's famous now, and after the way she was still upset about him dumping her, it's 'gotta be Mel."

Frank shook his head and pursed his lips. "That's enough of that, ladies and gentlemen. Maybe it's one of my customers I'm interested in! I haven't dated in a long time. Maybe I'm not meant to be with anyone. So, until I get the chance to talk to this person and see what she thinks, it may as well just be forgotten."

Josh and Penny chattered about Frank being too picky and waiting too long most of the morning despite his protesting. For lunch, they all went to a small, run-down diner in Truitt that, according to Frank, had the most amazing food in town. Penny needed to go home afterward to babysit some neighborhood children, but Frank and Josh worked the rest of the day, turning bolts and telling jokes. Frank waited until Josh left and pulled his secret autocycle project out from under the cover. He was too tired to work on it today and not yet finished with the car he was repairing, but maybe tomorrow or the next day. He had a week until Josh would be back, and he'd have to hide it from him again. Josh had a get-together planned for all the classmates still around. They were going to go to Radio Nation, a nice bowling alley in Truitt, of all places. He hoped he could get the cycle going in time to surprise Josh before that. He smiled again at how crazy it made Josh not to get to see what project he was spending his time building. "Maybe next week," he mumbled with a smile.

Meriwether walked in unseen and strolled up behind Frank, though keeping a safe distance from anything that could stain his white suit. He always wore bright colors, often white. His shoes matched his suit in a lively and shining white that caught the lights in the room and sparkled with a spectacular sheen only achievable with intense polishing on high-quality faux leather. His reading glasses sat low on his nose, and his thick white hair bounced as he walked. Had he been in public, he would have worn his matching white top hat, which he kept in the car. But in a mechanical repair shop, the risk of grime was too high to risk for a faux beaver pelt top hat. "What sort of oddity have you today, Franklin?" he asked, "Shall I play our guessing games, or have you a notion of indulging my curiosity?"

Franklin Greene looked up from soldering a copper preheating tube and into the bespectacled face of Meriwether Lewis, a long-time customer, smiling back at him. Frank had a long list of what he would refer to as close acquaintances—those folks with whom he was familiar enough to have a conversation but not close enough to meet for dinner or plan to take along on a cycle tour. Frank smiled a little as he drew back from Meri's face, which leaned in a little too close to his. Meriwether's interest showed that he enjoyed the creations that rolled, or sometimes flew, from Frank's after-hours hobby work. It was nice to see Meriwether. After having paid for a new roof that was not his own, Frank needed some cash flow. Frank did a good amount of business through his shop, far more than anyone would suspect by looking at his clothes, home, or vehicles. Still, he was a reasonably generous man, and even though he was not distressed financially, a little breathing room in the bank account was welcome.

Meriwether continued, turning to the partially covered secret project, "I don't suppose it to be an automobile; by the look of the frame, I would call it an autocycle or perhaps ... hmm, no, the boiler size is too small, and too similar to the one you seem to favor for piston engines. It must be an autocycle." Meriwether leaned back, satisfied that he had deduced what was the apparent truth of the situation.

Frank made a look and shrugged, "Perhaps," then finished his solder joint. Once finished, he extinguished his torch and stood. He stretched long and groaned from having been crouched to the floor for many minutes. He laid the torch on the table. "Meriwether, you get keener and brighter every time you visit. One of these days, you should look into turning that architectural engineering minor into something more enjoyable and draw me some prints." Frank patted his hand on his workbench as though there were prints there. The designs that were there were a few sketches of mechanisms drawn with an ink pen on dinner napkins.

Meriwether laughed his high-pitched laugh. "Franklin! You never work from anything more than a picture in your head, and I've no desire to enter there!" The two shared a small chuckle. Meriwether was much more relaxed with Frank when it was not a social setting ,particularly since Melody, the power-playing politician mutual friend, was absent. It was friendly small talk, and Frank loved to chew the fat over almost any topic when he was not trying to problem-solve a repair or under pressure to get work done. Meriwether was from a family of means. He spoke with a strange accent that was a mixture of Midwest drawl and English sophistication. Highly educated and well-connected, Meriwether made for interesting stories and conversation. He tended to speak too formally and seemed awkward to most. His dry humor was off-putting, and some would even say snooty or offensive. Frank enjoyed his different perspective and understood his humor. Fortunately, it was a good time for a break, so Frank was happy to hear from him.

"Do you have time for coffee?"

"No, I'm afraid not," Meriwether answered him. "I was merely passing by on my way to the Centre and thought I would see if you had been keen on fixing my Hydra."

Frank nodded and looked around the shop. Looking perplexed, Frank asked, "Passing through? You live at the edge of The City Centre, don't you?"

Meriwether replied, "Yes, I was in another town on business." Frank was glad that Josh was not in the shop today to get overly excited about the Rolls Royce. Currently, there were mostly his own projects lying around, in various degrees of completion: an autocycle, a customized Standard Steam brand automobile, pieces from a personal aircraft that no one knew for sure what it was but Frank, and the one repair that was not his own—a late model compact car that he was waiting on parts delivery to fix, now that the copper tubing was soldered together.

Frank rubbed his chin for a moment and answered, "Sure, as I turn you away, I won't have anything else for a month," he smiled at Meriwether warmly as he feigned disinterest. "I reckon that I'll try to see where the monkey wrench was thrown in. Bring the old girl in as soon as you get a chance, and I'll do what I can." The two shook hands. Meriwether thanked him and left for the City Centre.

Frank got work from people of every economic stratum in Eagle's Roost, including the workers in the Centre. Sure, they were power players in the local government and wealthy corporations, but he had reasonable prices and was as sharp as anyone could be when it came to steam, whether power generation or propulsion. He smiled as he returned the copper to the table as he thought about Meri's Hydra. The truth is, he loved that old Hydra. Hydras had been the "bee's knees" of luxury automobiles for almost three decades, back in the 1940s, '50s, and '60s, before falling out of vogue. While Frank tended to enjoy the raw power of the high performance or pulling power of heavy service autos, he could certainly appreciate the luxury of the first manufacturer to really bring reliable luxury to steam power.

Ford, General Motors, and Chrysler Corporation had held sway over all things automotive for several years, and The Kaiser's war in Europe only helped to propagate their rise to power as they each fought for a market share in the newly developing petrol-fueled automotive industry. Only Stanley retained their focus on steam power and its usefulness. As World War 2 began to loom on the horizon, the rush for more powerful weaponry roared technology forward.

However, in the process of discovering new weapons, nuclear power was discovered as well. The Navy realized the potential for nuclear-generated steam power. Nuclear bombs were invented but never used. The terrifying destructive force they possessed caused Dr. Oppenheimer too much concern. In the meantime, the power production of nuclear heat was realized, with steam-powered destroyers and aircraft carriers roaming around the ocean needing never to be refueled. This same awe-inspiring technology being adapted to recirculators and coolers for implementation in tanks and other vehicles, the war and the world were forever changed. The Allies soon had nuclear power in everything from jet aircraft to motorcycles. It turned the tide of the war for them, and Hitler was, you might say, steamrolled by the innovation. Scientists and engineers soon began to improve on the technologies that won the war for the allies.

It was then that Rolls Royce made the Hydra. It had a state-of-the-art recollector and a tiny nuclear reactor powering a twin-piston single-action steam engine. Despite their wartime use and testing, the public was hesitant about the nuclear reactors. There were protests, and propaganda posters, and newsreels showing, with comic inaccuracy, how a nuclear meltdown might appear. But when the movie stars started driving them, and when gasoline went from five cents to an unbearable twenty cents a gallon, the die was cast. Rolls Royce dropped their other production lines, unable to keep up with the Hydra's demand.

Stanley, who had barely hung on through the powerful alliance of Firestone, Ford, and Rockefeller, with the support of a few stalwarts and collectors, found that they, too, were suddenly in demand as "the everyman steamer." Soon, Stanley also had what they called an "atomic heater." These early reactors were shielded as best they could be, but the technology was young and not sufficiently tested. Henry Ford was, reportedly, so bitter about his company losing its hold on the marketplace that he was implicated, then suspiciously exonerated, for one of the only vehicular meltdowns in history. It was concluded that the core had overheated because a hole had 'developed' in the reserve emergency cooling tank of a military delivery truck that had left Detroit. While Ford escaped prosecution, it was not without injury. The public believed that he had played, or paid for, a part of the incident. Soon, there were video clips on newsreels extolling the virtue of clean atomic steam that showed burning, smoking, and sometimes exploding gasoline vehicles. Petroleum power was in decline. It was 1949, and the world turned on its head. Meriwether's Rolls Royce Wraith-Hydra, referred to simply as a "Hydra" since then, rolled out into a new and exciting world. Frank knew all this history, and he loved how the Hydra brought that world of some sixty-plus years ago to life when it popped its two large cylinders into his shop. He buffed his solder, now cooled, and smiled again.

Only two days later, Meriwether brought in the old Rolls. The Hydra was as clean as any new car and sounded like a percolating coffee pot as it chugged the long vehicle through the shop doors. Frank knew by the sound of it what was happening. It was a common problem in the older models. Meriwether got out of the car and grinned as he walked up. "It's always a joy to ride in the old girl. Even with its troubles, it's twice the auto of the newer cars!" he exclaimed.

Frank took a quick look underneath, then pulled up the side-hood and nodded knowingly. He picked up a hammer, reached in under the reactor, and smacked it with a good solid *bang*! Meriwether jumped as though he, instead of the car, had been struck with the hammer. "The retractor is sticking. When you are needing full heat, you aren't getting it. When you are done with it, does it sit and steam for a long time before it finally cools off?" Frank inquired.

Meriwether was still a little shaken but answered, "Why, yes. Yes, that is exactly how it behaves! I have had to refill the emergency chamber twice in as many weeks!"

Frank grunted a little and crawled under the car. After a few minutes of pecking around and then another *bang* that knocked more of Meriwether loose than it did of the Hydra, he crawled back out and began collecting tools. "Good sir, I believe you have a Rolls Royce Wraith-Hydra in good working order now. I'll have to make a quick adjustment, but it won't cost a bomb." Frank smiled at his slight teasing of the very proper spoken Meriwether.

"Bob's your uncle!" Meri exclaimed with a chuckle," if we are using British slang now. Where did you pick that up?" He laughed as he brewed, then poured coffee while Frank finished adjustments and cleaned up. As a gift, he had brought him some rare gourmet beans that he had ground personally.

Frank's eyes sparkled. "I get to work on the Hydra and a pricey brew as well? This is a day for celebration! I am not much for putting on airs, Meriwether, but you know, I do enjoy a good coffee!" As he poured, Meri laid some money on the workbench, knowing full well Frank was not going to turn it down nor ask for so much pay. When it was this easy to fix, he wouldn't demand payment.

"Franklin," started Meriwether, suddenly serious, "have you heard any of the news lately?" Meriwether was in the know on a great many things because of his activity on government contracts and the amount of time he spent in the Centre rubbing shoulders with high society. Frank thought briefly and sipped the coffee. The flavor was exotic and rich, with a smoothness that was thick and soothing. He looked into the cup, half expecting butter to be floating on top of the black, hot brew.

"Well, I heard the Penguins are playing at home this weekend. That's about it. And I heard that from a customer I was fixing a teslator for. I'm not really into sports, so I was only half listening. Besides, that's hockey. When the Kodiaks are playing ball, then I am a little more interested, not enough for a ticket, of course," Frank laughed.

Meriwether wasn't laughing. "Teslators are the issue I was referring to." Meriwether went on. "Apparently, a terrorist was able to break through the security at the Eagle's Roost Stadium using the energy transmissions from a portable one. The Penguins' game was last night. Once through security, the terrorists arced the power somehow to make the whole thing into a bomb. Franklin, there were over a hundred casualties, and twenty-nine died! There have been three attacks attempted lately with large portable teslators. You know more about these things than anyone I know. Do you think they are dangerous?"

Frank was aghast—first, that someone would kill so many spectators at a sporting event for no reason, and second, he was disgusted that when he had heard the boom of the explosion, he had thought a large truck had run into a bridge nearby and promptly went back to sleep. Third, and the one that seemed to be seeping into his mind and picking at another part of him that he wasn't sure he understood, the implication that teslators were to blame rather than the terrorist himself. Teslators were simply an adaptation of Nikola Tesla's electrical transmission devices. Someone had found that if you altered frequency and wattage a little, it worked, at least to a small range of access. Frank did not know the name of the person who made the discovery, but GeneVolt was the first to heavily market and mass produce the generators, giving them the name of Teslator that every other brand would be called by default. Many of the outer suburbs and rural areas relied heavily on teslators for backup power or just for powering their non-household appliances such as milking machines and shop lights. Frank had two himself for backup. Not only that but several of the poorer communities out in the Bull Run area that bordered Frank's shop, had no other in the Bull Run area bordering Frank's shop had no power than a teslator between three or four residences. He knew because he was called upon often to go and make sure they were working. He was something of a hero to those people. After the first time he donated a teslator repair in The Run he was driving home and said to himself, "When you make someone able to turn on the light to read to their little ones or to take a hot shower, and that's all they have wanted all day, the look in their eyes is worth more than cash on the barrelhead."

Frank was gobsmacked at what Meri was saying. "I, I don't think teslators are the problem. That's not even how they work," Frank looked at Meriwether, making eye contact as he explained, "The Teslators use a very small nuclear reactor to heat steam that spins an also tiny turbine to generate electricity. That's all they do. They make electricity and then broadcast it like a radio wave at an ultra-high frequency for a very short range. Even if someone adapted them somehow, I don't think they'd have enough power to blow up anything, let alone a whole stadium of folks. I know that anything can be used to do wicked things. But these machines do a lot of good. If they do nothing else, they keep lights on in the poorer neighborhoods, so people are safer."

Meriwether was ready with the reply almost within the same breath: "How can anyone be safe with a bunch of ninnies running around with nuclear bombs in their hands?" Frank stared in disbelief. Hadn't he just moments ago fixed the nearly sixty-three-year-old nuclear device in Meriwether's car? How could such a ridiculous statement be coming from someone he knew and liked?

"Meriwether, is that what people are saying?" Frank asked quietly.

Meriwether looked at Frank, seemingly surprised by the hurt and confusion in his voice. "Yes, Frank, and although I am not certain I agree, I think, perhaps, I may."

Frank sat and drank the rest of the coffee in relative silence as Meriwether went on about what the news programs had been saying. He was a smart man, though, and after seeing the expression Frank was wearing, he began to talk about the AC, as he called it, or the autocycle. Frank began to come out of his mental malaise, but something kept lurking at the back of his mind. There was a tickle there, a little indicator of trouble, and much like he could smell the rain long before he could hear the thunder from a storm blowing in, he thought he could smell something in the air. This time, however, it wasn't anything so good as a spring rain.

Chapter 6

Hazy Dreams

Frank awoke in a cold sweat from a strange nightmare. He had dreamed of evil-eyed men crazed with zeal. They stole his teslator parts and crafted a massive bomb. The next part was the part that gave him chills: they took that bomb to a shopping mall. Children played outside as a large black truck with a strange roaring noise jumped the curb and mowed down several of the children. The rest vanished in billowing smoke and dust. In his dream he saw the news reporting the incident, somehow live. The news reporter ranted on and on in an emotional plea for these weapons, the generators, to be taken out of circulation. Somehow experts were already on call to comment on the evils of the antiquated use of steam and the insane usage of nuclear power by individuals. In the dream Frank raged at the television about decades of people safely using nuclear heated steam, but he sounded crazed, even to himself. Frank wiped the sweat from his face as he tried to shake off the dream. He could not. He stumbled round his home and decided to go to the shop and make sure it was secure. It was not a long drive from his home but far enough to wake up and start to make sense of his dream.

When he arrived at his shop, the door was swinging open in the wind. Glass lay glistening in the moonlight in tiny cubes from the safety glass of the door. He rushed inside, convinced of the evil portent and accuracy of his dream. Why had he dreamed of something that seemed to be taking place? Confusion and terror gripped his heart, and it pounded like a drum solo in his chest. However, when he arrived inside, everything was in place. Every bolt, every bulb, every brass and copper fitting lay where he had left them. He walked to the door to examine it. It had been tampered with before the intruders had shattered the glass. The part that had him the most perplexed was the warehouse. The shop was in the old lobby and showroom of the automotive parts factory. The door that led back into the warehouse and manufacturing floors was propped open, and the antique emergency lights were on. Frank mostly used the old warehouse for his collection of outdated technical manuals and magazines. He had scavenged the few tools he needed for bending tubing or machining metal from the factory floor and left that part of the building essentially abandoned. It lay there, basically as he had purchased it, with all the tools and dies still laying around on shelves with all the old antique presses and stamps.

He began to carefully walk through the large warehouse. It felt mysterious, eerie, and somehow violated now. Outside, a strange rumble, then a roar, arose shaking the walls of the shop building. He had made it in time to stop the theft, but the intruders were still there, outside! He ran around the building's interior wall and into the shop, grabbing his shotgun on the way. He kept the gun in a small cabinet out of sight, but always at the ready. The tiny nuclear heater, no larger than a pinhead, cycled its one-way valve four times to build air pressure, and the superheated air was ready almost in an instant. He held it in his hands like he had on a dozen hunting trips, and his heart froze over. Even though he knew his life may depend on it, he was queasy and felt weak at the thought of using the gun against another human being.

The split-second passed, and purpose gave him legs again as he dashed out the side door to see an intimidating black truck throwing rooster tails of dirt, sand, and driveway gravel as it roared away. What was that strangely familiar smell? … Petrol! Its petrol engine roared like an unholy monster blowing its toxic hate-fumes in his face as he chased after it for only a moment. He coughed and choked, unable to pursue, unable to aim, too confused to fire, not actually in danger or convinced he should fire. The hazy exhaust smoke from the truck hung in the air like an evil spirit. He stared after the taillights as he gagged a little from the fumes. It appeared to be a Chevrolet pickup that was heavily modified. He couldn't be sure enough to give a good description to the police. He hadn't smelled petroleum fumes of any kind in years, but he knew that's what the smell was. He had worked with his grandpa all those years and smelled it. This was different somehow. Those engines typically didn't blow huge clouds of cloying black smoke. It was dissimilar yet familiar. Where did a petrol vehicle that new come from? Why his shop? Where did they find fuel? Were they really there to perform the acts of his frightened subconscious?

He walked, bewildered, back into his shop and turned on the news channel to have the comfort of other voices. It had been only two days since he had heard of the explosion, and he feared he had already enjoyed the calm before the storm. There was no chance of sleep tonight. He walked to the autocycle and picked up a wrench, looking around the shop again being certain all the teslator cores were, indeed, there. All the parts and units and all his gadgets lay there silently, delivered them from the madmen. He coughed, clearing his lungs of the petrol fuel fumes, and worked his confusion around a loose bolt.

He worked through the night into daylight and then into a sunny day as the moist morning air had given way to the lingering heat of summer. His old friend Melody had called and talked for what seemed like forever. She had gone on about the politics of the Centre and about her newest relationship drama, about her wealthy suitors, about grand political balls and banquets, and about celebrities she thought were not genuine in their actions. She called more regularly since the rally, though she didn't visit more often. Since their relationship in high school and as Mel began modeling, she had gotten married once, was it twice? Frank couldn't remember. Mel was always focused on the end game and had no intention of settling for anything less than the highest authority, fame and, wealth. She wasn't haughty or rude the way so many with that goal were, at least not to Frank. He was groggy during the conversation with Mel and began to wonder if he could sleep now. He was exhausted but unable to let his mind rest. There was just too much that didn't make sense. There was something he had noticed without consciously noting. Frank couldn't stop his mind from rolling things over and over in his head. The news video played on repeat, then the sights of the break-in.

There was one prescription that always helped—riding. This was not his first custom cycle, but it was his most powerful. His friends, Josh and Braegan, had begged to help. They both worked as machinists and were handy in the shop from time to time. Frank, however, had kept this one a secret and reserved all the work for himself. The turbine steam motor was salvaged from an industrial truck, the impellers shaved for quicker spooling, the housing machined, and he added coolers, etc, etc. He polished a bit of grease from a brass coupling, wiped his hands and began to feel instantly better. He hopped on his cycle and headed down the shop's short driveway and out into The Bull Run. He liked to ride the crooked and poorly repaired roads. The cycle was flawless in its performance. Its turbine engine whistled quietly and thrust the jet-black two-wheeler forward with a force like a locomotive. A twist of the throttle, and the world would rush past, leaving only him and the sound of a healthy jet of steam, the percolating of the steam condenser and slight gurgling of the cooler, the rumble of rubber on a cobblestone, then chip and seal, then pavement, then cobble, road, ta-tump, ta-tump, ta-tump, the tires crossed the cobbles and seams and small holes. *Shhhhhh* whispered the turbine as it whistled and gave life to the lively black and golden brass creation. It was heavenly to Franklin Greene.

"This is peace and satisfaction," he thought to himself. "Build it better than you can buy. Build it different than anyone else. Then enjoy it with all you have!" A completely happy smile spread under the darkened visor of his helmet. "I need to write that slogan down to put on the shop wall," he uttered quietly inside his helmet. There was another sound that repeated itself at every bump in the road. A quiet rattle-thump, thump, thump, as his short-barreled scatter-gun bounced on his back, slung in its custom harness.

Frank was not keen on the idea of violently defending himself. He had never once been in a fight, even with all those years working in The Run and Truitt. Violent crime was epidemic in those places, but he had always been able to avoid serious conflict. Now, he was horrified at the idea that he might have to actually use the weapon. Why had he brought it? He wondered to himself. Then just as quickly as he pondered the question, he answered it. Deep down, under the calming of work and the exhaustion, he was frightened. Uncertainty and a break-in had shaken him. Frank's shop was locked with only a simple lock, but he had never had a break-in, a vandal, or really anything other than pleasant customers.

The gun lay quietly in his shop, having never needed to make an appearance. He had thought several times of selling it. It was a popular model that predated some of the regulations in place now. It had a large shrapnel capacity with the ability to accept almost anything for projectiles, but he knew he couldn't replace it for what it would bring. He also felt it was better to have it and not need it than to need it and not have it. He seldom carried it and never rode with it. After the break-in, though, he couldn't feel comfortable walking into the shop knowing his only defense might be in a cabinet with intruders between it and him. So, the shotgun rode along this afternoon.

The sounds and the video of the news played over and over in his memory, stirred up by his dream, the scare of the shop break-in, and the images of the destroyed stadium and the carnage the news stations were all too happy to plaster all over the screen to get ratings. "Something doesn't sound right!" His thoughts returned to their circular working the information over and over. They would not let him continue to enjoy the warming day until they had been satisfied with some form of answer.

"Teslators exploding like bombs." He shook his head within his helmet and sighed. He looked distractedly across the cluster of houses to his left. There was a woman hanging clothes over the divorced heating element of a teslator "Freedom" brand generation kit so old that if you didn't know what it was you would never find a decal or stamp not rusted into obscurity. "The shielding on that old unit was far ahead of its time," Frank said in appreciation. His smile returned faintly for a moment as he watched these poor but happy people. Why was no one in the City Centre this happy? He thought about the people he saw there. No one ever smiled. No one sat and talked on the porch. He quietly chastised himself, "That's not a fair comparison. City Centre is business and manufacturing—power at work."

He pictured the part of town where the houses rose into the sky and made the sidewalk shady and dark during all but the noonday sun. He struggled to think of what those families looked like and realized that, although he occasionally saw a child on a bicycle in the driveway, there were never any parents outside, not even older siblings. Here, where they had nothing, they had everything! Family played together. Family fought together. Family simply was together here. A woman huddled over a basket of laundry then hung it on a line made of twine twisted together with old wires hung between a dead tree and old metal fence post as she stood over the heating element. It was hot enough that there was no need for the external heater, and Frank wondered if it was even running. She was standing almost on top of the unit as she reached for the end of the line. He almost wrecked his cycle as he turned his head, distractedly watching. "Wait, a teslator exploding like a bomb? How?" Why hadn't he thought of it before? There were so many safeguards against excess pressure, even on the old units like that 'Freedom.' Even if it did over-expand and rupture, there was nothing flammable!"

"Wires crossed, exploding, radiated fields ..." His mind was working and racing faster than the autocycle. The cycle sped up as he struggled for memory and unconsciously rolled back on the hand throttle. There was something in there, deep in his memory, an article in a technology magazine, a video, a radio broadcast, that fit the description. His mind was a fiery burner boiling thoughts and memories up that had lain stagnant in the tank too long. What was that device, what was its purpose, and where and why did he learn of it?

"It was no teslator at all!" he gasped as the thought rushed to the forefront of his mind and ran out of him. How could no one else have thought of this? He began to become more and more convinced, and as he mentally turned magazine pages, he became more and more distracted, releasing the throttle, slowing until he had to put his foot on the ground suddenly as the idling bike almost toppled in a mud hole. He had ridden until the lights of the city were far distant. How fast had he been going at first? How long had he tumbled the situation in his mind? Outside of town, past The Bull Run where poverty reigned and he had friends who knew his secret generosity, farms stretched out ahead of him. Dirt roads went in every direction between property lines demarcated with wire fences and to the north and west, Truman Forest, or "The Wastes" as so many called it, hid the river and the road leading to a mountain. It was a "no-go" zone, according to the police. He was not sure if it was illegal—nothing was posted—or if it was simply unwise due to blowing debris, trash from the city, and lack of police protection.

He stood now, straddling his newest creation of jet black and polished brass, at this boundary between the civilization he knew and the wild wasteland of lawlessness. Even this farmland was only regulated by the ability to defend oneself. He knew, however, that the folks on the farms were gentle and good people, but it was nearing dark when they would all be inside. He felt an odd thrill mixed with the twinge of fear. He had only left Eagle's Roost on roads leading to another town, never out into the forest. "Humph," he snorted to himself. He turned the bike around in the road and headed back to search his books and references. He knew sleep would not come before answers tonight.

The ride home seemed to take forever. Frank wasn't sure whether he had just paid more attention this time or had actually been going quite fast on the trip out. For the first time since the attack on the dome, he felt relaxed—not because everything had been resolved but because he knew he could prove that such a useful tool, his tools, his life's work, his charity, was not actually a death machine.

He shook his head disdainfully for the foolish ignorance, the gullibility, of people. Early dusk was coming. The sun was still high but settling in behind the city in the west. Soon the sparse clouds would be painted like a carnival across the sky even though the red-orange sun would be obscured from view. The trees and homes in The Run, in stretched shadows stood in graphic relief against the bright canvas that spread out before him. The citizens of the Bull Run were bringing in clothes, bringing in children, and locking doors. This was not a place to be after dark. It was not full of bad people, just poor. There was little or no lighting other than the light that bled through the shutters and curtains of the homes. These lights also went out very early to conserve the precious energy that the prosperous city refused to maintain or supply out here without additional taxes and legislation. It was not even a suburb or an outlying community, in the mind of the mayor and the elite. No, The Run was nothing more than a shadowy reminder of the city that had been there ages ago. The houses that had once seemed so stylish and picturesque were dated and fallen into disrepair, crumbling. The people of The Run mostly worked hard at menial jobs for low pay if they could find work. Most of all, these homeowners would come right up to you and talk, treat you with respect, and discuss hard questions about life. Deep conversations about the world and what mattered did not take place the same way in the city. Conversation there was all about your new apartment, your new clothes, the new fashions, what so and so the celebrity said, or who had made the winning point at some pointless game where the participants made more than a CEO of a moderately large corporation and yet had no responsibility to the community.

The Bull Run was avoided at all costs by the denizens of the city. As a result, it was also avoided by anyone with money. As a result of that, it was avoided by all but the most altruistic officers who were then, quite often, reprimanded for taking unnecessary risks … *BANG!* Frank was jolted out of his thoughts by what sounded like a gunshot. He looked around desperately as he slid his bike to a stop. "Oh, thank goodness." He said out loud as he saw someone pushing down on the hood of their car. Why was he so on edge? He took a deep breath, released his unintentional grip of the shotgun, and steamed away slightly irritated. "Lack of sleep," Frank muttered to himself unconvincingly.

The back room of the shop served as his smaller personal library for books and magazines he would still reference at times. It had been dark for almost an hour when he arrived at the door, and he was already picturing where the periodicals were that might have the science articles he needed. He couldn't help but walk around the building, both the shop and warehouse sections, and look for tire marks or other signs that the old, metal-sided, structure had been tampered with. Everything looked unmolested, so Frank opened the door, flipped on the light, and began his search. *Popular Mechanic, Science Craft Today, Engineering Monthly,* he pulled out magazines and periodicals and glanced at them to remember the contents. Finally, he had narrowed his search to ten magazines. He thumbed through them with fervor. His mind was racing, and he had already recalled most of the article before ever finding it.

Then, with two magazines left, the pages of an electrical generator hobbyist magazine fell open to the title, "Don't Sell Your Scrap!" This was it. He looked through the photos and found what he had been looking for—a handmade, homemade, bomb, crafted from leftover nuclear heater parts, hydrogen separators, and a mix and match of electrical components and … petrol. This bomb had the capacity to do massive destruction in small, confined areas. The article was nearly twenty years old. Frank stared at the article and the pictures. This wouldn't cause the damage that had been done in the video. Although he had watched it a hundred times at least, it was time to watch it now, this time, to compare bombs.

Outside the shop doors, the world lay quiet. Just down the road a few miles, the City Centre glowed from a million tiny lights, streetlights, traffic lights, headlights on autos, and emergency lights on police and medical vehicles. The streets hummed and roared in the Centre and its surrounding burbs, all hours of the day and night. In back alleys, illegal deals were being made, often with people of authority. In Franklin Greene's shop, the world was still and waiting. He turned on the old tube-type television, decades outdated. It crackled and came to life, and the poor picture quality and fuzzy sound began to improve as it warmed up. It didn't require scanning many twenty-four-hour news programs before he found the footage. It had been edited to eliminate the gore that earlier versions had shown. Black splotches now covered the blood, giving the whole affair a cartoon and live-action blend of lunacy. He paused the broadcast. There it was, picture-perfect. The contraption was nearly identical to the contraband homemade terror photographed and cataloged twenty years previous. There were new broadcasting antennae for the radio frequency interrupts, and there was some sort of tall extendable wire thing on the top.

He released the pause, and the video resumed. The security camera showed the man walking into a large group of people. He was wearing a long coat, already suspicious in the warm summer evenings. The bomb was set, but then the wind had blown. Inside the dome the wind did not blow often or with much force, but this night, it had blown for a glorious instant, and Frank saw something that brought tears. The teslator was the firing cap; it was the way it had been perverted that made a bomb from it. It took specific knowledge to do what had been done. Frank rushed to the phone and called the only person he knew with the connections to matter. "Meriwether," he said to his friend's voicemail," it wasn't the teslator! Come by tomorrow!" He hung up the phone, and exhaustion took over as he slumped into the shop's couch and thought until he fell asleep.

The clatter of metal parts hitting the floor brought Frank back to consciousness. He jumped to his feet facing the sound. There was no one there to explain why an old paint can, full of miscellaneous light metal rods, had fallen to the floor. Frank looked around quickly, but all the doors were shut, and he thought he could remember the gentle ground tremble and *thwop, thwop, thwop* of a helicopter passing over as the sunlight showered down on him. The old leather couch that customers sometimes sat on had been his bed, and it groaned as he rolled to a seated position and rubbed his eyes. He was groggy and clumsy as he stumbled in a circle to see the clock. Ten o'clock! He hadn't slept that late in years!

BANG BANG BANG! "Franklin! Are you there?" It was Meriwether. He had knocked the can off the wall by knocking forcefully on the door.

"Yes, Meriwether, coming." The door opened and spilled unfiltered, direct, sunlight into Frank's bloodshot and bleary eyes.

"Are you all right, Franklin?" asked Meriwether.

"Yeah, yes, I am doing fine. I just had a late night and overslept. Come here, I have something to show you." Frank motioned Meriwether over to his desk where the magazines lay scattered, and the decades-old article lay sprawled open like a centerfold.

"What's this about something not being something or other?" Meriwether began to query.

"Just look," Frank said, as he emphatically tapped his finger on the article to direct his friend. Meriwether was dressed in a suit and tie, as always. Frank had often wondered if the man actually owned any casual clothes. Not only were Meriwether's clothes all suits and ties, but they were vintage or styled to appear so. He was very wealthy and well connected. He knew politicians, movie and television stars, reporters, and business elites. If it was someone who held position or power, Meriwether knew their name and probably their number. He was not a major player himself but had hooks in all the goings-on of those who were. Now, though, he was out of his element.

"I don't know what I am looking at, Franklin. Did you phone me over here, sounding so desperate, to show me photographs? I was afraid something terrible had happened!"

Frank took the magazine, read a few key captions from the pictures, then said, "Look, see the shape of the tank? See the mechanism on the side and the antennae up top? That's what the bomber at the Bear's Dome was carrying. But look at the video!" He put in a copy of the video he had made the night before while reviewing it, "Right … there …"

Meriwether was staring open-mouthed. "I declare, no one has noticed that," he whispered. "I don't know all this other technical material you are trying to show me, but even I recognize a strapped-on explosive device! I will go to the City Council and the news at once! Let me have that magazine, Franklin! They have been looking for the wrong things! No wonder the copycat attempts with teslators have failed!" Meriwether seemed almost as excited about this discovery as Frank had been.

"Let me know what you find out, Meriwether. This has weighed heavily on me since it happened. I couldn't stand the thought of someone stealing a generator I have helped repair and using it for destruction. The idea of the fear of these things putting the people out in The Run in any danger has had me even more worried. It's nice to feel a little less responsibility in this."

"Oh, Franklin," Meriwether patted his back gently and looked at him with pity, "you were never at fault, no matter where the parts came from." Meriwether walked out of the shop and got into a brand new, electric, Rolls Royce.

"Where's the old Hydra?" Frank yelled.

There was no answer as Meriwether pulled slowly out of the driveway and disappeared down the road in his new luxury car. It was a beautiful day already. Things could only get better on days like this, he thought to himself. Surely everything would get back to normal.

Lines of Power

78

Chapter 7

Tall Tales and Steam Trails

It was a beautiful day indeed, and Frank enjoyed it. The stress of the past few days melted from him, and he went on a few service calls. He was thankful those calls were either in the incorporated suburbs or the city proper. It was always nice to get a paycheck from a satisfied customer. Frank seldom entertained but frequently met friends for dinner or to socialize. He had backed out of a couple of events during the days after the explosion, but now that his mind was more settled, he felt some laughs, and distractions were past due. It was summer, and summer was riding weather. A long bike ride was certainly in order. This weekend would be the drive-in theater with friends, and on Sunday he would catch up on paperwork after church. Frank went to a church outside the city limits at a tiny old-fashioned country church that sat in a lot cut out of a farm. The wooden rail fence keeping out the cows only a stone's throw from everyone's parking made him feel warm inside, as if he was returning to something pure just by sitting there. Although Frank would not consider himself religious in the way most thought of it, he was a deeply spiritual man and looked forward to that time of inner peace along with the other weekend events.

The sun was just coming up on an amazing Thursday morning when Frank's friends, Joshua and Braegan, showed up. The air was crisp for a morning in late summer, but it promised to be a beautiful, mild day. They both lived in the city and worked at an automotive parts manufacturer. They were only a few years younger than Frank but wore leather jumpers with aggressive sport bike styling and black helmets.

"Hey there! It's about time you two showed up! I was afraid someone with self-respect and realistic ideas would want to go for a ride if I stayed sitting in the driveway any longer! How much did those rompers cost? Rompers is right, isn't it? Onesies? What do you call a costume on an adult that would be leather pajamas on a baby?" Frank could never resist ribbing them for their style choices in riding.

They couldn't resist the friendly challenge and were always quick with an answer, "Hey, old man! Have you seen anyone around here with a cycle? We were told to meet a friend here to ride, but all we see is you in your jeans and quilted vest," Braegan replied with a wide smile. "Besides, my girlfriend likes my leathers!"

Frank rolled his eyes, "Girlfriend? What did you do with the last one? Do they know you have kids?"

Braegan just smiled and nodded, "I married one, and she has the kids. All these girls are getting is breakfast."

Joshua and Frank just groaned and sighed. Joshua looked at Frank and quipped, "Are those jersey gloves? I guess we can help you dig in your garden a little while we wait."

Everyone shook hands and laughed. Joshua had already walked to Frank's new bike. "Wow, Frank, this is really your best work yet," he said in quiet admiration. "I love how you used the brass for accent as well as for most of the plumbing. What does it weigh with the turbine motor? Is it lighter than our radials?"

Frank smiled broadly as he walked over and knelt down. He popped a side cover off just behind the motor to reveal an uncharacteristically large transmission. "It is lighter, a lot, if it wasn't for this. This is something of my own design. I had a friend in the Centre work out the details and do the work in exchange for some work on his factory's backup generator. It's a type of constantly variable transmission that lets me creep forward so slow you can barely tell you're moving, but it has a practically infinite top gear. I really don't know how fast this cycle can go, and I don't actually think I want to find out!" He laughed heartily, proud of his design.

Braegan was the more competitive of the three and snarked, "Well, you'd have to be able to ride it to keep up with us. So, I guess it doesn't matter so much! Besides, we could have done a better job machining your transmission parts." His mouth was curled into a challenging half-smile.

Frank was not in the mood for a race today, only a ride. He thought he had had enough excitement for the week. The three took off into the countryside, out past The Bull's Run, they sped. However, not through The Run and toward the mountain into the wasteland of 'bandits' and lawlessness, but past The Bull's Run on the highway and then the country roads that ran through farm country where people waved from porches and tractors and cows lowed in their mellow surprise at the speeding riders. The machines whistled along comfortably as the road provided its therapy and the wind its balm to the souls of the men who sat atop the metal horses. Stress and frustration were miles behind in stone and noise, trapped in its cages of worry and strife.

Braegan couldn't handle the restful pace for long, however, and from time to time would race far ahead, standing the cycle on its rear wheel. He was fidgety as they ate lunch at a tiny country cafe. "Hey, um, never mind. Well, when are you going to let me ride the new rocket?" He asked of Frank. Frank pursed his lips in false consideration and looked toward the ceiling as though doing some figuring. Both men were already starting to smirk, knowing what was coming.

"Well, I think," Frank began slowly, "probably not ever, never (he waited a moment more), ever, never, not once, ever. Ha ha!" The men shared his laugh, and Joshua slowly clapped his hands together at the predictable joke.

Braegan wouldn't leave it totally alone, though, and prodded Frank. "Well, how do we know it will run faster than 45mph? So far, that's all we've done. I have an antique, pre-war scooter that runs on gasoline that will do that!" He continued as he laughed, "it sounds like an angry bee, but it'll do 45, same as what you have today!"

Frank's face was dark as he asked in hushed tones, "Where do you get fuel? The petrol, rather … uh, gasoline? How did you find someplace that supplies that?" He tried to look nonchalant, but the look was dying, and his face was increasingly grim.

Braegan was taken aback. Frank could be very intense, even intimidating, when he turned serious. Frank was a big man and strong. He stood over six feet tall and was so broad in his shoulders that he filled up the doors of houses when he stood in them. In fact, it was not uncommon in some of the older houses in The Run, which had been equipped with much smaller than the modern standard-sized doors, twenty-eight inches or even smaller on those old homes, for Frank to have to turn sideways to go through them, particularly if carrying tools. Braegan hesitated slightly before answering, surprised at the sudden shift in the tone of the conversation. Frank's hands gripped the tablecloth tighter than he intended. "I, I just went to the vintage cycle shop, Frank. They have small cans of gasohol or gasoline just for pre-war scooters and bikes. It's ridiculously expensive, but they are fun to buzz around on every now and again." As he talked and Frank's face relaxed, Braegan kept talking as though the lowering tension was causing his mouth to bubble over like a boiling pot. "I have a membership in a classic and antique cycle and collectible club. We all ride into the Centre about once a month and just look at and enjoy the old bikes and scooters. There are a couple of old cars from the 1930s and 1940s …"

Frank interrupted, "But no modern petrols?"

"No, Frank, it's all antiques. All low power, oil leaking, smelly, antique gassers. They're fun and really retro chic. I like to wear my retro clothes when I go, and so does my girlfriend. We get a lot of looks and compliments on our outfits. You ought to see her in her polka-dotted …" Braegan could see Frank's brow lowering again as he had no interest in Braegan's attire or his girlfriend, "but nothing modern or powerful enough to even compete with a modern transport of any kind. Why, Frank? Something bothering you about the old petrol stuff? You didn't get another antiquated diesel generator brought in from Army surplus, did you?" Braegan tried to make a joke of it but looked awkward and uncomfortable.

Frank sighed and then smiled the half-smile he carried with him most of the time. He looked at Braegan and Joshua and began, "I had a dream, and when I woke up and went to check, it was happening …" This was going to be a long story. He was glad the diner had good coffee.

In the farthest corner of the café, Frank retold his story to the amazed audience of his two best friends. He felt relaxed enough to think he could tell the story without all the emotion. As he talked of the truck and the bomb design and all the details, it came rushing back. He was an animated storyteller anyway, and now, with the emotions charging out of him, he was using expression and had gestures. His friends and he laughed at his silly moments and stared aghast at the intense moments. When Frank had finished and looked around, the diners near them had caught bits and pieces of the story and were waiting to comment or hear more; three of the other people dining and one of the people working had eyes glued on him. He wasn't sure exactly what to do in response to the attention but was glad he had left Meriwether's name out of the story, calling him simply "a friend of mine." So, he continued and told tales about other things that had happened that were more fun and sillier. "It's not the first time I had a petrol nearly run me over," he started.

Josh chimed in, "That's right! Back when Gramps had the shop over past the scrag before you bought that property, you and I were working on something in the driveway and about got squashed!"

Frank laughed; any memory of his grandpa was welcome and warm, even if the old man had been coarse as sandpaper. "We were working on my old Federal Truck street rod. It was a good old hotrod, but we converted it to steam, and we're lucky we didn't blow ourselves up! B, why weren't you there?" Frank asked.

"I didn't ever work on your steam stuff, Frank. You always wanted to turn up the boiler pressure or do some crazy stuff to show off for your grandpa's hotrod buddies. I'm not good enough of a mech to be doing all that! Besides, you came and got me later. Josh still had grease on his pants from that truck," Braegan replied.

Frank continued the story. "That's funny you said that because that was exactly what we were doing. I discovered that I could increase the safety delay on the core retraction and get another fifty pounds of pressure in the lines. We were both up under the thing out there in the gravel, steam spraying us in the face, and we heard this noise."

Josh was already laughing quietly to himself, waiting for the story to go on. He could tell it, but Frank was fun to watch when he felt he had an audience like this. He didn't usually like being the center of attention, but when he was telling a story, it was a different story altogether. "It was off in the brush, '*chack, chackchack, chackchack,*' and I didn't have any clue what it was." Josh interjected, "We ignored it for forever, but ..."

"But then it got closer," Frank went on. "And now, we're up under the truck covered in thick grease and holding the secondary cooler up in this thing at a weird angle ..."

Braegan interrupted: "And why was it at a weird angle, Frank?"

Frank laughed a little. "I had to put it in at a weird angle to make it fit without sticking through the floor and still allow me to make that extra pressure."

Braegan was nodding, "So, again, you had to do something to it to make it faster, and that made it hard to work on."

Frank smiled, "Well, yeah ... if it can go faster and you don't make it, that's a lack of commitment and poor character!"

The diners all laughed. "Was it a prairie chicken?" One of the patrons, an elderly man with kind eyes and a stained beard, asked.

"No, but we thought it was," Frank answered.

"So, we're under there working, and this *'chack, chackchack'* noise is coming from the brush and coming closer to the edge of the driveway. Josh and I both think it's a prairie chicken, and we aren't concerned about it at all. It gets up even with us, still in the brush, still not making any noise like it's angry until it gets right by my feet."

Josh butted in again, "We're in the driveway, so Frank had pulled all the way over to one side. I still don't know why we didn't pull up beside the shop."

Braegan spoke up, "Because Gramps had told all of us that he would throw his spittoon on us if we made an oily mess by his door again, like the last dozen times. He'd do it, too! Then he'd have had a big ol' laugh at the three stinky boys! He'd done it once before!"

"That's just because you walked by while he was sleeping in his rocking chair and put a lizard on his chest—and you knew he didn't like lizards," Frank said.

Frank continued his tale, "So, my feet are only just a foot or two from the grass when out pops a roadrunner, you know, the long-beaked bird that the coyote is always trying to catch?" Everyone was listening, intently smiling or laughing. Roadrunners are not aggressive toward humans, but Frank's storytelling involved them all.

"Yeah, yeah, they stab their food!" said one of the patrons.

Another spoke up, "Oh, I haven't seen one in forever!"

Braegan said, "Well, they are probably all hiding in a cave telling stories about the crazy people they took turns chasing!"

Everyone laughed, coffees were ordered, and the diner was warm and friendly in the way only those old diners with the vinyl booth seats, and chrome-edged tables could be.

"Probably right, Braegan. Miss, could I get a warm-up on this coffee, please?" Frank continued, "This roadrunner pops out of the brush, making this odd clucking noise. I can tell by the way it's moving that it's hunting. Then it latched onto me with its little beady eyes." Frank held two fingers up, pointing at his eyes, and the room got quiet as Frank's voice became hushed. "I'm still working away at the boiler, but I can see this really strange look on Josh's face." Josh is making a silly, surprised, fearful look to accentuate the detail. "I turn my head and look, and here it comes! It dashes out of the grass, and *BAM*, hammers my shoe right on my ankle, poked through, and brought blood! Then it backed up and took another look as if it was aiming again! Well, I had no idea what was going on! I just knew that something had just driven a nail into the round bone on my ankle, and I wasn't going to lay there for more! That seemed like a downright unfriendly thing to do, and I was not in favor of another round!"

The diner was clapping and laughing. Braegan was laughing hard, smiling wide, and snorted a little through his nose, garnering more laughter.

"So, Josh is backing out, and I am trying to push past him to get out from under the truck on the side he is on, opposite where I was. The roadrunner is hammering away at my boot sole, the cooler is falling on us, and I'm trying to hold it up and slide under … it's mayhem, screaming, and banging. What we didn't know is that one of the pranksters who got work done at Gramps had just gone into the shop and told him, 'Those boys are about to light themselves on fire out there!' Gramps looked out the door, saw all that steam, and heard all the banging and screaming. Well, of course, he thought the gentleman wasn't joking but that he had reported an emergency! So, Gramps fired up his shop truck to come out and help. It was a long driveway. Back then, out between Truitt and The Run, lots of the shops and businesses had a very long driveway so you could put signs and flowers and such. Well, his driveway went so far as to make a huge U-shaped curve in the middle to make it even longer driving."

Josh spoke up now: He loved the history of the city, so he knew why or thought he did. "That was so you could see all the flowers and plants. That shop was built just after the war, and the more garden you had, the more it was seen as though you celebrated the victory. You didn't need veggies from anyone, and the flowers just felt happy."

Frank nodded as he continued, "Well, that was lost on Grandpa; he had put gravel in them all." Several people laughed again. "What he didn't remember, in his excitement, was that the years of wear had made the drive lower than the ground in the middle of the U. We finally get out from under the truck, and this poor bird has run around the end of the truck. We think it's after us—which it isn't. We're kids and don't know any better. It runs around and looks at us. We take off, running to the front of the truck. It did, too, on the other side. Totally like a cartoon chase! We meet at the front of the truck, and Josh screams like a little girl. It was hysterical!"

"I did not!" Josh protested. "I just … well, I thought this gigantic bird was going to stab us to death."

Braegan asserted, "They are about a foot tall at most."

Frank continued, "It was only then that I saw that a little frog of some sort had jumped onto my boot and crawled up into the cuff of my overalls. It must have been what the roadrunner had been hunting. As I lay under the truck trying to figure out what to do next, I wasn't moving my leg, and the frog just must've figured that was a safe place to be. After all the commotion, I bent over and picked that little frog out of my pant leg about the time that Grandpa's old 1940s model pickup hit the uphill side of the U and went airborne for about three forward feet. I shouted a bad word, scrambled to stand up, lost balance, and fell flat backwards!"

The laughter roared as Frank took a drink of coffee. Josh was sipping his tea and laughing into it. "I ran," Josh said. "I just figured if Frank was going to get hit by his grandpa, I didn't need to make two people run over."

Frank was laughing. "I struggled to my feet and could see it was Grandpa trying to get his truck under control as it hit the ground and started swerving back and forth, throwing gravel and dirt and rocks and clumps of grass. So, I tossed the frog into the cab of my own truck and dove over the side into the bed. I have no idea why I saved the frog. I guess I felt like he had already been through enough. Grandpa skidded to a stop even with my street-rod pickup and came out of it cursing and waving his hands, kicking at the gravel. When he could finally form words," Frank paused and chuckled once, "well, words you can repeat in public" (more laughter and a sip of coffee), "all he could say was, 'Why ain't you two on fire!' Red-faced and spitting tobacco juice all over the place, he drove back to the shop, and we could hear him cussing the whole way."

The laughter was loud and continuous for a good while, and several other patrons began to share stories as the three friends smiled and listened. They had shared their time, and it was time to listen to these folks. Some of the stories were obviously made up to best someone else's. The old-timers, though, had just seen and been through a lot, and the three friends paid them the most attention. Braegan was the first to speak again. After the thunderous laughter and loud storytelling had subsided, he said to Frank, "Frank, there is no possible way that big truck was running on the gasoline pints I buy for the scooter. They each cost what our meals here will cost, and that truck probably burned a pint just throwing the gravel in your driveway. I don't know what to say about any of the rest of it. I've never seen a petrol-powered vehicle with that much power, that loud, that big, or any of what you said." He shrugged his shoulders in helpless disquiet.

"I have," stated a gruff voice from nearby in the room. "I have seen a diesel engine with that much power. Before the nuclear reactors were used for steam in boats, those boats were all petrol, so were a lot of the really large industrial trucks," the old man related.

Frank nodded but was uncomfortable inviting the old man into this conversation. "Well," Frank began, "we had better head back if we're going to get back before it's too dark."

On the ride home, Braegan and Joshua goaded Frank until there was a race on the main highway. The wind roared past the three friends like a hurricane as the performance bikes screamed past the country scenery. Frank won easily and was waiting at the shop doors when they arrived. The radial motors on their bikes spluttered and bubbled as they pulled in and were silenced as they parked. "You know, Frank, if there had been any really sharp corners ..." Braegan started.

Frank immediately started to laugh, "Yes, I know, but you let me pick the spot, and I picked a straight one!" There was small talk and drinks, with no more talk of petrol or dreams. The smell of grease and engine polish filled the air when a breeze blew through the open windows. Frank was glad the topic was left alone. He felt like everything was going to work itself out now that Meriwether had taken the information to the people in charge.

"Do you remember the time you put bubble bath into the water tank on my dad's old station wagon?" Braegan laughed as the storytelling restarted.

Frank was laughing hard at the memory, "I had no idea it would dissolve the seals! The look on his face when he saw the bubbles floating in the air behind the car was priceless! Until it stopped running, that is."

"I remember," started Joshua, "when you replaced the nozzle tip on my old car in high school. Man, that made it faster, but it blew water everywhere!"

The laughter ran late into the night. It was good to relax. Maybe life would be normal now, and this week would only be one of those aberrant memories in otherwise normal life. "See ya later, old fart!" Joshua laughed as he slid his black helmet on to leave.

Braegan was just laughing as he waved and put his own helmet on. "Let me know when you want someone who can ride to show you what that monster cycle of yours can do," he said through his raised face shield. As they sped away into the night, Braegan rode a wheelie for a long time, and Frank shook his head at the daredevil. He was thankful for friends, and life seemed good.

Chapter 8

Of Mist and Pressure

Life seemingly did return to normal. Frank let the explosion sink into the back of his mind and waited on Meriwether to bring it up when they spoke. Meriwether, however, never brought it up. Meriwether was one of a stream of Frank's closer acquaintances that, along with those truly close friends of Frank's, came by to drink coffee and "hold down the sofa" in the shop. It was a comfortable hang-out spot for the men—and the two or three women who came by to chat. Frank had hung vintage signs advertising everything from new autos and lubricants to sodas and coffees. The sofa was comfortable, and the two rocking chairs that flanked it on either side were also very comfortable chairs Frank had hand-made using old sticks and barrel staves. There was a homemade light fixture made from the rear axle housing of an antique car and an antiquated old radio and record player that was usually playing new and energetic music much too new for the player but that Frank loved.

Business had picked up, but Meriwether had quietly, over the course of only a few months, stopped his visits. Frank hadn't really noticed. With summer being the busiest time for businesses and politics in Eagle's Roost, it was to be expected. Still, it would be nice, Frank thought, to have some confirmation that someone took him seriously and didn't just pat his head as an old-timey tech mech. The industrial complexes near the Centre had modernized their units, and the outlying business had been abandoned in the most recent modernization rezoning planning, forcing Frank to increasingly rely on walk-in business—people with cars or portable devices that needed repair. It was feast or famine for a long while, but now it finally seemed to be transforming into a busy and profitable venture. Frank's schedule was as packed as he liked it, maybe a little more. Monday, Joel Walters' Zephyr scooter needs to be inspected and certified. Tuesday, Bologna World's delivery truck needs the entire power train adjusted and parts replaced. Wednesday, clean the storage tank and replace the whole core unit on Walt Haltherstone's generator. Frank was happy doing what he loved and making a solid living.

It was another day of same old same old, "Turning wrenches and burning metal," he was known to say when Melody Maine walked in and eased down onto a cloth she had brought along and placed on the sofa. She was dressed in expensive casual wear. He was not at all offended that she tried to keep the shop dust off her clothing. It would hardly look professional to be seen in her political circles with the outline of buttocks in dust on her backside.

"Well!" Frank began in surprise, "This is a surprise! You haven't been by for months! Can I get the lady a drink?"

Melody sparkled her smile across the room like a lighthouse, "No, thank you, 'Steam King.' Did you know that's what some of the folks in The Run call you? Others call you 'Preacher' because you go around doing good and talking about how people 'oughta be.'"

Frank laughed loudly and shook his head. "I don't know why they'd do that. I just fixed a couple of units there is all. I have a job to do same as anyone else."

"Of course," Melody continued, "I can't stay long, but I wanted to talk to you about the explosion and see what you thought."

Frank stopped working momentarily and sat on his mechanic's creeper, looking at his old friend, now turned wealthy celebrity/beauty icon and politician. "Go on, Mel. I don't know what to tell you, except it's a tragedy."

Melody nodded her head thoughtfully, "Don't you believe that removing the generators that were used for this would help make it less likely to happen again?"

Frank was already shaking his head before she finished speaking. "No, Mel," he started, "I found some information on how it's done, and it's actually a technical process …"

Braegan, with his usual strut, walked through the door and stared in surprise at Melody. "Wow, Frank, I didn't know you were hob-knobbing with the upper crust nowadays."

Melody retorted, "He has to occasionally see the upper crust to recognize that he is not the bottom of the barrel."

With the conversation interrupted Frank returned to work. Melody and Braegan began to joke back and forth as Frank interjected a comment here and there. The conversation was soon interrupted again, however, by the television running in the background.

"This just in," said the television reporter," Police have made a discovery in the Eagle's Roost Stadium bombing." Frank's attention was immediately on the view screen with an outstretched wrench toward the work he had been doing. The Police Chief was stepping up to the very plain, black podium that had been dragged out of the station for the press conference. He cleared his throat and looked at some papers and, with a matter-of-fact, stern expression, began to deliver his newest findings: "We have determined that the bombing was not done by an average electron radiance generator such as is commonly called a 'Teslator.' Such generators are typically very stable and to keep them operational must be maintained in such a manner that precludes such malfunctioning."

Frank breathed a barely audible sigh of relief. "However, new evidence given to our investigators this week has shown that through intentional modification, virtually any electron radiance generator may be, with minimal skill and readily available plans …" With this, he held up a picture with plans of an explosive device. The picture was the same as in Frank's old magazine that he'd given Meri! Frank stared in shock and horror as the Chief continued. "…create a burst of electrical radiation that effectively rips hydrogen atoms from the surrounding air and then ignites them. This is the same type of device used to flash bomb the Eagle's Roost Stadium. We are continuing to work on finding where this particular reactor came from and where it was modified. We believe this to be the work of domestic terrorists who have been actively resisting the new regulations on home generation and centralization of power supply."

Frank was gobsmacked. Speechless, he stood dumbfounded as Melody Maine and Braegan uttered a couple of words to try to continue the conversation they had been having, then faded to silence when they looked at Frank. "Frank, Frank! Hey! Are you OK?" Braegan called,

"You're white as a sheet, dear!" Melody added.

Frank turned to face his friends, his head shaking in disbelief and growing angry. Meriwether had taken the information from the magazine and tried to get the story corrected in the media, and they had twisted it around to defame all those wanting to keep the energy generation cooperative bill from passing, including Frank himself! "Yeah," Frank said barely above a whisper. "I'm OK. Mel, did you know about any of this?"

Melody looked somber and replied, "Frank, our differences in policy never have set us at odds. It would be irresponsible to call any group of people terrorists over the news, anyway. Those are my voters, after all." It took a moment, but Frank shook it off for now. He returned to work, and Braegan and Melody returned to their conversation, leaving Frank out of it since he was slid under a heavy-duty pickup.

The rest of the day, Frank seemed to be in a haze. Melody left, Braegan left, Josh called and said something about bowling later in the week, a couple of new appointments called, and Frank went from disbelief to anger and then frustration and then back as he cycled through the feelings of helplessness and inability to comprehend why the case was being made against people who only wanted to be able to light and power their own lives inexpensively. Frank had been outspoken in the local communities and to reporters about the "Electrical Fairness Act" being anything but fair and instead being a power grab by the government. He had stated how it would quickly lead to the confiscation of Teslators, steam power in vehicles, and any hot air, plasma producing cores. According to many in the groups that dispute the bill, the whole reason behind the move is to remove the reactors from people to make them totally dependent on, and defenseless against, the government. At first, the media reaction was to make jokes about tinfoil hat-wearing conspiracy theorists. However, as the actions of government officials began to support the "conspiracy theorists," the media became more and more aggressive about labeling those not in favor of the bill with horrible names and labels. Now, the Chief of Police for Eagle's Roost and Raptor County's second-in-command officer had labeled them terrorists. There had never been an attack of any kind from them. The few violent acts that had taken place were blamed on them and quickly proven to be others, often supporters of the bill, and yet the stigma remained. Frank didn't believe the government was going to begin confiscation. He simply saw it as a dangerous precedent that could lead to more draconian measures in the future.

It was beginning to get dark a little earlier, and Frank worked late that afternoon. The sun had set, and the dim twilight was fading when he locked the shop doors and headed home in his service truck. The copper grill that allowed air to cool the core under the hood was tarnished a bright green and seemed to almost glow with the failing light falling on it as he turned out of the drive and onto the road. There were never cars out this time of night, too close to the Run. Tonight, however, Frank noticed the reflection of headlights and chrome parked on the roadside. Kids making out, he thought. The short drive home was uneventful, as always, but Frank felt uneasy, almost paranoid. Up the steps into the house with an eye over his shoulder, he again saw the reflection of chrome bumpers and headlight rings in the light. This time, the light came streaming from his own door. No doubt about it; someone had followed him home, but why?

Frank ate dinner and sat briefly in the den before bed, keeping an eye out the slightly parted curtains. When he checked the lock on the door before he went to bed and looked out, the reflections were gone. Whoever it had been apparently was not interested in him after all. Drug dealers or muggers, slum lords, etc., from The Bull Run, had followed him home in the past, thinking he was someone else. Frank dismissively thought that must be what it was this time. His Gramps built Frank's house, and since it had been near The Run for so long, most people knew whose it was. There were those, however, who got the addresses wrong, but there had never been any real trouble that he knew about.

Out on the lawn, the copper and steel tree sculpture his Grandpa had started and finished, twinkled in the starlight. It had a little sculpture at its base that seemed like it should have been larger. The whole thing, though, with the brown scale of surface rust on the steel and the green oxidation on the copper, the small rods that made up the limbs allowing the limbs to sway slightly in a moderate breeze, seemed alive. Frank had always loved the little thing. It only stood about head high to him and was modeled after some sort of scrub tree that made berries. He didn't know what kind. It was one of the only 'art' pieces his grandpa had ever had an interest in.

Frank wondered when he looked at it why his grandpa had built it. He wondered if his parents had been particularly artistic or crankier and more practical like his gramps. He certainly didn't share the same personality, though certain traits, like telling jokes and being stubborn, persisted. He could only barely remember his mother. She was a blonde woman and beautiful to her little boy anyway. His dad, he remembered a little more because he looked identical to him. The few pictures that were around were of Frank's dad at about the age Frank was now. The two were nearly indistinguishable.

Grandpa would never talk about what happened. He knew that his parents had worked in the City Centre and that something had happened one day, some sort of accident, and they had both died. He didn't know what they did for work, where they worked, what the accident was, how they died, or anything more than just that it happened. Grandpa and Grandma had raised little Franklin Greene until Grandma died of heart failure. When Frank was fourteen years of age, Gramps and he were all that either one had beyond friendships.

It was not quite light when Frank woke up. The alarm had not gone off, and he had no reason to wake up early. He woke up and stared at the ceiling in mild irritation. "Well," he said in the grumbling low morning voice, "I guess I will go to work early since I am going to be awake." Dressed and out the door in under an hour, he stopped at his mailbox. It was a sturdy design that he had welded from old boiler parts, and, in accordance with his craftsmanship, it closed and locked effortlessly and stayed that way. It had a slot at the top-front for the mail, and he opened it to remove the mail. This morning, though, it stood gaping open. There had been no mail there the night before, and there was none there now. He stared curiously at it and realized his "visitors" must have gone through it looking for money or personal information. He was irritated at the invasion of his privacy but shook his head, closed the box, and started the drive to work.

He had no radio in the truck, and there was no noise but the hum of the heater fan and the wind blowing in the partly opened window, allowing the fresh air to blow in. It was a busy day ahead. There was already a sports car, an autocycle, and another delivery truck parked in the drive at the shop waiting for his attention. The low steaming sound of the boiler shutting off ,the valves holding back the water, and the pressure as the service truck slowed was all he heard on the pavement. Then he pulled into the shop, and the gravel driveway crunched under the tires. The door was open again. He walked in cautiously and looked around. Again, no one was there. This time, however, no one was outside either. It didn't take long to find what was missing. A core outer shield was gone. A core is shielded in several layers of varying materials to eliminate any potential radiation reaching the serviceman or the owner. The outermost shield was nothing more than a cover that blocked a little microwave radiation and looked prettier. Still, the piece was stolen, so Frank called the cops.

The police investigators arrived just before noon. There was an older, tall, and heavyset man with a larger second chin than his first. He had a greasy bald spot with a poorly executed comb-over sticking off the left side of his head. The other detective was much younger and was well-dressed and keen-eyed. "Mr. Greene?" Said the younger man.

"Yes sir, the spot on the shelf is over there," Frank said, pointing to where the part had sat for weeks. "I've been careful not to touch anything around it or the inside of the door handle in case you want to pull fingerprints or whatever you need to do."

"Thank you, Mr. Greene," said the older man. "I have a few questions to ask you first, though, if you don't mind."

"Of course," replied Frank, continuing his work.

"Do you keep a lot of nuclear items in stock?"

Frank looked at the detective, slightly confused, "No."

"How many nuclear cores or core parts, including shields, do you suppose you do have?"

"I would have to get my inventory list to be certain," Frank replied, now staring with mild irritation at the older detective.

"So, you really don't know how many radioactive parts, or parts meant to shield from exposure, you have on hand," the man continued.

"Not off the top of my head. I keep a list in …" Frank began to reply before being cut off.

"And what sort of lock mechanisms do you have on the doors and windows of this shop and the back warehouse?"

"Look," Frank protested, "you saw the locks when you came in. You can see that the warehouse is all thick concrete block, and the windows are barred. Can you tell me what exactly these questions will do to help you find the thief?"

"If we can establish the amount of effort the robber had to employ, then we can narrow it from a random break-in to a career criminal thief or drug addict or whatever it may be," replied the younger detective, speaking for the first time since the questioning had begun. He immediately continued the questioning in the place of the older man. Although he was much friendlier, Frank couldn't help but feel that the questions were still directed to try to get him to admit to something he had neither done himself nor knew of anyone doing. "Franklin, can I call you by your first name? Thanks. You have some impressive machines here that you work on! Did you build that bike?"

"Yes."

"Wow, hey, Don, look at that thing! So, Franklin, do you ride or drive any of these customized vehicles around? I bet you get a lot of looks on it!"

"Yes, I actually have not had it finished for long, but yes," Frank answered cautiously.

"Do you think, just for the sake of argument, that someone may have seen the stuff you build and came looking for parts since you obviously have access to them?" the younger detective probed. Don, as Frank surmised was his name, was looking over the newest custom bike of Frank's as well as a couple of older creations, such as a light glider that used a heated plasma ducted engine. The glider was in the back because it would burn your legs if you didn't wear thermal-insulating pants. "Yeah," interjected Don, "Maybe you were out showing off your pretty little toys, and some jerk just thought he'd help himself to your goodies."

Frank really did not like Don so far.

"I'm sorry," said the younger of the two, "my name is Jeremiah Loving. It's good to meet you, Frank." He reached out to shake Frank's hand, and Frank did so dutifully.

"Look at all these manuals and magazines, Luv," said Don. "Yeah, I bet you could build a spaceship from stuff in here with the know-how."

Detective Loving laughed. "Frank, we'll look around The Run and Truitt to see if anyone knows anything. You'll be hearing back from us soon, I imagine," Officer Loving said, closing his notepad and snapping a few pictures of the warehouse and the books.

"Yeah, been a pleasure," said Don.

With that, both the detectives turned toward the door and walked straight out. Don grabbed a business card on the way, turned to wink at Frank, and mimed tipping a hat that wasn't there.

It was now about 1:30, and Josh pulled in on his bike as the detectives left. "What's going on?" queried Josh.

Frank looked at him perplexed, "I really don't know. I had a part stolen, and those were the detectives sent to check it out. But, well, I don't know what just happened, really."

"You, sir, have had a rough month! Hop in that old car or that bike, and let's go!" Josh exclaimed. "I hear there is a place outside the limits with a bowling alley and some of the best sushi you'll ever eat!"

Frank answered with a chuckle, "I can't just yet. Besides, you mean Radio Nation, right? We've been there before, and they don't serve sushi! Let me change the soluble lube in this guy's truck, and then I'll meet you."

"See ya!" yelled Josh as he went out the door and joked, "Be there by six or else!"

Frank finished up for the day and changed at the shop. Tonight, he locked even the bolts and slides he normally left alone. They groaned and struggled from disuse, but the door was secure when it was done. He barely made it by six that evening because he had made an extra stop. He had gone home and taken some clothes to the shop. "I think it's time I use the old upstairs apartment," he mumbled to himself as he contemplated the security of his home versus his shop.

102

Chapter 9

A Good Hard Strike Sets Things Aright

Josh had two lanes reserved, and all the old crew was there. Braegan Reynolds, Melody Maine, Akira Logan, Penelope (Penny) Hammonds, the steel mill worker, Archibald (Archie) Kilcarney, the car salesman, John Smith (who always hated how boring his name was), Peter Smith (no relation to John), and Emmett McDonell all sat around the pit lacing up shoes, selecting bowling balls, and bowling the first few frames. Emmett and Melody both had to try not to be seen if they wanted any privacy. The difference between them was that Emmett often wanted privacy, and Melody seldom did. Emmett had inherited a great deal of money and assets when his uncle died and willed him everything since he was the only relative who would rub his feet. Emmett had then wisely invested and managed that inheritance into one of the largest fortunes in the nation. He and Melody had become local celebrities and, indeed, national players in the political world.

Frank walked in, and his smile spread wide as he saw so many of his friends. In fact, this was nearly everyone he would truly call a friend. Franklin Greene had always felt that an acquaintance could be someone fun to hang out with and with whom you had a lot in common, but a friend was someone with whom you shared your life, someone you could count on when you needed them, regardless of what they were doing or what it would take to help. These were those people. Once, Akira borrowed a small plane and flew to Vegas with Frank, Melody, and Josh to stop Archie from marrying a woman Melody had discovered was a con artist with two other families. Another time, Archie had given John a car when John was unemployed. Frank helped them all with repairs. Emmett had held up legal documents at the judge's offices until fines were paid. The list went on and on of ways they had tried to help each other. They shared not only the tough times but the good times. Tonight looked to be another of the great memories they shared.

Akira had just picked up the spare on her first frame when Frank walked in. Josh had just guttered in the next lane. Frank walked into the laughter and camaraderie like a man walking into a refreshing summer rain. He bathed in it, feeling the stress and fear wash off his shoulders and ease the pinch in his brow.

Akira came up and slapped him firmly on his backside, "Hey, boy! What have you been up to?" Uncharacteristically outgoing as she was and uncharacteristically drinking booze, Akira's wicked smile teased, and her eyes flashed with a not-very-innocent flare as she slid an arm around him in a sincere and tight hug that pulled his waist into hers. Frank's throat tightened as he blushed at her attention. Archie walked up to shake his hand, felt the awkwardness, and began to walk away.

Frank called out to him, "Hey, Archie! Gosh, I haven't seen you in months!" Archie swung back around and clasped his hand, Akira still holding him tightly. "I was thinking of you at the dealership. We have a few old …"

"No work, Archie!" Josh yelled from the snack bar with an irritated look. "You can call his office on Monday for that."

Archie smiled apologetically and nodded at Frank.

"Archie! Your turn, man!" yelled John.

As Archie walked up to bowl, Frank eased over to his chair with Akira following him closely, settled into a chair, and began putting on the bowling shoes Akira had gotten for him. It was funny because it was not his normal shoe size, and he always forgot, but she always remembered. She had also ordered a soft drink and a cheesy soft pretzel for him. Akira always took care of him when they were out.

Melody sat across from Frank in the neighboring lane. She smiled at him as she sipped her soft drink with a straw. She had managed to slip away from the paparazzi tonight. She wore casual clothes, for once. They were still designer brands, of course. Melody had to be concerned with her appearance whenever she went out. She had used her looks to establish her name recognition for political office. This was not to say that she was just a pretty face. Anyone making that assumption soon discovered they had underestimated a keenly cunning official. She knew that a relatively small-town girl had little chance of being noticed or earning the kind of finances it took to get into the political game. She also knew that she wanted in the political game. It had been her goal from her youngest memories. She was calculating, and when she was successful in some youth beauty pageants, she began to work every angle she could to get into modeling, then acting, then politics.

As a result, the paparazzi were sneaking pictures of her, and it was important that she looked the role she was playing. Melody was blonde-haired, tall, and classically beautiful. Her mother was French. Her father was pure blonde-haired and blue-eyed European. Melody hit the genetic lottery, getting the best of all the genes in her background. Whenever she entered a room, the conversation would quiet, and people stared. She had always had a presence about her, a certain gravity. Out of the band of thirty-somethings, she was the one who had always had a direction, always had a plan. None of the group of friends knew for sure what her title was, but she had a lot of pull in the goings-on in the state. As she smiled at him and raised her left eyebrow, it was odd to Frank that she and Akira had always been rivals. He thought they had nothing in common besides their equally strong and stubborn personalities.

Akira worked for everything and worked hard. She had little respect for Melody's achievements as Mel always played politics and worked for popularity. Akira hated popularity games and envied Melody's childhood with a stable home and doting parents with plenty of money. Akira's father was a first-generation Japanese immigrant, and even though her name was typically a boy's name in Japan, her father loved Indian culture—and in India, it meant something about strength. She never knew what, exactly. Her mother had died in childbirth, and her father raised her to five years old. She was adopted by the Logan family when her father became addicted to drugs and overdosed, leaving her in an abandoned house in Truitt for weeks. Akira exhibited her quiet strength as she grew up with a family of different backgrounds and busy professional lives. She studied hard and played sports. She excelled at everything she did. The Logans were preoccupied parents. They cared about Akira but had little time for her. Joshua dated her in high school, but they had split and decided to remain just friends. He said she was too demanding; she said he would need a map and schematics to get a slice of bread from the bag.

Akira was attractive, her physique a counterpoint of Melody. Akira was muscular with dark-hued skin and quite curvaceous, while fit. She dressed modestly, almost prudishly, and practically. Akira was often embarrassed by the looks of boys that Melody had reveled in during school. Melody had flaunted and used her looks. Akira worked and worked hard. She had little respect for Melody's achievements as Mel always played the popularity game, and many things were given to her because she was well-known everywhere she went.

Akira had been shy and bashful. Over a decade in military uniforms had made her dress style business tactical or sweats and t-shirt comfy. Tonight, though, she had dressed sporty and stylish in form-fitting, stretchy clothes that showed her shape. She was thinking of Frank all day, and it showed. She wanted to get his attention. Tonight, she would tell him that he was always on her mind, that she hated being gone because it was away from him, that she wanted nothing more than to hear his voice. Akira was not a person comfortable with sharing her emotions in public. She had become so anxious that she had begun to drink a little alcohol while waiting and was acting silly in a way that few ever saw. She had felt like this for Frank since they were children on the school swing set, and even if it took some liquid courage to make her act foolish enough to do so, she was going to tell him all about it.

Frank got a bowling ball from the rack and stepped up to the line. With a nice approach and a swing of the arm, the ball sailed down the lane a fraction of an inch from the wood until halfway down the lane, where it touched down smoothly and began to spin. *BOOM.* It crashed into the headpin just slightly 'Brooklyn,' and the pins scattered into what looked like would be a 7-10 split before the wildly flying pins knocked down the two outliers.

"Strike!" yelled John and Braegan with their arms up like fans watching a good field goal kick at a football game.

Frank laughed and walked back to the ball return. Melody clapped appreciatively and leaned in as he passed to say, "Sometimes, a good hard strike is enough to set everything right, isn't it?" Frank laughed again and returned to his seat, where Akira sat next to him and leaned toward him. She was joking, saying things like, "Do you remember the time we snuck out of our houses and sat in the park all night talking?" and "Do you remember those cookies that your Grandpa burned?" The group grew more raucous as the night went on, but it was all in good humor, and even the other patrons at the bowling alley enjoyed their laughter and jokes.

Akira, however, became quieter and quieter as she drank more and more to try to get the courage to tell Frank her feelings. She never needed anything to help her do what she wanted before. She was embarrassed. "Why can't I just say it?" she whispered to Braegan late in the evening. Braegan just smiled sympathetically and gave her a gentle hug.

"Hey, Frank! Good to see you in something other than work overalls!" was the most common greeting. It was difficult, at first, for the friends to have much of a fun evening. Between Frank's customers, Josh and Braegan's coworkers at the lathe works (the largest employer outside the Centre), the various car customers of

Archie's, and all the other connections they had both joint and individually—not to count the endless stream of phone calls to Melody's cell—it was not exactly an intimate get together until well after dark. The pins were far safer than the snack bar as the balls often bounced down the gutters instead of down the lanes, but the snack bar got repeated visits.

Finally, people began to clear out, and the phone calls slowed and then stopped. John walked over to the jukebox and pumped in more quarters than any one man should have at once. He turned around, raised his arms, and announced, "It's jukebox sing-along time, finally! Hahaha!" The music started playing oldies and classics and even some of the more modern hits. They all sang along with varying degrees of skill. Braegan came to Frank just before closing and said, "Hey, I paid for your game, shoes, and your tab at the bar. I don't have much time since the girlfriend always wants me at home, and the ex-wife is always looking to gouge me for money. I know what you did for my Great Aunt Greta. Thank you."

Frank looked surprised. "I didn't know you two were related! She's a great lady, B." They shared a warm handshake and returned to the group. The evening went too fast for everyone concerned, and although it was late, it was too soon when they were again embracing and shaking hands as they left. Melody and Penny stood at the door, rolling their eyes and waiting as Akira stood close to Frank, leaning back sharply so she could look up into his eyes, not saying anything but staring at him as though she had something needing to be said. Akira had drunk more than she should have, so Penny would be giving her a ride home.

Penny finally spoke up in her serious tone and told Akira, "Hey, some of us hafta clock inta work before the sun comes up. Get in the car 'Kira." Akira mumbled something incoherent and told Frank again that he couldn't wait as long before the next time they got together and then, half sitting and half falling, landed in Penny's supers port, four-door car.

Melody came up to Frank while waving at the other ladies and began to talk to Frank. "Are you good to drive?" she probed. Frank smiled and wrinkled his brow in confusion, "Of course. All I ever drink is coffee or water." She continued, "It is a long drive, and it's late. Did you have enough coffee to stay awake?" She was sidled up tight against him. Frank knew her well enough to know she was trying to get under Akira's skin.

"I think I'll be OK," he replied.

Melody backed away and raised an eyebrow. "Well, I guess you will be just fine then. Do you think that Akira will be?"

Frank shook his head bemused. "I don't know why you two have always been at odds. She'll be fine," he answered.

"Are you headed home or to your metal darlings at the shop?"

Frank laughed loudly and sincerely. "My darlings? Mel, you have been around television personalities too much! I will likely go to the shop and check on things first."

"Well, are they not your darlings? You spend so much time there, even when you are not being paid!" she said as she looked around the ground. "I left my purse inside. Be safe driving home, dear!" And with that, she bounced and swayed back inside, trying to be just as cute and girly as she could.

Joshua and Braegan were the last two to leave, minus Melody, who was returning for her purse, and they were now waving as they got on their bikes. "Someday, you'll have to speak up so 'Kira won't have to, Frank!" Braegan yelled to him. He knew what B meant, but he doubted the validity of his statement. Akira had had years to express interest in him. No, they were friends, that was all, no matter how much he hoped it would be otherwise.

It seemed to never be too cold or too hot or too far for Josh and Braegan to ride. They rolled the twist throttles open on their bikes, and the steam engines made a rhythm into the night. Frank stood for a moment, drinking in the sound of their autocycles as they sped off, and then he dined on the silence. He walked to his old car, an old green wagon that he had repaired but left 'rat.' The old man he bought it from had been so appreciative when Frank bought it. He shut the door, clicked the activation button, and waited for a moment or two until the boiler warm-up light went out. He waited until he saw Melody wave him off in his rearview, then headed down the road through Truitt.

The old bowling alley lay on the outskirts of the poor and despondent suburb. When the town planning commission had opted to fight urban sprawl by simply moving all the important financial and industrial zones, the bowling alley had, of course, suffered. However, though retro chic recalled romanticized visions of the so-called glory days of steam power in the Industrial Revolution, in this latest revival of retro chic put the hipsters in old-fashioned airship goggles and leather flying vests and helmets that put pocketknife-sized bayonets on the pistols of the wealthy as a matter of position, and that drove the price of decorative copper and brass though the ceiling, people loved anything vintage. The Truitt Lanes became Radio Nation Bowling Alley and Parlor. Radio Nation was in huge, bright pink neon lights while the remainder of the lengthy name was in a fancy manuscript under it. The sign appeared very vintage 1950s; it may have even been vintage salvage, and everyone had taken to calling it "The Nation" or "Radio Nation," leaving off everything else entirely. It was a popular hangout despite its neighborhood. The two roads that met in front of it were the only roads in Truitt that were nicely lit. Driving past all the old, unrestored buildings fostered a sense of nostalgia for the "good ol days" if you will. Even though most of the hipster patrons had not been born when any of those buildings were in use, they dreamed of simpler times in their own lives and spoke of times when "folks were honest" and "a handshake was all you needed." The resulting slow gentrification of some of the surrounding neighborhoods to the Radio Nation drove up property prices for a few blocks and made those homes stand out like a fancy gown at a mud wrestling match. The homes were organized into small clusters of either beautified Victorian or some version of the Golden Age of Radio. The steeply pitched roofs and witch's hat turrets with their "gingerbread" ornately decorated porches were often directly across the street from run-down modernist-style homes that lay abandoned or in disrepair. Frank looked at the half dozen homes nestled on the two well-lit streets and snickered inside at the foolishness of people trying to be trendy. He had always worn the old-fashioned clothes, liked the old-fashioned styles, and restored the antiquated.

Going home meant turning right halfway through Truitt while the shop meant straight ahead on one of the city's darkest and worst maintained roads. He didn't much want to, but like he told Melody, he needed to check the shop before going home. The potholes would force him to drive well below the high speeds he enjoyed whenever he drove. He second-guessed his decision for a moment and looked up the road to home. "Maybe I should just go home," he thought. "But what if the thieves come back?" And, with that, he pressed on to the shop.

Where Truitt more or less ended—rather, where all the buildings had been abandoned, there were no lights. The street lay empty and still, a graveyard of hopes and opportunity. This was the section of road Frank knew well. He drove past this segment any time he had any business in Truitt. He remembered it easily because it had a certain haunting eeriness to it that Frank secretly enjoyed. The building that always caught his attention was an abandoned dress shop. Its mannequins stared out of the windows with blank stares in their various stages of dress, apathy on their faces, except for one. It was a dark-haired female mannequin, and the slightly opened mouth, combined with the way the sun had bleached away the painted-on eyebrows, gave the pop-art statue a vaguely surprised expression. It was like it was constantly observing something terrible or continually feeling shocked at its own abandonment. Frank could not stand to look in the direction of that macabre figure's stare, yet he always found he could not help but look at her. He could feel it as he went by every time, and a shiver would try to expand and creep up and down his neck. Tonight, the moon fell through the gaps between the buildings perfectly. The beam looked like a lone streetlight washing the pavement in front of the dress shop, Angelica's Dresses and Hosiery, in a pale white. The moonlight shone on the sidewalk and up the window, illuminating only one mannequin. Frank found himself staring at her. Mouth agape, she stared back with some terrible secret.

This was also the roughest section of the road, and he had slowed down far below needed, even for the cobbles and potholes. It was then that he heard a noise growing louder very quickly. It roared nearer, and he couldn't tell its direction, only that it grew nearer and louder. Then, it paused. It was a petrol engine, like the one the thieves had been driving. He passed the dress shop's corner and eased up to an intersection with broken traffic signals. The lonely red "Stop all ways" sign squeaked sadly as the wind blew. Frank stopped and listened. The petrol-powered engine could be heard quietly lurking in the shadows. Somewhere near, the hungry, slavering sound of the idling engine warned Frank. It was hunting. The roaring, smelly beast of a truck was hunting him. He had seen it. He had seen too much, and now the beast wanted to devour him. The hollow buildings threw the sound, and he couldn't tell if the vehicle was behind him or in front—or maybe even a few streets away.

Frank set his jaw and hammered the accelerator of the old wagon to the floor. The old car was never a race car, but it lurched forward with a loud chirp of the rear tires. Almost as quickly as he had left the stop sign, the huge black shadow of the large petrol-powered truck roared at him, and all its lights exploded into a blinding white brilliance. He was completely disoriented. Even if Frank had known to react, there was no time. With an enormous crash, it hit his old wagon. The car lurched sideways, tossing him onto the passenger side and slamming his head against the bumper of the truck as it smashed through the window. A confetti spray of glass enveloped him, sparkling in the glare of the truck's headlights, fog lights, and off-road lights. He could smell the odor of hot coolant spraying through the broken window onto his face, which had a sickly sweet taste. He immediately remembered it as the taste of antifreeze from years back when he worked on gasoline and diesel engines for Gramps.

The big truck's engine roared angrily, powerfully, as it pushed the old car across both lanes of the abandoned road. Frank was turned around in the seat, conscious but dazed as the car jolted against the curb, and he could see the mannequin, still staring, shocked, at the horror she was witnessing. The car began to turn, to roll, and the tires' screeching echoed in his ears. The truck engine revved higher as it, too, was out of control, pushing his car over while climbing and falling sideways. Steam sprayed from the antique auto's boiler up into the cab of the truck, and the driver could be heard screaming as he was scalded. It was all within a moment of time, but the wreck seemed to take forever to Frank.

"Oh, God," he prayed silently, "please not now." He braced himself, hands on the car's roof and feet pushing on the floorboard. The car stopped its movement, and the truck rolled down from above, itself on its side. The hissing of steam and the gurgling of leaking fluids from both vehicles were the only sounds Frank could hear as blood ran down from his head. "I have to get out. I need to get help. Where is my phone? I have to tell Kira," he whispered weakly. Or did he only think he whispered? He couldn't tell anymore. All he knew for certain as his consciousness left him was that he was badly hurt, and no one knew.

114

Chapter 10

Hard Landing on a New Reality

Akira woke up to the sun blazing in through her bedroom window's open curtain, making her shoulders and hair warm and heavy. Her eyes felt like sandpaper. She could remember Penny bringing her home and dropping her off but not coming upstairs or getting into bed. She felt a little foolish for throwing herself at Frank the way she had, especially in front of Melody. Frank and Melody had dated, and Akira imagined there must be some flame still alive. Had she even remembered to tell him anything? She remembered that she was going outside the bowling alley, but not if she had. She groaned loudly, and her obese Corgie, named Captain, yipped at her. She let her arm fall off the bed, and he licked her fingers, then ran in circles and down the stairs. "Silly dog," she smiled and mumbled. Out of bed and stumbling down the stairs with eyes squinting hard against the invading daylight, she made her way to what Captain wanted. She had left a burger on the counter, and it was starting to smell not-so-good. She usually did not feed him scraps but had forgotten to buy dog food. She dropped the greasy burger into the dog dish and started a kettle of water boiling for some herbal tea. She enjoyed green tea like no other, and today was a perfect day for just such a treat, even though it was not the curative herbal she had intended. The water was heating, and Captain was gulping down the burger, so she turned on the mid-morning news.

"A well-known activist against the Electrical Unification Act has been killed in a shootout with authorities after plans for explosive devices were discovered," said the reporter flatly. Akira smirked and wondered if Frank may have met this lunatic at one of the rallies he had attended. No doubt this home-bred terrorist was at all of them trying to radicalize the normal people Frank hoped to sway. She agreed with his ideology but felt the conspiracy theories he held were far-fetched.

"Thank you," said a detective with a greasy combover and raspy voice. "During a routine investigation, we discovered Mr. Greene had a large cache of materials, schematics, and other necessary items to create home-built explosives such as those used at The Eagle's Roost Stadium. When he was approached by a detective last night, Frank Greene produced a handgun, opened fire, and then fled. During the car chase, Mr. Greene lost control of his vehicle and refused to surrender, further firing on officers who then returned fire, and Mr. Greene was killed in the exchange."

Akira stared in shock as a tear began to find its way down her cheek. The tea kettle whistled, then screamed, as she stared at the screen. It showed the scene of a burned-out hull of a vehicle that she recognized as the wagon she had seen less than twelve hours before. No words would form. Her mind was muddled, and her arms felt heavy as stone. Suddenly, the room pitched hard to the right, and she stumbled and passed out on the floor.

"Akira! Akira!" It was Josh, and he was beating on the front door as if he might break it in. Captain lay next to her whimpering. She got up from the floor and let him in. "I came to check on you after seeing the news. You didn't answer your phone. Are you OK?" Josh asked with fear.

Akira nodded blankly and went to the kitchen to shut off the burner that heated the tea kettle. It had boiled almost dry, and somewhere in the back of her consciousness, she was thankful it hadn't been ruined. She sat at the table, staring blankly at the wall. Josh had no words for comfort. He had expected her to be angry, ready to storm the government offices and news stations proclaiming Frank's innocence to honor his memory. He had expected her to be boiling like the teapot, steaming up with an inner fire at her friend being disparaged in the media. He would, of course, calm her and remind her that little could be done. He would remind her of her good life and that no gain would come from throwing all that away in anger, no matter how much they loved Frank. She was stunned but was still the same cool-headed, strong woman she always was. She might get angry and be that way for months or forever, but for now, she was thinking, working it through. He had always known that she had been partial to Frank, loved him even. Josh's heart broke for her and the emotions he knew she was keeping in check. Now, he found that he had been holding back his own emotions, preoccupied with his friend's response to Frank's death. He began to cry. There, just outside the City Centre, they mourned in private. Josh stood in the kitchen doorway, head down, tears falling on his feet. Akira faced forward at the table, one tear falling slowly until it was no more, followed by another until sobs racked her.

"Do you think any of it's true?" After several minutes of silence, Akira finally said, barely above a breath of noise.

"No," Josh replied quietly. "There is no way Frank would have helped a bomber. If he even had those kinds of plans, they were in something else he was using to build a car or generator. There's no way he did any of that."

Akira straightened up slightly, and her voice returned to her, "I mean the shooting." Josh shook his head 'no.' Akira nodded, "We need to go see about the others. Braegan will be a mess and need us." She put on her jacket and grabbed her purse. She opened the door and looked with bloodshot eyes at her friend. Josh shook his head slightly and followed. How strong could a person be, he thought.

Braegan was on the phone when they arrived. He opened the door and ushered them in. "I'mmmmm on hold," he slurred. Josh and Akira both sighed. Akira closed her eyes and shook her head. They both knew who he had called and why he was on hold. From the piles of bottles and cans, he had obviously started trying to drown any pain or memory until he felt it would be a good idea to make a call.

"ER PD, how may I be of service?" Came the faint voice to their ears through the receiver Braegan was loosely holding by his head. He stood up as tall as he could and said in a slurred voice, "Yess, I would like to, to, to, talk to the officer that shot Frank Greene. I want to, innn, innnterrrview him for the Eagle's Roost *Democratic Gazette*."

The reply was polite but to the point, "Sir, you will have to call the department's media director, and sir, I think you have called four times already today. We understand your grief, but any more, and we will have to trace this line and take action. Thank you. *Click*."

Braegan was obviously not pleased with this response and yelled at the disconnected phone call, "You bring that dirty, lying murderer somewhere I can get my hands on him, or I'll come down there and find him myself!" Josh moved over and took the phone from Braegan, who sank into the couch muttering. "He's dead, Josh, *dead!* I went this morning to ID the body, and there wasn't enough to tell what it was. They said the car caught fire in the shootout, and he fell back into it when he got shot. Shootout, Josh, SHOOT-OUT!" He emphasized the last words. "Have you ever known Frank to shoot at anything other than a possum or raccoon that was already acting sick?"

Josh sat beside him silently. What was there to say? None of them believed Frank had shot at anyone. Not one of his friends ever would believe such a thing. The idea of Frank lending material aid of any kind to a terrorist was absurd. Yet, here they were, mourning their friend while the world was convinced that the tragedy in the famous Eagle's Roost's Stadium had been orchestrated, to some degree, by a boiler mechanic who donated his free time to helping the poor. What was there to say? "We'll find out who really did this and clear him," said Josh. He was destroyed inside, but what made him sicker than anything was that Franklin Greene would be in the history books as a terrorist, a murderer, and a coward who sent others to their death.

Akira was shaking her head in anger and disgust. "How, Josh? How do you think we'll do that? He's dead, and it's all over the news. Why, those detectives are the only officers …" Her eyes grew cold, and her facial expression turned blank. "Well," she said, "there just isn't anything we can do, is there?"

Braegan threw a bottle across the room and continued sobbing the tears of a mourner with too much alcohol to hold in his emotions. Little more was said for the next half hour as Braegan sobbed and then passed out.

"Poor guy," said Josh, laying the unconscious man's head on the sofa.

Akira scowled, "You mean idiot. Now the cops are going to follow that phone call, and he'll be under a watch for months. I know, I know," she halted Joshua's complaint with a raised hand and rolling eyes, "he is just grieving the only way he can. You don't think I would like to lose control and do something foolish? Frank was my best friend for decades. I loved …" her voice cracked, "Well, all we can do is move on from here. Let's go check on Melody."

It was nearing afternoon when the two rang the watch button at Melody's apartment building. A bored male voice answered, "Sunrise Manor, who may I ring for you?" Akira looked irritated; she hated the security and pompous attitudes in the wealthy sections of town. Akira didn't live in any poorer neighborhood than Melody. Where she lived, however, was all working families, and there was, at least a little, a sense of community.

"Melody Maine, please," Josh replied gently.

Anticipating the next question, Akira grumbled to the two-way speaker, "Akira and Josh, she knows us."

"Thank you. Please wait," replied the bored voice on the other side.

Waiting. Akira hated waiting. She impatiently drummed her fingers on the wall. She leaned, she stood, she leaned on the wall again. "What is taking so long?!"

"It's only been a couple of minutes, 'Kira," Josh said. He calmly continued, "Maybe she was taking a shower or a nap or something. It's probably been a stressful day for her, too. Everyone that knew him is keyed up."

"Frank," said Akira.

"What?"

"His name is still Frank, Joshua. I know it's easier not to say it, but if we let Frank become 'him' and 'he' in every reference, then he will fade too soon. Just … say his name every now and then. Just his name to keep him alive a little longer."

Josh stared at her. Her eyes had welled up, and her cheeks were flush, her lip quivered slightly.

"Just say Frank's name," she whispered with a small voice.

She had covered very well, thought Josh, but she was barely staying together.

"Your party has failed to answer her call," the bored man on the speaker replied. He read the script he was assigned with a hint of a groan, "Should I try again?"

Akira and Josh looked at each other with a touch of confusion and concern. Josh suddenly had a terrible thought. "Sir, is there any way you can send someone to make sure she is OK? An old boyfriend …" Akira stiffened, "of hers passed away this morning, and I am afraid she may react emotionally."

The voice on the other end suddenly sounded interested and even concerned, "Sir, if I send the building's medic to her room, and everything is OK, will you be willing to incur that expense?"

"Yes, certainly."

"I have dispatched our medic. Please stand by."

In moments, the voice came back on, sounding rattled, "You may enter. Our medic has found Miss Maine and wants you to come up to the waiting area immediately!"

The dark blue doors, Prosperity Blue, the city code called it, swung open with a magnetic hum. A dour-faced guard was waiting on them and motioned for them to follow. He walked fast. Akira had to take larger steps than normal to keep up, and Josh found he wanted for air when they reached the elevator, far distant on the finely decorated wall of the common room in this plush complex. The elevator was elaborately decorative in spotlessly polished silver and brass accents and mahogany wood. The attendant stared apathetically ahead into the mirror image of the three of them on the door. Akira thought she caught his gaze lingering on her a few times and instinctively pulled her shirt up. She figured she must look a mess, red-eyed and upset as she was. There was no way she would look into that mirror and explore her emotions displayed in her expressions. She knew how she felt; she just couldn't deal with that right now. The bell on the elevator rang out at each floor, a pleasant little chime briefly interrupting the quietly playing music, a hotel lounge remake of a show tune, punctuating the degree of Melody's removal from the more common levels of wealth on the lower floors. Melody's apartment was a penthouse suite. She lived in luxury like few her age could. The chime finally announced their arrival at the top floor with the same *ding*, and the doors slid open in near silence.

There was no hallway, per se, to Melody's room. There was a small seating area with one door to the north. Akira gaped at the extreme opulence, and wastefulness, in her opinion, of the seating area. The seats were silk cushioned and looked more comfortable than her own bed. The carpet was so thick that it also appeared more comfortable than her bed. She walked slowly across the room, followed by Josh, trying hard not to stare at all the lush extravagances. They both felt a twinge of guilt for even noticing the level of wealth they were standing in when such a horrible situation was what brought them there. Akira knocked.

No one had ever gotten the best of Melody Maine, not even her parents. Her name wasn't even Maine; it was Fausty. Melody had felt that the name made people think of deals with the devil, and since she had a desire for both performance and politics, it simply would not do. So adamant was she that they allowed her the name change while she was still a teenager, and after her success, they changed their own names to match.

Akira walked forward into the room, which was virtually abuzz with the private medical team and the noise of their equipment. And there she stood, aghast. No one had ever gotten into Melody's head. Mel had always had an exit strategy for every relationship. Frank may have been the only one to end a relationship before Mel, but it was only semantics. Melody had already moved on with her career and left Frankling Greene far behind. While she was tearfully saying goodbye, wiping her tears with one hand, she was waving hello to the next love of her life with the other hand. And yet, hanging from the ceiling fan, was a crude noose made from a belt. It was a stylish designer belt covered in sparkling sequins, but a noose was made from it nonetheless. Akira's head turned slowly toward the large leather chair Melody was reclined in. She couldn't take it all in. Melody laying back with a wide band of dark red on her neck, apparently from friction burn, the coffee table kicked aside, the medics packing up their things and preparing to leave, briefcases, files … there was too much to process and make sense. Why would Melody try to hang herself? She was moving up the ranks of Eagle's Roost politics. She was a nightly feature on the talk shows, telling how she was going to stop the Nuko-Steam terrorists, get power back to The Run, and revolutionize commerce. She was … better than this. Akira walked over to her rival and friend and gathered her composure. Melody looked up at her and smiled, but not the sheepish smile of someone who had done something foolish. It was different than that in a way Akira couldn't identify. Akira felt sorry for her.

"Hi 'Kira," she lilted. Akira was taken aback slightly.

"Hi, Mel, umm, what's new?" Stupid! Stupid idiot! Akira thought to herself. You can't ask someone who has lost a close friend, maybe even love, and then tried to hang themselves what's new!

"I am shocked. … We were, we were with Franklin—and just last night. Well, I didn't think he'd ever get to the end of the road. I thought he was invincible." Melody's eyes were cold and glassy. She stared out into space with a hard look for just an instant. Akira was speechless. Josh stepped up and took Melody's hand.

"You know where I am if you need me. You should've called. I would have been here." He choked up and looked at the ground.

Melody smiled wide, "Oh, Josh, everything will be alright."

Akira started to feel the tears well up with the rising lump in her throat. She knew Melody meant that *she* would be 'alright.' But, "Alright?!" No, they wouldn't! All RIGHT?!! Never again would anything be ALL RIGHT!! Her face flushed red, and she barely managed to croak the words, "I have to go, Mel. Please be safe. Josh, would you stay with her a bit?" Melody said something incoherent about a path or a walk or road or something else, very Melody-like and irritating.

Akira's tears started before she got to the elevator. She didn't notice the wealth of her surroundings, nor the men in suits meeting her as she left the Prosperity Blue doors and walked, then ran down the street. The tears came without any hope of being held back now. She was weeping, sobbing, wailing for a friend she would never see again. No, not just a friend. She began to say all the things to Frank she had never gotten to say. She didn't care about the stares of the people. She didn't care about the whispering and sidelong glances. She told him how she missed seeing him and how those road trips with all the friends were only fun because he was there, and finally, before she could no longer speak, she said, "I love you, Frank. I love you, you idiot. Why did you never notice and say anything? I love you, and I could never tell you, and now I never can!" She screamed it to her front door. She had run all the way to her house and fell, exhausted, on her floor. And there she slept.

Akira awoke at 1:00 a.m. to Captain scratching at the door to be let out. Poor guy, she thought, he's been in here all this time while I acted like a baby. So, she let him out the front door to the small yard in front of her house. She stared off to the east, out over the abandoned lot Frank had spoken at a few months ago. Through all the houses, through all the mess of humanity, she could picture his shop with the sign he had taken with him from Gramp's Garage leaning against the western wall and his own sign of welded metal and rivets hanging over his doorway, Greene Steam. She shook her head and then laughed a little as another tear ran down her face. He had always thought that was such a witty name, a play on words. He always was smart and good with words, much more than many of her other friends. She figured it must be from all his reading. Reading, something caught in her mind, as though there was something she did not remember but should. He read an awful lot when he was younger and still read when a mechanical problem stumped him. He had been talking about reading something, a magazine, or something that night at the bowling alley.

Captain was finished being an outside dog, and a neighbor's cat had hissed at him: more than enough reason for the pudgy Corgie to need to return inside after a last faux-threatening bark, of course. She put Captain in and fed him. He panted and lolled his tongue out as she scratched behind his ears while she thought. She couldn't relax. "Well," she looked Captain in the eyes as he cocked his head, "I guess I am going for an early morning drive."

She rounded the corners and eased through the lights, comfortably riding along on her little scooter. She owned a regular full-sized car but felt more like riding. Where it had been a cool summer night just last night (was it only last night?), tonight it was unusually warm, and if she stopped for too long, the sweat would start to trickle down into her eyes from her helmet. She kept an eye on the south and west to watch for storm clouds; unseasonably warm weather could mean a front was coming. She was out of the Centre now and headed out through the bypass that avoided much of The Bull's Run and took her almost to Frank's house. She cruised along, keeping an eye out for trouble. She was not terribly worried, in all honesty. If there was not an armed group, she was able to take care of herself pretty well. Still, she thought, it was better to be cautious.

Josh had left a dozen messages on her phone, and she was going over them all in her mind as she rode. Melody this, Melody that, we all know Melody is crazy as crap. ... Of course, she says it's all her fault. She feels like she has enough power to control the world.

"Of course, she is emotional, Josh," Akira thought out loud, "You are male, and the smell of testosterone makes her put on her 'get my way' act, and of course, you feel like you should stay to help poor emotional Melody Maine ... the damsel in distress ... always." She turned to the road near Frank's house and headed down by his shop. Lights? Why were there lights on at Frank's shop? Akira sped up in anger, thinking someone might be looting his shop already. Wait, she slowed quickly down again. That is more than his shop lights. Those are spotlights, police spots ... no, those are military searchlights and military vehicles. Local military? National Guard? No, this was ... SWAT? She didn't slow down but rode by and tried to see all she could without turning her head. Anti-terrorism unit,

Bomb Disposal and Explosives Team, Nuclear Accountability Agency. She didn't recognize the last two flat black vehicles, nor did she know to make a note of the two detectives smoking cigarettes by their car. She only knew that a well-known tech-mech was not reason enough for this much response. So, she turned down the road and sped off through Truitt, the back way toward Frank's home, full of confusion and concern.

Chapter 11

Forward Motion

Frank's house was silent and dark. It sat on an easy slope of hill just past the edge of The Run. The bypass around The Run came almost to his driveway from The Centre, then turned and went mostly East to the neighboring town. If he had moved his shop to his home, he could have taken the bypass to contract work he used to do on industrial generators. Frank always preferred the back roads from where the shop was now. His house was nearest The Run but didn't fit in with The Bull's Run at all. It was built before they moved the city. Gramps had disbelieved any chance that the voters of Eagle's Roost would allow such a bold and detrimental action. He finished the house, and the voting majority moved the city away from him, leaving his house and land worthless. Gramps was livid but grew to enjoy the peace and quiet. No one was around at night. Not only was the adjacency to The Run a deterrent, but there was little traffic from The Centre at night since the next town was rural, and the few small towns miles away were easier to get to by backtracking to the interstate on the other side of town, nearer the Centre, particularly at night.

Akira parked far down the road and walked the rest of the way. She kept to the shadows and off the road as much as possible, now, she felt silly for it. She sat in the dark, in the trees and shrubs, and stared at Frank's house. She ached inside. All the longing in her heart for him that had been pushed off into the back of her soul, hidden under a thin blanket of hope, welled up inside. The hope was that someday she would figure out how to break through the awkwardness, Frank would feel the same as she felt, and they would be together. That longing was working its way up from deep within and flooding through her mind.

She had a sad smile on her face as she looked at the artwork on the lawn that was definitely from Frank. There was a metal sculpture of some abstract something, lots of flowers and green things growing, but one thing mystified her. In the middle of the lawn was a sculpture of a tree made from hundreds of small metal rods varying from about an eighth of an inch to a half-inch in diameter. They were lined up and twisted together, textured, cut, and welded so that it looked so much like a living tree she would not have been able to tell the difference if it had not been more reflective where the lawnmower had polished off the patina of rust that had been carefully oiled to a, now, preservative finish. The branches were twisted iron and browned with rust, stretching out to smaller iron or steel rods bent to look realistic and lifelike until they terminated in small copper leaves that had been allowed to oxidize green.

Frank had planted morning glories and moonflowers at the base of the tree, whose vines had wound themselves up and around the metal tree and covered several limbs. It was breathtaking and a brilliant blending of nature and man-made art. How much of the metalwork tree was done by Gramps, and how much was Frank? At the base of the tree was a concrete stool shaped like a stump. It was also well crafted and, although not as realistic and awe-inspiring as the metalworking in the other tree, still impressively done.

She remembered the stump from her childhood very clearly. On the few occasions that she visited Frank after school or came by before they went bowling with friends, or whatever other occasion, it had been here. The metalwork tree, though, she did not recall. Had it really been so long since she had visited Frank at home? On the back of the stump was a tiny machine shed with a tractor Gramps had placed there years ago. Also, inside the shed sat an old model steam-powered sawmill from the turn of the nineteenth century. It made her ache with mixed emotions. She already missed Frank more than she could emotionally process or express, and antique steam equipment was something he loved passionately.

She reached down and picked up the little model, not even large enough to need both hands, even though it was made from cast iron. There was an audible *click* when she removed it from its magnetic base, and the cast iron flywheel turned a quarter turn. She smiled a half-smile as she watched its pushrod slide slowly out. She turned and looked at the tree again; it appeared to dance in the moonlight for just a second, the same way a real tree moves when disturbed by the wind. The stationary steam engine was slightly tarnished from outside, but the model machine shed kept it in working order.

Akira placed the model back on its base with another click and walked over to the tree line rimming Franklin's yard. She could hear a light thunder in the distance, only perceptible because of the calm and quiet here. The sky was clear overhead. The clouds were far to the East, and any storm was moving away from her. Leaning back in the dark against a much more natural tree, a large red oak, she thought. She stared at the metalwork tree, and her thoughts drifted to memories of herself and Frank. They had spent hours laughing and talking. She could still hear his voice in her mind as she fell asleep. Morning sneaked up on her from behind Frank's house, where the sun had been blocked from view until almost 9:00 a.m. She woke up sore, cold, and stiff and rubbed her muscles to get limbered up again. She took a long last look at the house and walked away down the gravel drive and the old side road to her scooter. She needed to check in with Josh and see how Melody fared.

The morning sun shone through the windows far across town from Akira and sparkled on the blue walls. In the penthouse suite, men were already hard at work writing speeches and preparing press conferences. In a video conference, Melody sat at her computer in her room, doors closed. Josh had returned to check on Melody; her security team, recognizing him from before, had allowed him entrance. He stared at all the hustle and bustle and was overwhelmed with the clamor. It was inspiring, he thought, to watch all of the activity of her political work happening. Here, in a lush apartment, amid the crystal and fine art, people were on the phone with utility companies and donors building support for the energy bill tied so closely to her name.

Josh found a seat on the couch and moved aside briefcases and papers that had pictures of street scenes from an old security camera, presumably in the areas dealing with unreliable electricity. Unintentionally overhearing a conversation about a damaged store front, the businessman was talking about how the store couldn't be used because of damages or something or other. He figured it was insurance stuff and tuned it out. An office aid came by—a kind-appearing man of about the same age as Josh and Melody—carrying a cup of coffee. Joshua assumed that meant she must be nearby.

"I don't care if you have to fly strike helicopters and bombing dirigibles over that site and video every insect that twitches, you are going to find it, or I will find you a detail out past The Run raiding illegal porta-johns!" Josh heard Melody's voice as she appeared from the bedroom doorway into the sitting room. "Wow, I've never heard that from her," he thought to himself. He sat and wondered what she meant by strike choppers and bombers. Surely, she didn't have access to that sort of thing. He figured she must be using hyperbole and was talking to the media about their helicopters or something. Melody came red-faced through the door with a folder held above her head like a war banner. "What are you people doing with your time? How can something like this happen, and no one knows anything about it?!" She was livid and hadn't noticed the only non-governmental employee in the room. Her aid handed her the coffee, cleared his throat, and side-eyed Joshua. "How the …" her face flushed with frustration and anger. She noticed Josh for the first time.

"Thank you, Brian, for the coffee. Joshua, I did not know you were here." Her tone softened immediately when she followed Brian's eyes and saw him. She walked over to Josh, who stood to greet her. Melody quickly gave him a friendly embrace and simultaneously retrieved the files and photos from the sofa, slid the files together, placed them in a side table drawer, and then closed the drawer. "I apologize. I am passionate about some projects, and I would never want you to have to see me when I am out of sorts," she tittered and laughed comfortably.

Joshua felt an uneasy awkwardness in the room and assumed it was because he was not meant to be privy to political actions. "It's OK, Mel. I just wanted to see how you were doing. You were pretty upset yesterday and then buried yourself in work. I wanted to make sure, you know, just to check on you."

She looked him in the eye with a searching gaze as though looking for something in him. After a moment, she smiled again and told him, "I'm doing well, Josh. Thank you for checking on me. Please, though, call me Miss Maine in front of my employees." Josh looked at her with perplexity. "Umm, really? OK, I can do that. Umm, Miss Maine. I guess respect and professionalism are important."

She smiled again. "Thank you, Josh. I really am busy. You are welcome to wait in the adjoining room if you like, but I have to get things going for the day." He shook his head and was about to speak when her phone rang again. Melody smiled warmly at him, "I have to take this," she said. Before he could answer her, she was on the phone and walking briskly away.

Brian, her aid, was at his side, seemingly from thin air. "Joshua, sir, would you like to move to the dining room? We have a continental breakfast that no one has touched. I can bring you a beverage if you would like, or I may escort you out if you prefer not to wait. Miss Maine's calendar is quite full for the day. I cannot guarantee when she will be able to receive you in a manner more pleasant," he offered.

Josh nodded his head, answering, "No, sir. I appreciate the hospitality, but I think I need to let Akira know that Mel, Miss Maine, is OK." Brian escorted Josh to the door and walked him to the elevator, where he continued out, unnoticed by anyone but the doorman, who nodded politely with disinterest at his passing. The weekend would be gone soon, and there would also be plenty of work on Monday. Maybe focusing on work would be the healthiest thing for him, anyway.

The next week went about as normally as it could for Joshua and Akira. Braegan and Melody were hard to keep track of, like normal. Josh worked extra hours while Akira flew a quick freight transport. When the weekend came, Josh called Akira and asked if she'd like to get together and just talk, "Just … you know, because." There was a trendy café at the edge of the City Centre called "The Verge." They had met there before, though it was difficult to find time to meet, with their schedules seldom matching up. This was one of the few places uniquely theirs. Frank hadn't cared for robots or being surrounded by so many people. There were coffee shops and diners farther out that he preferred. So, Akira, Josh, Braegan, and Penelope would come to The Verge and reconnect from time to time. The two friends sat quietly at a table in the back of the café, which sat on the corner of Promise and Prosperity.

Prosperity Boulevard ran from the incorporated housings into the Centre and right up to the Capitol building, while Promise Street was effectively the drawn border between the City Centre's sprawl into the supporting industrial buildings and The Meadows, an upscale, high-rise residential zone. Why it was called "The Meadows" was beyond any of them as it had no grass that was not in a pot and no trees, not in the tiny garden area of the high-rise complexes. The Verge was an ultra-modern shop where your food was ordered on a touch screen and then delivered by tiny robots running on a track suspended from the ceiling. They would whiz along, then lower your plate to the table on tiny, plastic, mono-filament wires. Overall, the atmosphere was relaxed but not quiet with the sci-fi space travel theme, the news channels running on televisions recessed into the tables, and the robot servers.

Conversation came with difficulty for the two. Each wanted to talk about Frank, but neither wanted to talk about Frank. So small talk was the order of the hour. "I have a trip to China coming up," Akira lazily shared. "It's always kind of nice there. The people are friendly. It's interesting not to be the only one named Akira in the airport, haha!" Her laugh was forced and non-committal.

Josh wondered if she had made up that part just to have something to laugh at. He smiled politely and offered his own small talk. "Your airship is amazing. I know it's an older one for a commercial fleet, but I love it," he intoned. She smiled politely, hollowly. Her dirigible was, in fact, one of the nicest in the fleet, which explained why it was still being flown at its advanced age. It was a relic by all standards of machinery life expectancy, but she loved it more than she loved most people. It was less efficient in its propulsion, and its frame and ballonets were larger than even the largest of the more modern commercial zeppelins. All these things would seem to make it less desirable, but the size and design of the frame, long and smooth with a sharp point at the front, making it one of the smoothest and fastest flying ships in the fleet. It was adorned with silver skin that reflected the sun like a mirror. The cabin was old enough that it was back in style: retro chic by original design within its polished wood and brass passenger area. It had been kept as the premium luxury liner of the fleet. It was, without a doubt, more difficult to fly. All that extra bulk made it more vulnerable to overcorrection while docking. Too much throttle could cause it to pitch or yaw unpredictably at takeoff. Akira was the only pilot currently employed who had never damaged *The Silver Cloud.*

"My machine shop has been turning parts for the government this week. The computerized mills have been running 24/7, building plane parts for StratoJet," Josh half-heartedly continued. Then, the two sat in the quiet and listened to the whir of the robots and the other meaningless discussions around them. They sat a little closer than normal and made less eye contact than they had in the past. The quiet was comforting. Joshua stared at her and wondered what was going on in her mind. The military pilot training, the years of flying commercially in a hot air dirigible, and all her life's hardships and ups and downs gave her a perspective and depth that he didn't feel he possessed. Suddenly, her eyes opened wider, and she began to turn up the volume of the tabletop television. Josh looked too, and there was Franklin's shop on the news.

"… Military and police have cordoned off the site of Franklin Greene's garage and warehouse and have declared it a sensitive government location until a pending investigation into its former owner's actions can be completed. We spoke to a neighbor, who wished to be kept anonymous, about why." The reporter said.

A blurred figure with voice-changing technology spoke up, "Yes, I knew Mr. Greene for many years. He helped me on several occasions with my steam repairs. He was always building some crazy confabulation and sending it out the door without a care in the world! I think folks should be more intentional and precautionary when they are dealing with things that could be dangerous!"

Akira's face turned red with rage, and she stomped out of the café. "'Kira! Akira, wait!" Josh followed her. "Akira, you knew that people would create connections even if there were none. That's why I have been thinking," Akira looked at Josh now as he spoke, her jaw still clenched tightly shut, "We need to check into this on our own." Josh stated.

Akira looked at him, nodding. "How, Josh? The only place we can access is his house if they have left it alone," she loudly replied. Josh motioned for her to quiet down, which never worked." Akira, please, I … I don't know. Braegan has a crazy plan and some even crazier ideas about the whole deal. He sent me a letter like in the mail! I guess he was afraid other things could be read by people he didn't want to know. Let's go see him and find out what he thinks."

Akira thought, then nodded, "Let's go."

The birds in the yards and those sitting in the trees were singing and flitting about as Josh and Akira rode past into the incorporated housings. Akira had to drive because Josh had ridden his cycle. Braegan worked with Josh, and the two of them could have been roommates in an upscale apartment complex in City Centre, but Braegan drank a lot. They pulled up behind B's tiger-striped, orange, radial-engined autocycle, the only licensed motor vehicle he owned, and parked. Braegan was immediately out the front door to greet them. Surprisingly, he had not been drinking yet tonight. "Come on in, guys. I guess you got my letter?" he said to Josh in tones, quickly turning hushed. Braegan whispered to them both at the door, "My girlfriend is here, so, ummm, be quiet. She's in the den at the other end of the house. We'll go to the garage."

The garage was a 'man cave' for Braegan. He had autocycle parts and posters with women posing with sodas or whatever other drink they were trying to sell. Akira had an idea that B didn't even know the product represented in any of the posters. There was a pool table that sat in the middle that, more often than not, was covered in whatever Braegan was working on, whether machines or paperwork. Braegan had several newspapers laid out on the pool table desk, and after asking if either of the two would like a beer, he motioned them over to it. "You see this?" he began, "This is an aerial photo of Frank's shop the night of the wreck. It's about the time we were bowling. Did you ever see a truck or anything like that?"

Josh and Akira looked closely and then, in unison, answered, "Where?"

Braegan pointed to the far-left corner of the picture, almost under the streetlight. "Right there, the streetlight makes a big shadow there because of Frank's sign, and the truck is in that shadow. It must be black or dark gray."

Josh looked around with a pointed finger. "I still don't see it," he said. He looked up and could tell by Akira's face that she did see it. Akira moved in a little closer and described what she saw: "It's hard to tell much about it, but there are the headlights and the bumper; it's a big vehicle. I've never seen one quite the same. It looks a little like the police truck but without the box on the back and none of the markings. OK, Braegan, so what is it?"

Braegan took a moment and smiled with satisfaction that at least someone else saw the picture. He then pulled another paper over and pointed without saying a word. Josh's mouth dropped open. This time, he saw it too, and it was in the bowling alley parking lot behind a car, captured on the security footage used in still photos for the news report on the bomber, Franklin Greene. "And finally, here," Braegan continued as he pointed to the final picture where the truck was shown in an aerial photo of the bowling alley by a trashy news rag getting a supposed scoop on Melody Maine going bowling.

The three stood silent for a moment. Akira whispered, "Why? Why was someone following him? Do you think they may have seen the wreck and shootout and know what really happened?"

Braegan shook his head and started to speak, but Josh was already forming the words, "You think they *were* the wreck. You said that you thought there was more going on than the news is saying."

"Shhh! Shhh, Josh. My girlfriend doesn't know or care about any of this, and let's just leave her in the den watching sappy movies. I do think this truck was involved," Braegan confirmed. Akira was shaking her head in disbelief. Braegan went on, "I called Emmett and then went to the dealership where 'Carney works and took the pictures. Archie said he's never sold or seen a truck like that."

Josh looked puzzled. "So why did you need Emmett?" He asked. Braegan smiled. He was not usually the one to have schemes and plans. He was very proud that this time, not only had he noticed something out of place but had taken action. Braegan lowered his voice conspiratorially, "Frank had the deed to his shop held by a lawyer since he doesn't have any family left. I knew Emmett would know the lawyer and be able to find out what's what. We were all going to get the first bid on it. So, I had Em buy it."

The two-person audience stared in disbelief, then erupted in "What?" and "Why?" and "What were you thinking?"

Braegan hushed them again. His girlfriend opened the garage door. Her eyes were glazed, and she seemed out of touch. "B, I don't freakin' care what you and your two idiot friends are doing. Just keep it quiet so I can concentrate on my shows," she mumbled/slurred. Akira gave her a death stare, and the young lady stumbled back into the house without another word.

"Think about it, guys. Em is rich..." Braegan continued.

"He hates being called Em, Braegan," Akira interrupted.

"Whatever," Braegan dismissed her, then explained, "Not only did he inherit a pile of dough; he has invested it everywhere and is *sooo* loaded. Now, he's connected with every politician in the state, right?"

The two nodded.

"So, if you were a politician trying to crack down on a terrorist, would you lock up, or destroy, or bring a lot of attention to a warehouse owned by a major campaign financier?"

Akira laughed hard as she spoke, "Can you imagine how angry someone is going to be when they get that call? When did you and Emmett even do all of this? They announced it was roped off today!"

Braegan was chuckling as he spoke, "Today, 'Kira. I have been following the investigating officers after work every night that I can. We all stopped for donuts, and I heard one of them say that some big something or other from the government wanted to dig around in it and had already sent repairmen into the old factory. A couple nights ago, they said they were going to barricade the whole place for good, not just have cars parked outside. I couldn't leave it alone anymore."

Akira rushed to him, hugged him tightly, and held him for a long time. Josh clapped him on the back, impressed and appreciative. It had only been a week and a day since Frank had been killed, and out of Franklin Greene's closest friends, only the drunk had kept a head about himself to actually take action. Suddenly, Akira straightened up and looked at them both. "Fellas, we have to break in … tonight!"

Both men stuttered and replied in turn, "What?!" Josh continued, "Are you out of your mind? They'll be told to leave tomorrow anyway, and we can't get his things. It's crawling with all kinds of people with guns tonight!"

Braegan smiled and clicked his tongue, "You're right," he said, "tonight's the night. They will have moved any evidence by the time they leave tomorrow. Besides that, I said I have been following the investigators; they pulled all the other government agents away when they fenced it off today."

"Come on, Josh," Akira said, taking him by the arm. We'll discuss how on the way to my house so I can change. Josh stuttered and protested, but there was no changing Akira's mind once it was made. Braegan began putting on his riding leathers. "I'll be a few blocks away waiting on you two." Akira shook her head. "Wait until dark to leave. I'll call."

With that, the three newly forged spies parted, and hasty plans were put into motion. Akira was unsure if she felt relief that things seemed to have taken a small turn in their favor or just that they had some direction for action. Maybe, she thought, it's simply knowing that the media story could be proven false. Regardless of why, she smiled the whole way home with thoughts of burglary in her mind. As she opened her door to Captain waggling all around in front of her, she wondered, "Am I only happy because I feel like I can get some petty revenge in this?"

The police tape surrounded the entire shop as though it were a fence keeping an animal at bay. Perhaps, Josh thought, Akira was the animal, and that orange fence and police tape were to keep her out. They misjudged that! She was smiling and energized. She had tired of killing while in the Air Force but enjoyed the challenge of pitting herself against other trained personnel. He smiled a little, glad that she was no longer showing depression, noticed her looking at him, and wiped the smile from his face immediately. He looked at her when he felt her gaze lift. "You're a close friend," he thought silently, "but you scare me right now."

She was watching, watching the guards, watching for cameras, for drones, for dogs. She whispered, "They think no one is going to challenge them. Look, Josh, one guard outside the front door and one at the corner watching the road into The Run. There are no dogs, and the only camera they put up is on the same road they are guarding."

Josh dramatically whispered the cliché, "It's almost too easy." She rolled her eyes at him in the dark. They called Braegan once they had gotten there, and he was just arriving. Akira knew he would ride up and alert any guards, so she and Josh walked up from the darker side of the shop bordering The Run and then told B how to do the same and not give away their hiding place.

It was a perfect night for mischief. The moon was occluded by clouds and only occasionally gave off the faintest of shadows that toyed with the mind. The guards, having been there and tuned out the shadows that intermittently danced across the landscape, would never notice three more. They skirted the fence until they found where one joint had been tied to another. Akira produced some wire cutters from inside her dark brown aviator jacket and cut the wires. None of the bandits wore all black. Braegan was in his riding leathers, which were mostly black, and he had put black duct tape over the colorful portions of them. Josh wore a dark gray, long-sleeved, t-shirt and sweats, and Akira wore black leggings and her dark brown leather, fur-lined aviator jacket, the darkest jacket she had. It was apparently good enough costuming because the guard had glanced in their direction when the *snap, snap, snap* of them cutting through the orange fencing had whispered through the light breeze. Like rabbits being eyed by a predator, they sat motionless, not breathing. He turned his head this way and that for a moment, then spit and looked back toward the road.

Onward, they crept, moving slowly so that the crunching of the gravel underfoot was barely audible even to them. The huge warehouse complex that was the back of Frank's shop stretched out before them, a gray mountain bluff, impassable and impenetrable. Braegan looked up and down the length of it and began to climb onto an air conditioner to look in a window. "*Psst*, get down," Josh whispered. He pointed down the wall, and everyone went in that direction. Josh had spotted an old railing and hoped it was around a door. He had never been in any of the buildings except where he and Frank did repairs.

They crept silently, slowly. The railing was coming into better view. It was made from pipes—old, rusted, and broken. Josh closed his eyes and prayed without a sound moving his lips, "Please, let that be a door and not a safety railing for holding paint or something stupid." He opened his eyes just in time to see a large rock and he tripped on it. Down he went with a thud. All three stood stock still. They waited. They could hear the guard by The Run stirring and moving. A beam of light shone out past the corner of the building, and Braegan picked up the large rock as though he'd use it as a weapon. A night bird called out in irritation at the flashlight disturbance and flew off from its perch. The light turned back the other way, and the movement stopped.

Braegan put the rock down, helped Josh up, and then continued to the railing. It was a door. Now, how could they open it without being heard? They tried the door, and it was locked. There was a window, but it was too small for anyone to get through, even if they forced it open. Braegan whispered, "Rock?" Both of the others shook their heads. Josh held up a finger and pulled his wallet from his sweats pocket. Akira snorted lightly. Josh gave her a small frown and took out a credit card. The door was not a typical industrial door. It looked, judging by the framing, that it once had been. It had broken or rusted at one time in the past, and either Frank or the previous owners had simply shimmed in a standard residential door with a standard residential lock. Josh slid the credit card into the clumsily hung door and tugged on the handle. With a quiet *click*, the door swung wide open. Joshua, Braegan, and Akira were now not only trespassing on a crime scene, but they had also officially broken into a government-controlled building.

The warehouse was massive. Somehow, it appeared even larger once inside than it did from the outside, as if the sheer scope of the outside caused the mind to not encompass it all, while the inside had so many items there was a sense of measure and comparison. Braegan wondered why Frank had never taken any of them back into this graveyard of old manufacturing. For a split second, the thought crossed his mind, "What was he hiding here?" and then the thought was banished with a scowl as quickly as it had arrived. Dust lay on everything. There were parts of machines and assembly line pieces from when the warehouse and factory were in full production. It was nearly impossible to tell what anything was because, even as dark as the outside had been, the inside was an inkier black. The tiny slivers of moonlight that occasionally broke from behind the clouds only served to prevent their eyes from ever fully adjusting. Then again, can eyes ever fully adjust to total darkness?

Akira struck a match. It felt silly, but the light it shed was enormous compared to the consuming pitch-blackness of the warehouse. She quickly found an old headlight that would have been mounted on a fender and fashioned something of a lantern from bits of ragged, oily cloth. The headlight and mounting were conical, and with the glass in it, she could let the smoke come through the top of the metal cone, and the glass let the line shine only in a downward beam. She felt very satisfied with her ingenuity, and the two men accompanying her were quietly impressed. She made sure to be careful not to cast any light upon the walls in case there were holes, and they crept along at a snail's pace inside the huge floor space.

They just wandered and wondered for many minutes, not knowing what they were looking for. Eventually, the warehouse's storage changed to the machines and apparatus of the old factory floor. They could see several machines glinting in the low light of the makeshift lantern. They knew this meant they had been recently cleaned, or the dust would have made them dull and non-reflective. A bat flapped overhead, squeaking as it went. All three jumped and then nervously, quietly giggled at their nervousness. The ceiling-to-floor racks of parts loomed behind them, and the rails of the assembly line with the machines stretched out before.

Akira sighed and began walking. Braegan tugged at her coat sleeve. He pointed to the other side of what, according to the faded paint on the floor, was assembly line A. There sat a nearly completed truck, much like the one in the pictures. Whoever was responsible had taken this old factory and refitted machines to build these powerful vehicles. They walked over to it shakily. Yes, it was very similar in style, but this one wore thick armor plating and had weapon mounts.

Josh picked up a piece of paper and handed it to Akira to put in the light … blueprints. They looked through the stack of prints at a glance. There were different types of trucks, a light personnel carrier, and the most terrifying print, bearing a stamp marked 1B1A2 February 10th, A tank. It was months away still, but a tank was in the plans for this factory. Akira held the paper out in front of her in anger and turned, shaking it, toward Braegan. As she swept her arm to the left, she bumped something. It smelled strong, burning their eyes.

Braegan gasped, "Petrol, it's gasoline, Akira! Put out ..."

It was too late. The fumes from the splashed liquid had gotten on her lantern and flashed, causing her to drop it, and then the entire gallon, now spreading on the floor, was aflame. The area was no longer a coffin for dead vehicles; it was a firelight bazaar with dancing lights on all the walls.

"Run!" she choked out. Run, they did. The door they had come through was now thrown open, and the guard yelled, "Stop! Stop, or I'll shoot!"

They did not stop. They ran. They hurdled over pallets of new and used parts, they slid under railings and threw open doors, and when they reached the distant door into what had been the office of this factory, the door to what had been Franklin Greene's shop, shots rang out. The report of the pistol in the dark, concrete, and metal building was perhaps more shocking than if they had been hit with the bullet. It echoed off the walls and sent dust falling off shelves. Josh kicked open the door to the shop. Light streamed through the door, and the surprised guard, who had been about to open the door, was bowled over backward. With both guards in pursuit, the three would-be spies ran through the shop's front door, and Braegan yelled, "Scatter!"

Akira turned down the road toward Frank's house, Josh ran straight out into a field, and Braegan headed back to The Bull's Run. Only Josh was caught on camera, and all that could be told from the footage was that someone wearing gray tripped and fell often when running over rough ground at night, and that same someone had a piece of paper in his hand. The camera couldn't see the others, but as Braegan ran through the poorest parts of a community left forgotten, no one cried out, and no one alerted the shouting guards. When the sirens from the police screamed at the abandoned shop of the Steam King, no one told them that a crazy-eyed man in leather ran past with a handful of blue-colored papers and a smell they couldn't place.

144

Chapter 12

Strange Meetings in Familiar Places

The break-in was all over the news. At first, it was reported that thieves from The Bull's Run had broken in looking for scrap to sell; then, the reports became more frightening. Apparently, according to the unrealistically attractive newscasters, a group of anti-government, right-wing activists had banded together with "NukoSteam" terrorist bands, so-called because of their resistance to the regulation of the government-run electrical cooperatives. These terrorists had raided Franklin's garage to steal his plans for devices like the one used at the Eagle's Roost Stadium during the Penguins' game. Akira, Josh, and Braegan all watched the news closely that day—Akira from home and Josh and Braegan keeping small handheld televisions nearby as much as possible. Braegan had such a good plan, Akira thought. We mucked it all up by getting impatient. Besides, what good does it do for us to know they were building trucks that run on gasoline?

Midday rolled around, and anxiety was making each of the three short-tempered when Emmett McDonnell appeared on the television. Braegan stopped his metal lathe and started trying to read lips, the machinery grinding out parts too loud to hear over. In the break room, Josh drank cola and tried to nonchalantly turn up the television there while Akira, across town in her quiet neighborhood, settled into her sofa.

"The new-found owner of Franklin Greene's former garage, Emmett McDonnell, has called a press conference regarding last night's break-in as well as the investigation ongoing into Franklin Greene's connection with domestic terrorism," came the voiceover. "We have cameras on the scene. Let's go now."

Emmett looked every bit the ultra-wealthy businessman that he was. His pressed suit glimmered clean against the dusty backdrop of the mechanic shop. He was a genius. Pictures of Frank doing charity work on top of roofs and working on generators for the poorest of Eagle's Roost hung on the wall behind him to his left. To his right were pictures of City Centre businesses and office buildings where Frank had come in and repaired their emergency power.

Akira's eyes welled up. Emmett was trying to remind people that they knew Frank and that he was no terrorist without extending himself too far politically. Emmett was standing stoically behind a small podium that someone had pulled into the open shop doors where Emmett stood. The effect was that the shop's interior, including the clever propaganda pictures, could be seen behind him; the wind was cut from his microphone, and he shone like a representation of purity and respect in an atmosphere of down-home reliability, regardless of the situation at hand. It was calming, peaceful, and brilliant.

Josh smirked and commented quietly, "He didn't get rich by being stupid, I guess." A few breaths of time had passed while the reporters on scene had clamored about shouting questions to Emmett, who stood unresponsive. Finally, when the noise had turned to silence, he cleared his throat and began his speech.

"The last few months have been nothing short of horrifying for those of you who have been affected by the Eagle's Roost Stadium bombing, and to be clear, we have all been affected. For those of you who knew Franklin Greene, the past week has held confusion, anger, and betrayal. Many of you have received help or service from him and remember him as a charming and capable repairman. His willingness to call out at any hour to keep a business running or a house warm and lighted is no secret to anyone. It was with shock and dismay that many of you heard of his alleged ..." Emmett paused slightly longer than normal here causing the word to sink in, "involvement with the terrorist attack on the Eagle's Roost Stadium.

The investigation has not been definitive, and I encourage everyone not to jump to conclusions until it has reached completion. I have purchased Franklin's possessions and holdings and will cooperate fully with all investigating officers until such time as the inquiry is terminated."

Reporters quickly began shouting questions, asking how he had acquired ownership so quickly and if his connections in politics put him in a conflict of interest with the investigation. Emmett simply smiled and nodded to the reporters until they quieted. "Regarding last night's break-in, while evidence is still being reviewed, it appears this was nothing more than some young people's thrill-seeking, and nothing of any hazardous nature nor of any use to any activist was taken. Thank you."

With that, Emmett McDonnell shook his jacket back straight and smiled at the crowd of shouting reporters as he turned, walked away to his waiting limousine, and left. His personal security was briefly on camera, closing the doors and shooing away reporters.

What happened next couldn't have been more beautiful to the three conspirators if they had personally crafted it. The commentators and newscasters began to talk about Emmett McDonnell, the wealthiest man in the state, who had political connections and business relationships in every field. Pictures of Emmett with dignitaries and people of influence and affluence were on the television for hours as the discussion was how such a connected individual wouldn't allow a business with which his face was now associated to be identified with terror.

Josh and Braegan couldn't contain themselves and cheered quietly with fist bumps and high fives. Alone in her home, Akira smiled and pondered, considering their next move. Emmett had run blocker for them, making himself far more involved than any of them had intended; they would need to capitalize on this and make his risk worthwhile.

Akira's cellular phone began to ring almost immediately following the report. She knew who it would be even though the number was anonymous. "Hello," she replied with a smile.

"I trust you saw the breaking news?" Emmett said with only the slightest hint of sarcasm.

"Yes, I did, Thank you so ..."

Emmett cut her off, "Please, no names, no need of thanks. Meet me tonight by the tree."

With that, he ended the call. The tree? What sort of cryptic nonsense was this? Emmett was a major player in a world she knew nothing of, but this cloak and dagger, coded language, and secrecy seemed a little unneeded. Who would be listening to their conversations? Static electricity from a generator could interfere with a cell signal and even easily intercept the conversation; that's why cellular phones have largely failed in most cities. *Maybe that was why he was so guarded*, she thought. His name coming through the television on feedback from a generator in Truitt or The Run would make anyone's ears perk up.

The phone rang again; this time, it was work. JetStar had a flight booked, and she would be leaving in the morning for Europe. They were filling the zeppelin with water and performing all the pre-flight maintenance now. "Why does everything have to happen at once, all the time?" She groaned. "At least London is a short trip, and I can autopilot nap most of the way."

It was just turning dark when she pulled up to Frank's driveway on her scooter. She had timed it so she would be able to ride without lights all through town and most of the way there and still be concealed by the darkness of late dusk by the time she got there. She couldn't imagine that the police wouldn't be watching his house after all the drama surrounding this ordeal, and she wanted to be sure the last mile or two would be driven by moonlight.

Emmett hadn't specified a time, so she figured dusk was as good as any, and then she could wait. The engine hissed a little pressure release as the steam currently in the expansion stroke was bled to the atmosphere, and then she heard another hiss—this one from over by the metal tree sculpture in Frank's yard. *Good,* she thought. *I did guess which tree was THE Tree.*

She walked over slowly, smiling. She could tell that there were several gathered in the shadows where she had fallen asleep just over a week prior. Emmett was the first to speak as she walked quietly toward the tree. In the moonlight, the oxidized leaves seemed to illuminate pale green as though charged by the sun and were now releasing that cool light into the cooler evening air.

"We wondered if we ought to postpone our continuance or continue without postponement," he said in a hushed but light tone. Akira merely smiled. She was taking in the scene before her and wondering what would play out next. With only a few exceptions, this was the same group that had been knocking down pins at the alley the night of Frank's ... accident. She scanned the group, nodded, and smiled at Josh and Braegan, who sat paired up under the tree against which she had fallen asleep so many days earlier. Penny sat on the stone surrounding the flower bed. Archie was smoking a cigarette and slowly pacing the dark side of the house away from the drive, back and forth slowly and thoughtfully. John and Peter leaned on a fruit tree in the shadows on the edge of the yard.

Emmett cleared his throat and motioned everyone to the crafted metal tree. With his hands at his sides, he began. "I know that none of us believe Frank started shooting at police officers. Please, no interruptions, Braegan." Braegan's mouth closed from where he had not yet given voice to the words in his mouth. "So, the questions must be posited: who wanted Frank out of the way and why? Please, B ... let me finish." Again, Braegan sheepishly hushed. "I have many connections in every local and state government level and even several at the Federal level, and I cannot get any information. This means I have been shut out purposefully." There were many quiet gasps and surprised, even angry, looks from the listeners.

Braegan would not be hushed this time. "Then it's time we take the fight to them! If they, no Emmett," Emmett's hand was up trying to calm Braegan. "If they are blocking you out with all your visibility and money, then they are doing criminal stuff, and we need to flush them out somehow!"

There were many nods, and the small crowd degenerated to ideas on where to hit first and how. No one was too keen on violence, but Archie thought they blockaded the police with old cars, and Josh thought they could try to sneak into some different places to find evidence. Peter was, surprisingly, the most aggressive, stating that it would not be hard to put a person in place in several locations within the local investigative headquarters for the FBI and then lock the place down through an 'accident.'

Emmett raised his voice slightly. "Enough! You do not have the manpower, know-how, or commitment to wage a war on city hall for something about which you don't have any information!" Emmett continued, "This is not unheard of, although it is uncommon, for me to be left out of the loop precisely because of my visibility and means. Melody was not invited tonight, as many of you have already noted in your conversations around the yard. I do not believe she has any involvement, but she may unwittingly know someone who does, and I couldn't risk a power player locally being informed accidentally. Furthermore, if I am being shut out of the loop, she most certainly is as well."

Nods of understanding ensued, and Braegan mumbled, "Get her a few drinks, and she'd tell everyone."

Emmett frowned. "We know that the government—at the state level at least—wanted the metal fabrication plant that was basically wasted space on the back of Frank's shop. We know they had blueprints to build weapons, thanks to some resourceful, albeit irresponsible, thievery. Quite honestly, I don't know what we can do. I have taken ownership of the shop and warehouse, which includes the factory. That will give us some time to figure out whatever we can, but it won't last long. There is no way this will be allowed to stand. The property will be condemned and taken, and seized as part of an ongoing criminal investigation."

Braegan whispered, "Emmett domain, you know," he waited on the punchline, "instead of imminent ..."

Emmett shot him a dirty look but didn't miss a cue, "and we will have to vacate it without collecting anything. Therefore, my first plan of action, if someone is willing to do it, is that Frank's goods, all his tools, manuals, magazines, research, and all raw materials be moved to a storage facility where I am a silent partner outside of town. If this is agreed upon, then I have the paperwork here to grant Akira clearance to enter with whomever she deems acceptable and a pass card for her. Before anyone objects, she was the one to whom Frank left the keys to the shop in an envelope, and I feel she is the one least approachable to the authorities. She is a pilot, and although she doesn't talk about it, she is a well-respected veteran for her military service."

John spoke up now, "Can't you just have some movers load it all up? If there is that much political heat over it, I'm not sure I want to be associated with it. I have kids I have to think of."

Peter similarly expressed his uneasiness over the plan now that it was not merely contracting a third party.

"I can bring a van and help load it all up if you need," Archie said.

"No, I don't think any of you should be involved, really," Josh began.

Braegan nodded and added, "You guys were his friends, no doubt, and I hope none of you feel insulted, but Josh and I were the ones that were stopping in there the most. Even Akira was too busy to make it down very often, no offense, Kira."

Akira choked out a barely audible "None taken."

Emmett looked solemn and raised his hand, "Then all in favor of Braegan and Josh cleaning out Frank's belongings and Akira being the caretaker of those in my own storage—I'll also provide the truck, Archie, so it doesn't come back on you—raise your hand." It was unanimous. "I cannot be personally involved with this any more than I have already pledged. For now, until I know who is pulling the strings, I cannot move my own chess piece lest I lose the checkmate later. Having my name connected with the shop and simultaneously connected with so many political and professional celebrities is about the most protection I can give you for now. Akira, the papers and card will be in your mail tomorrow." With the plan settled, Emmett turned to leave.

"Wait," Akira said before she thought. "That's it? This isn't much of a plan, Em. We're cleaning up. That's all your plan is? We're going to clean up his things and … what?"

Emmett stopped and looked very sad as he looked Akira in the face in the partial moonlight. "I don't know any more than what I have said. There isn't enough information to make a plan. Think Akira, you've trained to respond to horrible situations, but you always need to know who your enemy is. We don't know, and time is not on our side to find out. All I am trying to do now is to preserve the memory of Franklin Greene and hopefully stumble on the evidence I need to show he was gunned down for something he knew. Think of it," his tone turned to a hush as he stepped closer to her, "out of the millions of possible manufacturing plants that were left standing full of vintage equipment capable of building what those prints showed, they chose the one, the only one, with a well-known backyard steam builder and inventor who had recently made regional news opposing something so seemingly politically unimportant as single source provided electricity. Why would they choose that, or him, Akira? I believe there is something in that library or his notes or lying on his shelves that answers that question, and I wouldn't recognize it if I saw it. But Josh and Braegan might."

Akira awkwardly replied, "But there is so much government posturing and media behind the electrification bill. I thought …"

Emmett shook his head, "No, 'Kira, I doubt the union lobbyists and lawmakers for the electricity bill thought he was so much of a threat. Quite honestly, as the city expands toward the river and away from the rural districts, they will make just as much without investing in cables and installation of the system in the lower-income areas. It would be slower, but that bill in itself is not the reason." He straightened up and stepped back. "What I will do while you," he cleared his throat and looked at her from under his brows, "clean up as you say this is," he paused for everyone to hear, "I'll use my connections in the police to try to get traffic cameras and other footage to see what happened that night. I know, Josh. I saw what you were telling Archie about, and I can only assume there is more. Goodbye, all of you. I hope to see you again soon by the sun and with better news."

Marie, one of Emmett's security attachés, handed Akira a thick yellow paper packet, gave her a nod, and the four walked off to his car, parked out back where it would be nearly impossible to see. Archie, John, and Peter followed suit after giving Akira a quick hug and a disappointed, half smile.

It was raining and cool when Akira, Josh, and Braegan arrived at the shop to begin sorting things inside. She had called in sick to work for the first time in several years. Josh and Braegan had done similarly and had been told not to make a habit of it. They walked in quietly and stood just inside the doorway, staring around the place in silence. During the lockdown, the police had rifled through everything. Papers were strewn about, and items had been knocked off shelves and not picked up. It was not like a movie scene so much as a sloppy teenage boy's room. It was depressing and overwhelming to the three who knew this place so well. Frank might have left a few things lying around, but the shop stayed neat more than not. There was a distinct absence of freshly brewed coffee smell in the air, and there was no music playing. No customers were chatting and laughing with the always happy mechanic. No one was asking why he disliked the idea of the government taking generators away from people. There was no banging of metal or sizzle of the torch when it hit the soldering. Akira looked around the shop and thought it looked like death had pillaged it. She knew it was not death but rather someone in the government—someone with plans to build tanks, someone who thought Frank knew something or had some information more than anyone else, someone with dangerous motives and little reservation.

"So …" Braegan sighed loudly, "I guess let's get started. We can't find anything until we look." They started in the shop where Frank had done most of his work and where the customers had stayed to relax. Magazines, newspapers, and parts that none of them recognized lay here and there in Frank's haphazard organization. Josh said what a few of them were, and Braegan rolled his eyes and told him he thought he knew more than he actually knew.

After a lunch break, they moved on to the office; the main shop had not taken as long as they thought, and they were beginning to enjoy having something to do even though the stories about Frank and the memories sometimes brought tears to their eyes. The office was where Frank had the makeshift apartment. It was not kept as neat as the shop because it was meant only for himself. This space, too, had been gone through once before by "inspectors." Personal effects, nothing of any interest to anyone but Frank, were all that occupied this space. After looking it over with a smile, Josh grabbed Frank's favorite coffee cup and slipped it into his duffle bag.

"Hey, what are you doing?" Braegan asked.

Josh looked at him with a shrug. "If we are going to store all of this, I don't want to let this go to storage and get lost. Do you remember when he got this? We had all gone to a Valentine's Day mixer thing for singles. It was horrible!"

Braegan shook his head, laughing, "No, I didn't go; it was you, Akira, Melody, and Frank."

Josh smiled wider, "Oh, that's right, you were already married to your first wife. We didn't go as couples, but everyone there thought we did, so no one talked to us for half the night until Akira walked up to some random guy and told him I thought he was cute. I could have murdered her! But it did get the conversations going!"

"So, where'd the cup come from in all that?" Braegan asked.

"Well, they had silly and sappy gifts for the supposed lovebirds on the way out the door. They also had a few more sarcastic gifts, so Melody bought this one for Frank. It says, 'So you're bitter. Everyone loves coffee, and it is, too!'"

Braegan laughed hard, and Akira softly cried but laughed at the memory. The cup had a picture of a sour-faced older man with a fedora pulled low over his ears. Akira remembered Frank making that face to her several times in the past when she was down. It usually brought a small smile to her face, just like it was now.

After much time and effort, the office and the shop were pretty clean and neat. They were not yet boxing things up. Akira felt like they needed things back where they had been before boxing them away again, and Josh and Braegan didn't really know what to do, so Akira led, and they followed. They opened the door to the massive library of old manuals and technical data, fearing the worst. The 'library' was in the warehouse portion of the automotive factory. It still had an eclectic collection of parts from when this had been used to build petrol and steam autos during the interwar period, and Frank had stored some of his more valuable or unusual parts in it as well. However, most of the shelves had been left with only a scattered selection of parts that Frank had moved to fill the racks farthest from the shop. On the racks and shelves nearest the shop, or what had been the factory's office, Frank had a collection of technical manuals, mechanic's digests, popular scientific and whatever other sort of magazine appealed to him or that he thought he might get some use from. It was in these rows upon rows of journals and periodicals that Frank had found the mention of the bomb, the hydrogen gas bomb that was used at the Eagle's Roost Stadium.

Akira groaned inside herself as they opened the doors. What would be of all these papers if the shop and the office had been so messed up while someone had snooped? The door slid open easily, and rows of neatly boxed books lay before them. Whoever had been doing the snooping had planned to take these somewhere else and go through them more slowly.

Braegan and Josh shook their heads. Akira crouched down to a squat and stared at the books. "Call the trucks, Akira; we found what they were looking for. Now we just have to find which one," Braegan said.

Akira nodded, "I think we should go through them ourselves. I'll bring in some other boxes, and we'll take anything that looks suspicious or interesting and move it. Then I'll call the trucks." Josh and Braegan were exhausted, but they knew time was of the essence. With a moan and a sigh, the two men began opening boxes to see what could be found. They worked late into the night, and finally, all three fell asleep reading magazines. No one knew who had fallen asleep first or who awoke first because they simply resumed their research when they awakened.

About halfway through the next day, Braegan wearily addressed the other two: "I think we have at least glanced at every book and magazine in here. There is no way we are going to make smart decisions as tired as we are. Let's have Em haul this stuff and put it away. If we missed anything, we can come back to it later." Akira and Josh nodded their consent, barely able to form words in their sleep-deprived stupor. Maybe they felt that the sooner they had some answers, the sooner they could grieve. Perhaps they just clung to the memory of Frank so desperately that stopping their work would let the day-in, day-out drum of life erase him. But all of them shared a sense of urgency, an inner need to find whatever could be found or to know for certain there was nothing to find.

Emmett's trucks came the next day, and the movers started loading box after box of Frank's things. Akira had to leave for her flight. She hugged Josh around the shoulders, and Braegan patted her back as she left. Josh stared as they hauled away the entire contents of the office, shop, and finally, the library/warehouse. He sighed, "I feel like we have put Frank in the grave for good, and I'm not even convinced he is dead."

"Say that again?" Braegan intoned.

Josh repeated his thought a little louder but still in hushed tones: "I feel like we are burying him, and I am not even convinced he is dead."

Braegan nodded slowly, forming his thoughts. "I feel the same. I wonder if it is because all this drama over his work has kept us from planning a, you know ... a funeral," he trailed off into a whisper.

It took a half dozen moving trucks to get it all, and that did not include any of the equipment from the factory floor that no one really knew what to do with. The two of them silently watched, silently thought of Frank, and then silently left.

As Braegan had noted, the group of friends that surrounded Frank had all been so stunned and so confused by his death that no one had planned a funeral. The phone rang in Akira's apartment that night, but she wasn't there. The call went to voicemail, but no message was left, and the caller did not have a recognizable number when she got home to check it. She expected Emmett to be calling, discussing the storage, and letting them know everything had arrived safely. Her trip to London and back safely in the bag, she wondered whether they would call again. Exhausted, Akira fell asleep on the couch with Captain in her lap.

It seemed she had only closed her eyes—though it was actually just over two hours later—when the phone did ring again, and Penny spoke from the other end: "Hey 'Kira, I know you've been busy, but some people at work that supported Frank are wondering when there will be a funeral or memorial."

Akira rubbed her eyes and felt exhaustion begin to take over again. "Penny, I have never planned a funeral. I don't know any of Frank's family, and I am exhausted. I know we need to have one, to honor him, to let the people grieve … or if they are among the morons on the news, rejoice," she spat out the words angrily, "but I just don't know where to start."

Penny was nodding as she answered, though Akira couldn't see. Her grandparents had passed away only a few years earlier, and she had taken care of their memorials. "I'll take care of it, 'Kira. I haven't felt like there was anything I could do up to now, so I'll gladly do it." They discussed details, size, and location, said thanks, and hung up the phone. It was time for some much-needed playing with Captain. Akira threw his yarn rope, and he brought it back until she began to smile. Dogs know love; they understand it. *Dogs know loss and miss you, she thought. I wish we could be more like dogs. We could just live our lives without a care, and loneliness could be cured with a rope toy.*

Scheduling a funeral turned out to be very difficult. Penny tried several different dates, but Melody was swamped with official city business, and Emmett was also very difficult to find at a free moment. Even Akira's flight schedule was nearly impossible to coordinate with anyone else. Summer was slipping by quickly. The uproar over Franklin Greene's shop and shootout, as well as the bombing, had started to settle a little. Penny finally got the funeral scheduled, skipping the church ceremonies and choosing a graveside ceremony with little production. Just a few friends would share memories and then have a dinner at Franklin's shop in his honor. The newspapers reported that it would be a "small family and friends" type of event. The evening news was kind enough not to refer to him as anything but "a controversial local mechanic" when they announced the proceedings. The news and authorities, however, were not kind for long.

Franklin's friends arrived in plenty of time to chat and comfort one another but were surprised that there were already about ten people gathered. John, Peter, Akira, and Josh all drove separately but arrived within moments of each other. As they began to console each other and tell stories of Frank, the small group of bystanders moved in and began to share their own stories of him. "I hadn't had any food for a month. I was dumpster diving for my food because I had no power to store anything, and I couldn't afford to buy any to replace what had spoiled when my power went down. Franklin Greene was out riding that bike he made and talked to me. While I was gone the next day, he fixed my breaker box and my generator so that I had backup power." Several of the others were nodding about the similarities in their stories. "Then he filled my fridge with food. Since I had enough food for the month, I was able to start looking for work every day, and now I ain't had to be broke since. He saved my life."

The stories continued for nearly an hour as more of the close group of friends arrived and more of the residents of Truitt and The Run crashed the funeral. Sometimes Frank had worked for free, sometimes he had temporarily given the person a job to pay him back, and sometimes he had just given them an open-ended time on when they could pay him.

Josh was openly crying. Braegan was red- and wet-eyed but still as sarcastic as ever. After the ceremony had officially begun, he leaned in to whisper to Josh, "A gravesite with an empty grave. Frank would find this ridiculous." Josh smiled amid the tears. Melody, who had arrived in a limousine, was wiping mascara frequently. Only

Akira was not tearful; she was smiling. She smiled and worked to memorize everything that was being said about Frank. She definitely would cry, but it would be when these memories and stories came back to her in the quiet times as her silver airship floated over the oceans, and there was nothing else to do but think. Emmett had ridden with and stood near Melody as she shared her own memories.

Eventually, the minister began to speak, quoting the 23 Psalm: "He makes me to lie down in green pastures ..." As Josh was supposed to speak but couldn't pull himself together, one of the residents of Truitt told his story of Franklin's goodness to him. Akira hugged Penny close and thanked her.

"Would you like to ride with me to the shop, 'Kira? I think Josh is. He certainly shouldn't drive with the way he is upset," Penny offered." Akira thought for a moment and then nodded. It wasn't all that far, and it felt good to be around friends for now.

The procession was short. The cars snaked through side streets, moving slowly. People lined the street from Truitt and The Run. Akira noticed Josh staring at the gravesite and turned to see what had his attention. There, beside the headstone, was an odd group of people, four or five, dressed in black but not like any of the rest of the mourners. They didn't look poorer, though certainly not any wealthier than those of Truitt; they simply didn't fit in. The clothing was not Victorian vintage. It was older styles before the retro-chic movement of the last decade. The oldest man in the group caught Akira's eye. He wore mostly black with denim jeans and brown leather boots. His jacket was an older-styled Western casual jacket with pearl snaps on the breast pockets. Akira figured it was some of the farmers from the country church that Frank attended and smiled faintly. Most Truitt and The Run residents had returned home or were walking along the roadside. It was only those close to Frank personally who were driving there. Melody's limo was in front, of course, with her and Emmett.

When they arrived at the shop, there was a group of about fifty of Frank's former customers, all being kept at a distance from the shop by police tape. In silent opposition, the city SWAT stood armed and armored inside the tape circle.

Meriwether stood with the customers, angrily phoning everyone he could think of. Melody and Emmett got out of her car and quickly ran to him. He held up his hand for a moment as he finished his phone conversation: "Yes, yes … I understand that, SIR. But this is outrageous, and hello? He hung up? He hung up on me!" Meriwether was completely out of sorts and angry.

Melody was indignant. "What is the meaning of all this, Meriwether? Have you found out who authorized this?" She demanded imperiously. Meriwether replied equally indignantly and royally, "I, Madam, haven't a clue, and the Mayor just hung up on me!"

Emmett was stoic and emotionless as he watched his old school friend, Melody, and this other player from the city flail their arms and act in frustration.

Josh and Braegan got out of the cars they were riding in almost simultaneously. Akira could be heard telling Josh to stay in the car, but he was not listening. Expletives began to flow loudly from Braegan's mouth as he and Josh pushed through the crowd to the officers behind the tape. "Drop that gun and see if you can keep me out!" Braegan immediately threatened. The SWAT officer did not reply.

Josh was even less deterred in an emotional haze and simply jumped the tape and kept walking toward the shop. "SIR, stay behind the line, Sir!"

The officers began yelling at Joshua over each other. "ON THE GROUND!" came the next unheeded command. One of the officers broke away from the pack and stopped Josh with a tackle maneuver. He began to get up, so the officer slipped cuffs on his hands and feet. "Stay down!" The officer commanded. The crowd was having none of that. The yelling became a roar, and bottles began to arc through the air. A police loudspeaker blared through the din, "Please disperse and return to your homes!" The crowd became quieter in response. "This business is a crime scene. Please disperse!"

Akira was furious. She looked at Emmett with fire in her eyes, and he shook his head sadly and with an unspoken instruction. Melody and Meriwether stared for a moment, then shrugged and returned to their cars. Braegan was not calming down but was at least not becoming physical. "Emmett, there is nothing for us to do here. Let's go get on the phone at my office, and we'll do what we can. Come along!"

Melody called to him. "A moment, Miss Maine," he replied.

Emmett walked over to Akira, leaned in as though to give a comforting hug, and whispered to her, "This is all very suspect, but exactly what I said was likely to happen, correct?"

Akira nodded almost imperceptibly. "Gather our friends before they are charged. I hope you found some information in all his things. I fear the plot has thickened." With that and a quick hug, Emmett went to the waiting limo with Melody Maine and drove away. Akira sighed and kicked Braegan in the back of the knees just enough that he dropped a little. She helped him up and, before he could start yelling again, told him, "Get Josh, if you can, and shut up." His eyes burned, and the rage in them was obvious, but he knew she was right. He also knew better than to argue with her.

One of the officers came over with Josh at her beckoning. "Ma'am, we'll have to book him into the jail for the night." Akira shook her head lightly and looked at the helmeted officer, "Sir, we just came from our best friend's funeral. Emotions were already high, and then all of this. We're taking him home if you will allow us. I know you don't want to do the paperwork. You can see he isn't a troublemaker. I mean, he didn't even fight you when you knocked him down or when you cuffed him. I was an Air Force officer, and I understand procedures and orders. But, please, officer?"

The officer stood for a moment, holding Josh by the arm. He began to nod slowly, then spoke: "You know, we're just doing our job. I liked Frank. Take this guy home, and don't be seen anywhere tonight with him." The officer released Josh, and the three walked to Penny's car. Penny had never left the car; she was still weeping in the front seat and didn't utter a word as she drove them back to their cars and then left for her home.

Chapter 13

Emmet's Cogitations

Emmett had lost Frank's shop, at least temporarily. Emmett was a godly man and tried to remember that if that's what was going to happen, his Lord must be behind it. Nevertheless, it rankled and bothered him that something was afoot, and he had no idea what it was. The last thing he wanted to do at this moment was to attend a charity banquet, but that was exactly what he had to do. Going maintained the appearance of business as usual for him. It allowed him to listen to the elite's scuttlebutt, and the banquet was in his honor. Even though it was held in his honor, he did not feel honored; he only felt saddened. He felt this way at nearly every dinner of this sort. The elites from around the world would arrive in their overpriced and glitzy autos and be escorted across a red carpet while the media flashed pictures of them in their excessively expensive outfits. There was always back-patting, handshaking, and fake smiles.

He self-checked his cynicism and the mild depression that always ate at the back of his thoughts. There were some true friends there, at least as much as true friends existed in the Hollywood and Washington elite circles. Ronald McIverson was as solid as a stone, reliable, and funny, Emmett thought. He always enjoyed Ronald's jesting and barbed sarcasm, which often targeted himself and the ridiculousness of being wealthy in this country and what that brought with it. It was well known that Emmett had inherited his 'starter wealth,' as many called it. From there, however, Emmett had been a shrewd investor and businessman. He was well known for having an intuition about where to invest and how. Most credited his intelligence and research, which didn't hurt, to be sure, but Emmett gave prayer and meditation all the credit. He had learned, though, that sharing this with his circle of acquaintances only hurt business without furthering his opportunities to share his faith. His reputation was also that he was always fair, even kind, and generous without depleting the bank from whence that generosity flowed. This reputation gave him more opportunity to talk about his Judeo-Christian beliefs in kindness and giving. That was why this banquet was held with his name attached. The only reason he attended was to generate money to start a trust that would buy leftover food from local restaurants and deliver it to the poor. Less food waste in the garbage and fewer hungry while also obtaining better food than the normal donations they might get was good for everyone. Emmett believed in the cause, so he tolerated the self-important along with truly altruistic guests.

Emmett wasn't a dour sort of person, not at all. No, indeed, fighting mild clinical depression had caused him to seek out spiritual avenues for dealing with his inner turmoil. He had tried a multitude of religious avenues and, for a while, even alcohol, but he had found peace in the more traditional midwestern values of the Bible and began to have real joy instead of the day-by-day dragging doldrums that afflicted him previously. This, in turn, made him even more of an oddity among the elite who sought out gurus and eastern traditional meditation. Emmett was private with his faith and lifestyle choices tonight. He had endured the mockery of being called a Bible thumper and holy roller by his associates. He endured speculation about his sexuality due to his single relationship status and that he was never seen dating anyone. The truth of the matter was that he preferred time alone in the quiet rather than out socializing. This made it hard to meet anyone and get to know them. He and Frank had always bonded over their faith, being single, and a desire to help people of lower station. They would laugh and joke for hours when they were younger. It was Frank who had introduced Emmett to his faith and the possibility of a meaningful and enjoyable life. Frank's death was heavy on his mind tonight as the funeral lay just a few days past. He worked the room, talking to patrons and guests, making and maintaining connections. He knew his business and how to gladhand. That's what kept the billfolds open and investors happy. That's what kept one informed on important politics and what kept investment advice coming. You had to keep up a persona and be a people person. *People invest in you*, he often reminded himself, *not in your businesses*. He figured that questions about acquiring Gramp's Garage and Franklin Greene's shop were inevitable. He was correct.

Ronald sauntered casually and firmly shook Emmett's hand in greeting: "Hey Emmett! Man, good to see you. I think you and I are in the minority of people who know what this whole shindig is about!" Ronald laughed. Emmett had been listening, almost eavesdropping, in the room, and there was little discussion of the poor, of food, or even of donations. Most of the donation talk was comparing the amounts to be given. Ronald continued: "So what's with buying the steam repair shop? I heard he was a friend of yours and left it to you. Weird times, man. Still, I guess it's a decent enough real estate holding."

Emmett was gathering breath and his thoughts to answer when another guest, Diedre Pulman, swooped in between the two with a hand outstretched in a similar greeting. "Emmett, old dear, HOW have you been?" she queried with unneeded flair. "I heard your name on the news the other day and had to stop my online spinning class to see what it was about. How dreadful! And that man was one of your friends? Did you even know? And now you own his old building?! Whatever do you think is inside?!"

Emmett replied with a strained smile, "Yes, I've known Franklin since we were children. How is your husband, Diedre?" She laughed an uncomfortable laugh, waved her hand, and swooshed away as quickly as she had interrupted.

Ronald excused himself, "Emmett, I hope we can talk later, not about anything of importance. I have to go see that gentleman over there," he said with a nod and a pat on the shoulder, showing he understood that Emmett wasn't wanting to discuss Frank's shop.

Emmett looked in the direction Ronald was walking, and there he saw Meriwether sipping a glass of wine and puffing on a thin cigarette. Some state political lobbyists were in the group. Emmett couldn't remember their names immediately, but after thinking about it as he milled around, he was sure he'd recall them. Emmett had a glass of ice cream-filled punch as he walked about the room. He would talk a bit and then sip on his punch when others spoke. That way, if they said something he had to think about, he could sip a bit before speaking.

"Emmett, I have missed you so!" came a lilting greeting from Patricia Corniss. She approached him confidently. She was in her early thirties, roughly the same age as Emmett, and wealthy by her own making. She had made a fortune in tech, coding games for cell phones. She was dark-haired, for now, and a beauty. She swayed up to Emmett and snaked an arm around his waist, leaning in a little too closely. She had been drinking the complimentary wine. Emmett smiled sweetly at her. "Em, Em, I was so glad you bought Frank's shop! I have wanted to buy that place for a long time. It's right on a major route! Well, once the city has expanded to the river, it will go back that way, and the route will become a major one. You could do sooooo much with that place! I don't think any of what they say about him is true. You aren't friends with anyone that could hurt anyone. Well, except Maine, she seems dangerous, HA! Too much ambition, I think. She does good things, though. More than I can say for those guys over there!" She drawled out her southern Arkansas accent as she jerked a thumb toward Meriwether Lewis and the lobbyists. Emmett wasn't sure how to answer; she was not usually so blunt. He leaned in close to her ear and felt her become tense. Flushing red, he whispered to her, "Patty, you are more lovely tonight than normal, which is saying quite a lot, but you have had more wine than you realize. People will think you are jealous of Miss Maine. I'll call a cab and check on you later if you like."

She straightened up, leaning back more than she intended, and looked into his eyes, staring deeply as they made contact. "Thank you, Emmett, but I own this hotel. I think I will retire for a couple of hours. Please do check in on me later," she answered with a wink. "Oh, and Maine doesn't have anything on what I have!" she flirted with a sway of hips and a pose that any model would envy. With a wave of her hand, an attaché had come alongside to walk her upstairs. She waved warmly to all the guests as she left and promised to return shortly, though she had no intention of doing so.

Emmett smiled despite his embarrassment; he had never been able to talk to women. The fact that she, a single woman, was openly flirting with him on yet another public occasion left him feeling even more awkward. Many nearby had been eavesdropping in and now returned to their disinterested chatter. Clearing his throat, he managed to navigate the room to the lobbyists and Meriwether. The names returned to him as he had expected; he had trained himself to remember names. It was a must in his position in life. He quietly shook hands as they welcomed him into their conversation.

"Emmett! Good to see you! It must be quite a hoot to have this whole banquet named after you! Say, will the leftover caviar from this go to the homeless?" one of them joked.

Emmett smiled politely as he answered, "It wasn't my idea to be sure, Troy. I also doubt that any of tonight's food would keep well enough after being exposed to all this hot air." Troy roared in laughter while the others merely smiled. Emmett addressed them each in turn. Troy, Peter, Herbert, and lastly Meriwether. They shook hands despite Meriwether wearing the typical white cloth gloves that he wore when driving the antique Rolls Royce to a prestige event.

Meriwether immediately turned the conversation to Emmett and the repair shop. "Emmett," he began," do you intend to put a mechanic in Franklin's old shop? I don't have anywhere to go with my Rolls. You know it is rather unique nowadays." Emmett merely shook his head, but Meriwether wasn't finished. "Well, what do you intend to do with it? It's hardly a valuable holding, and from what I understand, there is a bit of pressure to close it permanently due to

… you know, all the … things about it … now." He trailed off purposefully, seeming awkward about the situation.

Herbert picked up the baton of sensitive subjects, just like Meriwether had hoped someone would. He coughed and asked, "Ahem, yes, Emmett, that must be a dicey situation holding the property of a friend that is now considered, well, I guess it's no secret that he's been branded a terrorist. I'm sorry, Emmett. I know he was your friend, but it's all over the news. You surely didn't know what he was making in there, right?"

Emmett maintained a painted-on smile as he answered, "He was a friend and not a terrorist, nor did he craft a bomb. There has been a great error in reporting. The property is only being held while his possessions are being dealt with according to the police investigation and his will," he calmly intoned.

Troy interrupted, "Heard there was some sort of break-in. Did they get away with anything?"

Emmett just shook his head. "I don't know. The police are looking into that."

Peter snidely commented, "It seems that someone with underworld connections wouldn't want to leave his workshop to someone with political connections that could get him caught."

Troy barked, "Well, he's dead, so he's not worried about getting caught!"

Emmett stared at Troy, who looked only slightly disappointed that no one laughed. "Gentlemen, I think I will continue my social duties. Good evening. Remember to try the *hors d'oeuvres*." He nodded his head slightly and walked off. He suddenly had an unshakeable feeling that something was even more wrong with the situation than he had thought previously. The night stretched on for Emmett, and although few were as brash as the self-important lobbyists and Meriwether, all the conversation pivoted to be about

Frank and him. Peggy Ulberth asked if they were close. Sal Haddis asked if the shop would be for sale and on and on through the night. It was clear that he would need to distance himself from this as much as he could while still being true to his friends. This was going to be a tightrope walk; something more seemed to be going on. Too many people not in real estate but very involved in politics were concerned.

Eventually, he felt it was allowable to duck out of the crowd. The wine had been running freely, and the speeches had been completed, congratulating the attendees on their excellency of character for their donations and support. Joseph Glit and Phoebe Shumacker were always good at stroking egos in a speech and generating support. Emmett shook the last hands he felt he needed to and found the elevator. Though he would not check in as she had meant, perhaps he would leave a note for Patty. "Dear Patricia," he wrote in his most ornate script, "The pleasure of your company was most welcome tonight. Would you be interested in another evening soon without the wine but with a sunset?" The elevator door chimed and opened. He walked the plush carpet to the penthouse suite, where Patricia would be napping off her excess wine. Standing at the door, he could not make himself push the note through the mail slot nor leave it on the table. Anxiety began to work at the edge of his mind, and he could feel his heartbeat step up. With a deep sigh, he turned and walked back down the hallway. "I have nothing to offer her that she does not possess already. Why should she care to give up any habit just to be in the habit of seeing me?" he thought to himself.

A hotel porter appeared from a supply room door almost on top of Emmett as he walked, and they exchanged surprised gestures. "Sir," the porter bowed his head dutifully. Emmett returned the gesture, his mind running over a dozen reasons for why he was up here, though he knew no reason was necessary. The porter waited silently, looking at the note in Emmett's hand. "Please deliver this note to Miss Patricia," Emmett finally blurted out, trying to sound businesslike.

The porter took the note and placed it with a handful of cards on a tray containing bottled water and aspirin. "Yes sir, anything else?"

Emmett shook his head, smiled politely, and went to the elevator. The doors shut, and he closed his eyes, calming his mind. "On to other things," he whispered as the conversations and questions about Frank began to force back into his mind. He hoped the driver would have something else to talk about on the way home.

Emmett sat in his study in the dark. The charity gala had been stressful, and he had kept quiet and shut away from the media ever since. He couldn't say too much in public without hurting his bystander status in all this mess. The funeral's mayhem had stirred up suspicions already brewing for him. He slowly tapped a gold and ebony pen against a notepad on his desk as he stared into the shadows along his library wall. He liked it dark when he was deeply thinking. There were no distractions. The antique grandfather clock ticked as it sat along the wall, the pendulum swinging lazily back and forth. *Tick, tock, tick, tock* … Emmett's own heartbeat slowed to match. Peaceful, deep concentration had settled in over him. It was meditative. Many of the items in the study were from his uncle, but it was not nostalgia that had made Emmett keep them. Though he was wealthier, by an order of magnitude, than his uncle had ever been, these items were beautiful and of high quality. The chair that was of thick and supple leather, the desk of mahogany and cherry, the bookcases that matched the desk, jade decorations, and the crystal serving set on the wet bar well reminded him of his uncle's eye for quality. The crystal tumblers often caught the moonlight during the summer evenings and happened to be in such a place that they drew his attention when he reclined in his chair. Tonight, there was little moonlight as the light clouds floated over the sky, muting its brightness and casting only a pale glow on the landscape. *Tick, tock, tick, tock.*

Emmett was disturbed by the events that had unfolded around the death of his friend. Frank was just a mechanic or a good ol' boy to most people locally. Emmett was not most people, though, and knew that Frank's everyman image had struck a chord with the voting public. His willingness to comment on what he viewed as the government's role had angered many in government much higher than Eagle's Roost. Emmett knew for certain within his heart that Franklin Greene had been murdered to silence him and to intimidate those more powerful who agreed with him. Franklin was the most recognizable of the people who spoke out about the electrification bill if that was even where the connection lay. No, that had to be the connection. Where do all these pieces fit together? *Tap, tap, tap, tap.* How come Frank and not another mechanic and not another shop? Frank was obviously the target because the newspapers and tabloid television had kept his face and name in front of people. He was the face of … what? A revolution? Resistance? Rebellion? Why his shop? Why had the local and state governments seemed to take an interest in the shop itself? What was unique about his shop? It was the front of a years-out-of-date automotive plant. There was machinery in place that might be used to build pre-war-style autos. That didn't seem like enough to make it politically or economically valuable, but that had to be why Frank's shop was so quickly locked down. It was all that separated it from any other repair shop. *Tick, tock, tick, tock,* the grandfather clock synchronized his heartbeat, and his pen tapped in rhythm. His mind rolled the puzzle pieces over and over. More and more pieces seemed out of place, and more and more questions arose within him. Emmett tapped his pen slightly faster as his thinking and heart rate sped up faster than the clock's ticking: *tap, tap, tappity, tap.* How did the city and guards quietly organize the shutdown of the shop, factory, and warehouse and get it done so quickly during the funeral? *Tap, tap, tap, tap, tick-tock, tick, tock, tap, tap, tap,* someone had to be connected between all the parties involved. *Is someone using my connection to Frank?* he pondered at a murmur. *No,* he answered the thought. He was aware that he knew very little of Frank's business. He wouldn't be of any use for anything but a cover, and no one had covered with his name or presence yet.

The clock continued to pace as he took a drink of cool water to calm himself. *Tick, tock, tick.* His pen continued to tap just slightly out of rhythm with the clock, *tap, tap, tap, tap.* Who had he seen at all the events? *Tap, tap, taptataptatap.* That person would be the go-between if there was a common connection. That would be the person who is too conspicuous to be the plotter, the planner, the mind behind the movement. *Tick, tock, tick, tock.* But that would be the person … *tataptataptatap* … that ties the city to the shop. But … anyone with any experience in politics like that would not have the same connection to the military and guard units … *tick, tock, tick, tock.* That person, though, would be obvious … *tatappatatappatatappa* … someone who would fit in with the City Centre but also be familiar enough with Franklin Greene's shop that no one would particularly notice—or if they noticed, no one would care that a City Centre socialite was at a steam shop on the edge of The Run … *tappatappatappatappatappatappa* … that … *tap, tap* would make logical … *tap, tap, tap* … sense … *tick, tap, tock, tap, tick, tap, tock.* Now then, who are they talking to? Emmett laid down his pen and looked at it thoughtfully. It was time to sleep. He had names to check on in the morning. Maybe things would become clearer with some rest.

Chapter 14

To Love and Have Lost

Akira wandered about her home quietly, thoughtfully, the beige Berber carpet in the living room, silencing both her own steps and the padding of Captain's feet as he followed her into the kitchen. She was not the type to find comfort in food, but she realized that the summer's emotions and its events had been causing her to lose weight unhealthily. A chicken sandwich would be comforting even though lost in thought again today. Captain watched closely to help clean up anything that fell to the floor. She had never been the political type. That had always been Melody. Frank was passionate about a few issues, but he was not 'political.' Not her, though. She had fought too much for politicians and had too many bad dreams from when she was serving her country. She didn't regret her military service—quite the contrary. She appreciated the opportunity to show her love of her country. She reveled in being at the top of her class in AIT. She bragged to military buddies about being able to best men twice her size in hand-to-hand combat despite her height and female shape, which most saw as a hindrance to fighting. "Eye candy," she remembered one sergeant calling her before she put him in a submission hold. She was well-decorated for her time flying and deserving of even more accolades. A small shadow box on the wall held her medals and awards and a folded-up uniform. She was proud of her success in the Air Force, even if part of her success was killing when needed.

This time, however, she found herself in the arena of political posturing and deception as she tried to figure out what had happened to Frank and his shop. Had Emmett not become involved and said all he had—and implied even more—she would likely have not continued to dwell on it. She would have mourned and moved on, allowing Braegan to have conspiracy theories and be 'crazy.'

Things had simply happened very fast since Frank's death. Not only did she feel that things had happened too quickly to be chance, but she felt they had happened in ways that seemed orchestrated by power players to not *appear* to have been orchestrated by power players, even though those players were obviously involved. *Now I am confusing myself even more*, she thought. Where was the motive, who were those players in power, why Frank, and what did Emmett mean about his shop being only one of many with equipment? There were just too many questions.

Josh had ridden his autocycle home, angry, bruised, and hurt in more ways than physically. Sitting down on her leather sofa, she pictured Josh in her mind. Akira sighed, and Captain briefly turned his attention from her sandwich to her face. *Why would anyone be sad while holding a sandwich like that?* He seemed to ponder as he tilted his head to one side. In her mind, she could see the boiling anger and confusion in Josh's eyes. That didn't bother her much. Josh was always happy, but everyone gets confused and angry from time to time. What really bothered her and what kept coming to the forefront of her memory from the evening of the funeral was how sad his eyes were. Sad may not even be the right word. Defeated. They had known that Emmett's hold of the warehouse and shop was temporary, but it had seemed like a glimmer of hope. It felt like maybe they could sort some things out and properly deal with the death of Franklin Greene. The news may say he was a terrorist, but no one believed it. Those close to him were not being allowed a chance to respectfully mourn, and it had felt like they might get that chance—and even a chance to clear his name. Then that chance was gone, and the police were, apparently, instructed to forcefully control anyone who stepped out of line. How could they hope to make any forward motion on any sort of investigation or anything with the police involved and seemingly not helping?

That was the look Josh had in his eyes behind the anger— defeat. Helpless defeat. It was the sorrow of being wronged and impotent, having no power whatsoever to right the wrong. She hated that look. She had seen it in other countries when the military had picked the wrong target. She had seen it in other countries when the people had learned helplessness from decades of oppression. She had helped deliver entire areas of the map from that look. She had also been 'just doing her job' or 'just following orders' and caused that look. She sipped her tea and took a bite of chicken. Captain panted happily in anticipation. She was not happy about the times when mindlessly following orders had caused others hopelessness. What can you do, though, but follow orders? Those were the memories Josh brought back. Now, she sat on her sofa, with Captain laying against her leg as she thought, and this time, she began to feel helpless.

Tears again began to well up in her eyes. "I am tired of crying. I'm not a crier," she mumbled to herself. Then, the tears flowed in floods. She had expected to focus on the memories from the funeral high in the air after a long flight had settled into autopilot. "Frank was always so sweet. I think he made so many friends, his substitute family, because his family was all gone ..." she mumbled, then broke into yet more tears. "I didn't focus on work because I didn't care about his life. I wanted to be in his life! I wanted it to be our life ever since we were ten, and he was the only one in that low-income school who didn't think Asians all ate dogs, had the bodies of little boys, were naturally mathematicians, and should be avoided. We were always so close, but I was too afraid to lose a friend if we dated. We rode bicycles, raced cars, rode autocycles, plinked with guns on the weekends, went to the drive-in movies ... did everything together. Even when he and Mel were dating, we always hung out. Why didn't I tell him? He probably never thought of me as more than his tomboy friend, one of the guys. I don't have Mel's flashy blonde hair and smooth speech, and he didn't really chase many girls anyway. That's part of why I went away. I couldn't stand to be his buddy when I always wanted him with me. Maybe some of this could have been avoided if I had just toughed it out and stayed around."

She sighed. "Even if I had been in his life more, I might not be able to piece things together. Josh doesn't seem to know anything I don't, and no one was around him more than Josh. Braegan might know a little something, but it's all just him making guesses. Besides," she sarcastically laughed, "he's always finding conspiracies in the government. Obviously, something is going on here, but I can't believe that the government is involved. Melody is too busy being Miss-Up-and-Coming-Politician to care. She wouldn't be able to say anything even if she found out. She'd surely say something if the city was in the know. I hate her so much. Why did she have to get in the way every single time I tried to talk to him? She's always had everything she wanted, which wasn't enough unless she had a little of what I wanted. Well, you had to get cosmetic surgery to get some of what I have, and my being Asian made it sting that much more, so there! Akira snorted out loud to her silent thoughts. Well, Mel, now you can't take up his time! If I had been around him as much as you had, he wouldn't have been driving home alone, that's for sure!"

She sighed and leaned back on the couch. "It's not her fault. It is someone's fault, but not hers, I guess. Even if I had been with him, or if," she rolled her eyes, "she had been, there'd just be another body in the smoking wreckage … wait." She stopped for a moment and looked at Captain while she thought. Captain cocked his head to one side, and his tongue fell out to the side of his mouth. "No one has seen any wreckage, or bodies, from either vehicle …" It was too late for her to call anyone, and she didn't even know what to do with this question that was building in her mind; there definitely was a question there gnawing at her, though.

"Who do I know who would have access to the towed vehicles, the fire and EMS or coroner's reports, or anything related? The news has only played the same video of the wreck and the 'shootout' according to them. There is only one car, and it isn't right. I guess I'll go see Emmett tomorrow," she decided. "Maybe he can tell me where to look." Captain laid his head back on her leg, and she leaned back into the sofa again, thinking and turning things over and over in her mind until she fell asleep.

The phone rang early in the morning. The taupe walls had a warm glow in the morning sun as it came in through the orange curtains. She wiped her face, felt where she had been drooling in her sleep, and wondered whether it had run down onto the matching orange throw on the dark leather couch. Outside, she could hear people driving off to work. The *psshhht psshhht* of steam-powered scooters and the steady hiss of steam turbine autos were familiar to her but lacked comfort. It irritated her that the world went on as normal, but nothing seemed normal in her own world, well, almost nothing. Breadcrumbs covered her lap, and Captain lay on her with a glob of dried mayonnaise on his cheek. That was normal.

She had a trip to Tokyo scheduled for that weekend, but apparently, thanks to this call, she would also be busy all week. Jetstar had scheduled a series of tour stops. It appeared that she was to be the featured flight in a sightseeing tour of thirty-five passengers all over Europe. This was not an unusual tour to give in the old dirigible. *The Silver Cloud* had that certain ambiance that made it perfect for European holidays. Maybe she could make a few calls on the way. There had to be pictures of the car wreck, right? If there was smoldering wreckage, someone had to have taken pictures for the police report, right? "They don't just have a shootout with someone and burn down two cars, and no one takes a picture, do they?" she asked herself out loud. Captain cocked his head to the other side and then licked from her wrist halfway up her arm while wagging his rear end like Corgis do. She laughed at him and shook his head gently back and forth. "You are gross, my little friend, but you are at least funny," she said as she wiped dog slobber from her arm.

Chapter 15

Into the Wild Blue Yonder

The morning was warm, with bits of early Autumn scattered here and there. The trees were still green and would be for over a month, but the grass was becoming less robust, and the air had a feel to it that pointed to the upcoming cooler temperatures. A cardinal flew over and landed in a cedar tree. Some neighborhood dogs had found their way into the surrounding field at the dock and played chasing rabbits while in the distance, a boy could be heard calling them. The dogs, totally engrossed in the chasing of the rabbit, paid him no heed whatsoever; apparently, their names were Grover and either Puppy or Putty. Akira couldn't tell for sure.

The airship dock was outside of The City Centre in an industrial section of the incorporated housing zones. It was one of the poorer lots inside of the zones, as always. This was so the property value of the land was low and wouldn't be affected by the coming and going of a large airliner. *The Silver Cloud* sat ready and fueled with the little bit of water it needed for extra thrust at takeoff. After liftoff, it would generate plenty of thrust simply by heating the air that it drew into the huge circular air intakes that protruded from the gondola on flying buttresses. She loved the confused look first-time fliers had when they observed the gondola. Most passengers were much more aware of jets than dirigibles. This made them assume the gondola was where people rode in *The Cloud*. In reality, the gondola was where the crew rode to mind gauges and fly the ship, and it was where the extending portion of the stairs retracted to be protected from debris or birds. Inside the huge zeppelin is where people rode. There was a row of windows, just above and behind the gondola-cabin, that gave away the location of the passenger cabin to the very observant. The color of the ship's skin and its reflective quality made the windows blend in and appear as part of the rest of the ship. The kitchen and crew sleeping quarters were in front of and in back of, respectively, the passenger area.

Akira met the chief engineer at the base of the stairs and saluted. He waved back, "Old habits, right?"

She smiled and laughed, "Haha, yes, I guess they do die hard. How is the old girl today?" she asked.

"All systems are primed and operational. All safety checks are green. The ballast and weight are pre-set and ready. All adjustments are within tolerance. It's enough to make you bored when you check. This old ship never needs anything but polished, and right now, even all the old oak and walnut smells of fresh polish." The pride in his voice was obvious. It might be more hassle to operate an antique; it didn't have the automatic landing and docking systems or any of the electronic flight controls, but it was rewarding. There was a brief hiss as the condensers that gathered moisture from the interior of the skin collected enough to push it to the ballast, and the ballast was already full and set, forcing the condensation to be expelled in a small jet of pressurized water.

The wind was calm and warming. There was supposed to be a storm later in the day, but they'd have already left and headed east toward the Atlantic Ocean before it rolled in. The storm could catch them if they had to slow down for other air traffic or passenger trouble, but it was not likely. The calm breeze carried the smell of rain, and she could feel the moisture on her cheek as she pulled her hair back into a ponytail for the official dress of the airline. She put on her white captain's hat and stood at parade rest by the stairwell.

The stairs into *The Silver Cloud* were a work of art in their own regard. Typically, a zeppelin's stairs were purely utilitarian. This was not the case on *The Cloud*. Its stairwell had brass railing and polished aluminum treadplate steps. It glittered in the morning light like the stairway to heaven. The safety lighting along the stairwell was made of brass fixtures designed to look like old steam train lighting with a woven wire cover and brass surround. *The Silver Cloud* was still—even all these years after its design—the epitome of opulence for passenger flight. It always amazed Akira how much weight was wasted on the folding staircase. She loved the weight and inefficiency of the luxury passenger ships like *The Cloud*. Such excesses would never have existed on a military vessel.

Pssssst! The ship discharged more condensation. On a morning like this, with so much moisture in the air and the weather changing, it would have filled all its ballast and hygienic water tanks quickly even had they not been filled earlier.

Her co-pilot came across the walkie, "Captain Logan, good to see you. The flight crew is ready and at preflight stations. All positions reporting in."

Akira reached to her shoulder, where the microphone was clipped, and pressed the button. "Acknowledged, good to hear you're awake, Captain Morris." It was uncommon for there to be any surprises on *The Cloud*, and Captain Davyn Morris had been her co-pilot many times despite the untraditional situation of having two captains on one airship. Because of the crossover of dirigibles being both Air Force and Navy, it was more common to have two captains, one from each branch, than on any other vessel in the military. As it turned out, Captain Morris was, in fact, Navy.

After a fairly boring wait, the long, ultra-modern limousine carrying the fares for this trip eased slowly to the parking slab. Akira had ceased being impressed by wealth many years ago. Not only did she quickly identify the wealthy as the aggressors in her overseas combat experience, but she had also seen many wealthy tourists and political elite who were simply reprehensible people. She no longer saw anything in their excesses beyond a desire to project a non-existent superiority. It was warlords and oligarchs who tended to destroy countries, and all it took for most wealthy people to shoulder up to that sort of person was an opportunity to profit from it. She wondered whether Emmett had ever invested or profited from dealings with horrible people in bad places. Emmett was different, though, at least to her. He didn't flaunt his wealth, and although he used it in politics, she didn't think he bribed and bought politicians.

The doors on the limo swung open, and the suits, ties, and sunglasses started to emerge. She could tell by their movement and level of situational awareness that these were well-trained security. Either they were secret service or ex-military or something quite similar. She stayed in top condition but could tell from their motions that she would not want to be on an opposing side if a fight ever broke out. "And now the money," she whispered almost imperceptibly to Chief Engineer Marcus Holman. It was airline policy to have the Senior Captain and Chief Engineer meet the passengers, and a flight attendant would then walk them up to their seating. The flight attendants almost never stood by the officers out of respect. Today was no different, and the attendant stood dutifully on the other side, trying to hide their awe of their passengers' wealth.

Marcus barely smiled at her sarcasm. He was not as cynical as she and was curious about what sort of celebrity they had for the day. To their surprise, a man in his mid-forties, in a department store suit, popped out of the limo like a bizarre jack in the box that had just been cranked. He fiddled with his luggage and adjusted his jacket. Then, turning to the awaiting crew, he waved happily. Akira wasn't sure how to react. She looked over at Marcus and shared a puzzled look, and both of them, totally interrupted in their expected protocols, waved in return.

Akira looked at Marcus with perplexity, "That it?" she whispered. *The Silver Cloud* could seat forty-four passengers, less than half of the modern airliners. Travel on a dirigible, though, was never about numbers, seating, or speed. It would take ten times as long to make this circuit to Tokyo, over Italy and southern Europe, over to New York, and back to Eagle's Roost as it would take in even the slowest airliners. It was called an aerial cruise. You could rest in comfort. You had huge, plus-sized seating and an onboard movie theater with lavish meals. Your seats were all window seats and would fully recline with plenty of room to sleep. As such, it was not uncommon to have small groups, twenty to capacity, and sometimes a couple of extras. One passenger with a couple of aids and four security was unheard of unless it was a celebrity of great wealth. It was not uncommon for the airline to not give a passenger list for flights even without anyone of special note like celebrities, so Akira and Marcus had no idea who this was or how he ranked to book such a flight. Even the highest of the political sphere didn't fly solo with Akira; if they could afford it, they usually had their own plane.

Marcus gave her a bewildered look and shrugged. The man walked up quickly to them. Setting his luggage down, he began patting his pockets in his pants and jacket as though to make certain he had remembered everything he was going to need. He smiled with some nervousness as the security detail with him stood at the car, each unloading their own small carry-on-sized bags. The gentleman had only two aides or assistants; these were also removing luggage from the car and appeared much calmer than this somewhat flustered-looking passenger.

"Good morning, sir." Akira began. "All systems check out, and we are ready for flight," she reported in official tradition.

He smiled at her and Marcus again and, with a hand on each breast pocket of his jacket, replied, "I forgot my pen. Oh well, I guess it's a small matter. Good morning, Captain. They told me that the engineer on the flight would be here as well, so that must be you, sir. I have never flown on a blimp before! I'm actually a little excited! Wow, she's a beaut! What's her name? I assume it's a ladies' name like on ships. I'm to give a lecture to a clothing supplier in Tokyo. I've titled it 'Why Ties Survive.' I guess you don't really care about neckties. I'm sorry, I tend to prattle when I am excited."

Akira managed to only allow a very small smile at the edges of her mouth as she corrected him, "Dirigible, sir, or zeppelin. Blimps don't have an internal frame. It's called *The Silver Cloud*. Many just call it *The Cloud*. I'm glad you are excited about the flight. There is a game room on board and many amenities. You may board when you are ready. Will there be more joining us?"

He turned to look at the five people walking up behind him. "No, no, this is all of us. We'll be enough to handle for you!" he laughed. "Oh, my name is Peter Walker."

Akira cast a sidelong glance at Marcus. Something seemed off to Akira, but Marcus still had the same slightly bored expression he always had while greeting passengers. Peter Walker walked up the stairs into *The Cloud*, and his security team, with their brisk pace and no-nonsense brief nods, followed quickly. The personal assistants to Peter brought up the rear, handing over papers, passports, immunization reports, and the customary medical paperwork in case there was an emergency. None of them introduced themselves. Most of the time, the assistants were like this if they were not flying: completely business, overworked, underappreciated, and slightly annoyed that 'the boss' was flying on a fancy airship and they were not. This time, however, all the normal attitude was there, but they were flying along. Akira quickly checked the papers to make sure they were correctly stamped and then said, "Welcome aboard, enjoy your flight."

With that, the duo ascended the stairs simultaneously, and Akira leaned to Marcus and whispered with a smirk, "People are weird." Marcus just shrugged again and went up the stairs alongside Captain Logan. He was ready to make the engines sizzle and feel the huge ship groan against the wind.

"Good morning, Davyn," Akira said as she entered the flight deck.

"Good morning, Akira. I haven't seen the passenger list, but I didn't see very many people either. Did corporate screw up and forget to send a VIP list?"

"No," Akira responded flatly. "He's just a salesman for a clothing company, from what he says. I'll admit that something seems off."

Davyn looked at her, amused. "A salesman? He must be the best salesman in the nation for them to send him and some friends to Tokyo on your boat!"

Akira lightened, "Now that is the truth, sir. Are docking tethers released, Marcus?"

Marcus was waving through the window at the ground crew. "Aye, Madam Captain, tethers released. Radio and visual confirmation. Power systems are ready. The wind is at 8.3 knots and variable. Permission to fill ballonets and begin the ascent, Ma'am?"

Akira took a quick look at the gauges, "Aye Chief, fire the engines, inflate the ballonets, fourth over static. There's no reason to pop up too quickly with seven people on board. We've got more crew than passengers. Heat the engines and set thrust at one-third."

The Silver Cloud had a brass railing shaped in a semi-circle in the middle of the flight deck for the captain to stand in during docking and undocking. It had brass grab rails that hung from the polished oak veneer ceiling and was slightly banked around the perimeter to help you keep your footing. The intent was supposedly for increased visibility during those times. The real reason, according to Akira anyway, was for nostalgia. She usually sat in the large, leather captain's chair that was up by the windshield. It had been installed decades after *The Cloud's* inception but had been carefully matched to the other interior elements in the ship, and no one could tell it hadn't always been there.

Davyn nodded at the commands, and as Marcus turned the dial for the ballonets to inflate, he threw the levers for the thrust. Even from as far away as they were, they could hear the loud sizzle of bugs and condensation being burned from the sudden heat in the engines. The skin of the ship creaked as the pressures inside changed, and steam rolled out of the engines as the water was injected into the engines to force the heated air in the correct direction. There was a slight, low-pitched whistle as the air was drawn through the dozens of engine venturi, heat instantly, and expelled through the thrust nozzle. She leaned against the rail and felt the gentle push forward coupled with the slight feeling like an elevator had just started to ascend. Tokyo, here we come, eventually … Akira thought silently to herself.

She loved Tokyo. Japan, in itself, has always been an exciting place to visit. The only thing she did not love about her ancestral country was repeatedly explaining that she knew her name was normally a boy's name, that her dad had wanted a son, that he knew he would have no other child, and so he named her the name he had intended for his little boy. Gender-specific names had begun to fall out of vogue in Japan in recent years, so the puzzled looks had become less and less frequent. She still found herself telling the general public all about her name more often than she liked. She loved the food, the lights, the excitement, the nightlife, and the people speaking in Japanese, even though she did not know anything more than greetings. She had always felt so many expectations here at the foothills of these small midwestern mountains. In Tokyo, Akira got to be either a bombshell or a nobody, whoever she wanted. She was slightly taller than most of the women they met, and in her white button-up uniform and skirt, men declared their love for her and offered gifts just to sit by her and watch a ballgame at a grill or diner. It was a very welcome change to not be the tough guy or girl, as it may be. She would admit to herself that she got plenty of attention from men in Eagle's Roost as well, but she always felt overshadowed by her rough childhood and broken family. In Tokyo, she was mysterious.

It wasn't all about the morale boost that she gained, however. It was seeing the country, at least a portion of it, where her mom and her dad had been from, where they had met. She imagined what their lives must have been like as educated and professional people before her mom died and her dad started trying to drown the pain of that loss. Japan also had an exciting level of advanced technology unseen in Eagle's Roost. There, the robotics industry was growing by leaps and bounds. Most of the automated machinery in the United States had been designed either in cooperation with Japan or entirely in Japan. The two countries, however, were not on equal footing in technological development. Anywhere you went in Tokyo, it was likely you'd see slightly larger than human-sized robots walking about, clicking servos and clattering clockwork mechanisms internally, driven by a combination of steam and the reception of radiated electricity from teslators stationed around the city. Their articulated aluminum and stainless bodies and oddly sculpted heads went about the daily business of repetition that was too costly to employ a human to do, and they made an odd counterpoint to the bamboo and wooden carts and wagons being pulled by humans selling their goods. These robots were not entirely practical for every use yet but were awe-inspiring, nonetheless.

The flight deck radio crackled, "Captain Logan, there is a man here who refuses to identify himself but says you two had a mutual friend, and he needs to speak with you, and it's urgent."

Akira picked up the microphone, "If he won't say who he is, then how can I know if we share any contacts?" Rolling her eyes, she put down the mic.

"He says he doesn't feel safe saying the name on the radio," came the reply. The airship was already high in the air, so she had to use a pair of binoculars to see the gate where the old pickup was parked as the man spoke to security. She could see the guard with the radio, and there stood a man in old-fashioned, out-of-style, and threadbare clothing. It was one of the people who had been at the funeral alone. Her heart beat fast. She had no idea what they could want with her, and she knew the mutual friend was Frank.

"Tell him that it'll have to wait until I get back. Please keep the line clear for emergencies," she told them.

The guard acknowledged, and she could see the driver of the pickup kicking dirt and getting back into his pickup. Davyn and Marcus were looking at her when Davyn asked, "Problems?"

Akira just shook her head. *The truth is*, she thought to herself, *I don't know*. She looked at the gauges and told Marcus, "Level us off in low flight. I imagine they'll want to see the sights." Then she went back to address the passengers. The passenger cabin was lush with leather seats, walnut polished accents, and brass railings. New passengers were always up admiring the ship as soon as the initial jolt of ascent had subsided. The game room to the rear, past the cabin, had shuffleboard and billiards. She almost always had to make her greeting over the intercom. Today, however, everyone was seated and reading. Not one passenger was out of their seat, and only one secretarial aid was even looking around. "This is going to be one of those odd trips where everything is backward to the norm," she murmured.

"Attention passengers, thank you for flying with Jet Air. I am your captain and pilot, Akira Logan. This is *The Silver Cloud*. This airship is the oldest and finest in the fleet and is the most luxurious. It was commissioned in 1945 and was meant to represent all the hope and prosperity that would take place in the post-war era ..." Akira continued the brief visual tour of the ship and pointed to exits, amenities, and safety features. Only the aids seemed interested. The security, she assumed, knew about airship safety. The salesman was busy sending messages back to corporate on his tablet. In the air, away from the static of teslators and the buzz of the city, wireless communications worked just fine, and he was taking full advantage as he typed away madly.

She pointed at the surrounding areas now visible through the glass sides of the passenger bay. No one took notice until "... to the north and west is Truman Forest. Folklore and urban legends say that bandits live there." All eyes were expectantly upon her. "I think it's all a bunch of hooey, but if you know a good story, feel free to share it while we fly."

All eyes went back to their previous tasks. Returning to the flight deck, Akira was shaking her head. "Marcus, Davyn, this is the oddest group of sales reps I have ever seen. I guess they wanted ghost stories about the woods, and I don't have any."

"Well," Davyn replied, "They say that's where all the city's and surrounding areas outlaws and exiles go. I bet there are plenty of stories floating around."

Akira raised an eyebrow. "Do you know any?"

He chuckled. "Only that there are apparently bands of them, gangs, I guess you could say, and they live entirely by stealing and killing," he claimed.

"So, really, no, you don't know any stories," she laughed.

He began again: "I remember in Iraq we ran across a band of nomads, good people. There was a band of robbers terrorizing them…" It was going to be a long time in the air, and the war stories had already begun between Davyn and Akira. Marcus enjoyed listening, even if he had heard the stories before. Sometimes, he would interrupt to remind the tellers of the tales and how much the story had grown since its last telling, and the three would laugh.

Elsewhere on the ship, maintenance was cleaning wires and sweeping floors. The kitchen staff was preparing chicken cordon bleu and sauteed mushrooms. The smell permeated the entire airship, and everyone's mouth watered. Akira felt relaxed and at home. She only wished the airline had not disallowed her from bringing Captain with her. He used to travel along on every flight and sit in her seat. His name had been Reginald, but she began calling him Captain as they flew, and he always answered to it. After an allergy scare, anaphylaxis, they called it, she was not allowed to bring him aboard for fear that someone allergic to dogs might be onboard.

She sat back into her chair, set the autopilot, dismissed Marcus and Davyn to their quarters, and ached mentally and emotionally. The memories of Frank's jokes and jibes. The memories of him and Josh and Braegan riding cycles and laughing. The memories of all those late nights sitting out under the sign of his shop, watching the sun settle early, down behind the city, and drinking coffee. The memories of gunfire and wondering if he would understand why she was gone if that was to be her last day. Would he have missed her as she missed him? He was her brother, her friend, her confidant. Now, she was filled with regret as she remembered the stories about how he had done so much good for so many. She regretted that she had always been too afraid to be told that Melody had a better future. She regretted that she had always been afraid that she would be told that a man like him only wanted a woman with a stable family background. She regretted that she had always been afraid that he might think she was not pretty enough.

Many of those fears had died on the battlefield, but when she returned, there were new fears. She had decided that life was too short and precious and would not let anything stop her from being honest with him and herself about her feelings. But, at the grill and a thousand times before, she found that she was afraid that he would think she was too rough, too much 'one of the guys,' and so she choked back on her heart's reins. If being friends meant she could see him and they could be together from time to time, well then maybe time would make something happen.

She began to sob as tears rolled down her cheeks and wetted her uniform shirt. She wiped her face and cursed softly under her breath. Looking up at the altimeter, she caught a glimpse of white to her left. Embarrassed, she looked over at Davyn, who was seated at the copilot station silently. He didn't look her way.

"Captain Morris," Akira said sarcastically. "I didn't hear you come in."

Still not making eye contact, he said, "I'm sorry, Ma'am. My personal cabin was too quiet, and it was too early to sleep. I … I just wanted to come and sit up here and watch the sky pass by."

Akira nodded slightly, "It's what we have spent our lives doing, I guess." She gave a small snort through her nose in sarcastic derision.

"Can I help with anything? I didn't mean to intrude in whatever. I know we aren't exactly friends, but you're the coworker I like the best," he stated.

She took a long, quiet breath. Without turning to him, she began quietly, "You know, Davyn, Franklin Greene was very close to me. I had dozens of close friends in the Air Force. I'm one of the few survivors from my squadron. Oh, not in the jets," she corrected. "No, the jets, we streaked in, did what we had to do and left. In the airships, though, the payload was always high, and they would barely stay afloat until after we unloaded. The cargo airships were no different. In the bombers, well, I got shot at a lot in the bombers. Those metal-clad monsters, though, nothing was bringing them down. We floated in silent, and by the time anyone knew to shoot, the bombs were falling, and the whole sky would be bright and beautiful like the sunset. Underneath, the ships would look like hell had risen from the earth's core, but the sky behind us was beautiful in its destruction and death reflecting off the clouds and glowing in the sky."

Her eyes were hollow and far away, her voice flat and joyless. "We called ourselves The 7th Plague. Remember the Bible story? Thunderstorms that dropped fiery hail on Egypt. That's what we called ourselves. We were a plague." She paused. Her face had gone dark, and her eyes glassed over in memories she held close in safekeeping. "I retired from combat flight after we wiped out three large villages in one night. Intel was unclear, and I still don't know for certain that the buildings we destroyed were storehouses for weapons and not civilians." She laughed a dry, hateful laugh. "Intel was bad, Davyn. Intelligence … I decided to train hand to hand combat. I excelled at it. I trained in small arms and excelled and became a trainer for both. My S.O. decided I was wasting my talents training and suggested I become an EST officer. I figured that base defense would be a good way to help the Air Force and still not be killing anyone I didn't know deserved it. My heart was in flying, though, and I kept longing to soar, to float, to see the sky from above the clouds. So, I started flying an aircraft carrier, a ship almost exactly like this one."

Davyn looked at her in surprise. "I had heard that the Air Force had used bigger dirigibles to haul very small fighters. That's a very odd idea; did it work well?"

Akira shrugged. "It worked. It was a little larger than *The Cloud*, and with none of the brass decorations, of course, but the controls and design were the same. It was about the same age, too, in the postwar 1940s. The micro fighters would be released from a modified gondola and drop out upside down. I am told they could reenter, but I never saw it happen. My training in hand-to-hand and small arms set me apart from most of the pilots, and we'd spar for fun when things were slow. We were close," she paused for a moment with a far-off look on her face. "I flew over a region that was supposed to be at peace at the time. I heard an allied jet request permission to engage hostiles." She was shaking her head slowly. Her tears were dry, and her face stoic as she related her story.

Davyn knew that he was being told something no one had ever heard before. Akira kept her happiness on her sleeve, but these dark things were kept buried.

"My pilots deployed on orders to eliminate all threats. The ground erupted in small arms fire. My airship had no guns other than the four security officers with combat rifles that rode in the hold. They leaned out the windows and opened fire on anyone that moved. My pilots rained down missiles and gunfire. The villagers and the rebels in the area were scared and confused and started firing at us. They used my radio positioning to target better. Isn't that ironic, Davyn? I was just flying past, and someone who didn't know what was going on started a firefight, and we burned that whole village down," she laughed bitterly. "I told the supply airships to abandon the mission and vacate the area. There were only two left. The other nine had already been hit with surface-to-air fire. I emergency inflated the ballonets so I would rocket straight up like a submarine coming to the surface. We were escorting a shipment to rebels that we support. We weren't told. I was a decorated war veteran before due to my time in the jets and bombers. It was a disgusting scene for the morning news filming."

Davyn interrupted, "I have heard you called a hero. Whenever I heard of you, it was just stories of those times you fought off attackers on deliveries and building infiltrations. You're not known for any of what you're saying. You're known for being skilled and tough and for always getting the mission done on time. I always thought they should have called you 'Post Office' or something," he said, trying to lighten the mood with a strained chuckle.

Akira, however, was not in a light mood and was too deep in dark memories to be brought back that easily. She sighed heavily, "I kept my own mouth shut about the military killing hundreds of villagers on accident and nearly losing an entire squadron of airships. They gave me credit for killing terrorists with radio positioning help. Suddenly, I became a 'war hero' in the news. I don't know. Maybe there were some insurgents there."

Davyn sat silent. He had heard rumors to the effect of this story but assumed they were anti-war propaganda.

"You see, Davyn, Frank was my friend, and I loved him. I was too shy when I was young, and now, all that horrible stuff I did is why I couldn't tell him I loved him. I couldn't leave it all over there. I thought the killing, dying, and terrorists were all on another continent or another planet, it seemed like. I had just spent the evening with him and drowned out my feelings to keep my mouth shut, and then, just like all my friends that were also important to me, my battle buddies, he was killed by … somebody."

She saw him with his head down in respectful quiet.

"Oh, I know. The news says that he was a terrorist and that he started a gunfight. He owned one antique old shotgun, Davyn. If he ever shot it, it'd fall apart. He had a lizard living in the walls of his shop because he didn't think there was any reason to hurt it if it was eating bugs and only sometimes pooped in his coffee pot at night." She laughed even more sardonically. "The man didn't shoot at anyone." She smiled at the more pleasant memory before falling back into her sadness. "No, he didn't shoot at anyone, and innocent friends of mine dying around me was supposed to be in the past."

Davyn pulled a small flask out of his jacket and poured a little into a coffee cup. "I'm on call if you need me," he said.

She shook her head slowly, "I'm flying, not drinking. Thank you, though. You're welcome to stay. I've never told anyone that story, and I'm pretty talked out, but you can stay and watch the sky if you like. The clouds ahead of that storm are beautiful. I think I'm done for now. I'll just watch the sky; it's peaceful and clear."

Davyn lifted the coffee cup he had meant for her in toast, "To peace and peaceful skies."

She replied softly, "To peace."

The hot air of the engines made a barely audible *whoosh* of the air being drawn into the intakes. The gentle rocking of the airship was peaceful, and Akira was lost in her thoughts.

Davyn, too, was lost in thought. His thoughts, though, were about his wife and kids—how lucky he had been that he made it back to them. He occasionally glanced at this normally strong, powerful woman. Today, she had reminded him to be thankful.

Between the passengers being weird and Akira being different, I wonder what stories I'll have to tell my kids when I get home from this flight! All they wanted were pictures of me with giant robots, Captain Davyn Morris wondered to himself.

198

Chapter 16

The Workaday Blues

Josh walked into work amid stares from coworkers. His cheek had a noticeable bruise on it from the officer taking him down. He was lucky he wasn't arrested, even though it was difficult to consider himself lucky with the big bruise showing for the workplace rumor mill. Braegan sauntered up to him as casually as he could and began the normal joking that he did as the two found their way to the machinery: "Hey Josh, when are you gonna get out that slow bike of yours so I can outrun you again?" he jibed.

Josh only stared at the floor as they made their way back.

Once out of the workplace view, Braegan asked, "You alright? I imagine the cheek isn't the part that's the toughest to deal with, but still."

Josh nodded emptily, "Yeah, I've got a few bumps and scrapes, but mostly, I am just confused and angry. Do you think Emmett will get it back soon?"

Braegan nodded, "Oh yeah, probably either today or tomorrow. You know he won't let that go without some phone calls and pulling some strings; having his fingers in so much of the nation—not just here but everywhere—he'll make it happen. If this plot, whatever it is, is just local, then they don't know who they're messing with in him. I know you don't watch political shows or read many magazines, but he was on Forbes Top 20 this year. He invested in Cybernews early, and they have been the number one producer of personal electronics and the number one news source for three years running. Just that investment made him wealthier than a Rockefeller. He is in pictures with the President. He's quiet and humble about it, but the man is connected. The fact that he doesn't know what is going on blows my mind."

Josh smiled weakly, "Good. The idea of Frank's old shop being swarmed over by police acting like those acted. I know they're just doing what they've been told, but it isn't right." He gently felt his cheek.

"Don't be too hard on the officers, Josh," Braegan began, "I know I batty fang them a lot, but they really are just trying to provide for their families. Besides, if we didn't know Frank, what would we think from watching the news?"

Josh looked at Braegan bewildered. He never defended police officers and couldn't believe he was hearing it now. "B, surely they know ..."

"How would they?" Braegan interrupted, "Who, other than poor people from the crime and gang-infested part of town and a half dozen nobodies—that's us and two politically connected people—have said anything good about him? And really, with the media saying he had used funding from who knows where to bring together a gang of steam terrorists? Well, the rich people unknowingly funded their friend so he could get those poor folks to follow him. It plays into the narrative their making. No," he answered Josh's reddening face and shocked expression, "No, I don't like it. It makes me so mad I could spit nails! That those mutton shankers are holding his shop hostage for who knows who or why. I'm beyond furious! But I can also see that it's someone in a much higher place than those officers. And, Josh,"—he looked Josh straight in the eyes—"we'll find out who. Just because you copped a mouse on the cheek there, that doesn't mean we're beaten."

Chank-Chank-Chank-Chank ... the steady beating of steel-toed boots rang out long down the concrete floor. "That's the Super, B. We'd better get to stamping out parts. Thank you, though. We're not beaten at all, maybe just being toughened up a bit."

The Supervisor, Greg Watson, strode around the corner with a clipboard in hand, nodding blankly as he checked gauges on machines and more closely inspected a couple of dials. Still looking down, he waved in greeting to Josh and Braegan. They were both reliable as clockwork, and he had become nonchalant in making the rounds near their machines. He nodded at the two as the machines chugged out metal plugs, then looked over at Josh as he began to walk away. Greg had learned long ago that most things are best left unquestioned at work, so when he saw the large shiner on Josh's cheek, he raised both eyebrows in surprise and mouthed over the loud machines and hearing protection, "You OK?"

Josh nodded and gave a half-hearted smile.

Greg wrote something on a piece of scrap paper and stuck it to the machine between the two friends. "Investigators came: Asked after you both. Only wanted a work schedule. Come by HR if we need to talk." With that and a hearty clap on the back, Greg disappeared to continue his rounds.

Greg Watson, who had never violated company policy as far as either man was aware, had just violated company policy in a matter of privacy and that involving the police. Both men were shocked but knew they could not quit working for longer than it took to quickly pull down the memo. They talked at their break time and decided it must have been to follow up on Josh and be sure he was at work and not out causing trouble. Still, what if the police were investigating all of Frank's friends? What if there was more to this than just a routine visit or innocent question? The possibilities and portended doom roiled in both men's minds as the day progressed until the weight of concern left them both exhausted by day's end. They walked to their cars slowly, drained of energy but keeping an eye on their surroundings. Nothing seemed out of place. There was nothing more threatening that they could see than their imaginations.

Waving to Braegan, Josh half mumbled, "See ya."

Braegan turned back to him with concern and stated, "I'm going to call some of the bunch tonight. Something feels wrong. Be safe, Josh, be safe." With that uncharacteristically serious goodbye, Braegan got in his car and drove slowly, thoughtfully away.

Josh watched him go and thought to himself, *I will be. How do I take care of you, though?*

Archie could not shake the events of the funeral from his mind. Every day, he sold his cars just like always: Smiles, handshakes, and fair deals, just like he'd always done. He went home to his wife and three kids just like always, but something in him was decidedly different. He had stood on the other side of the crowd from Josh and the happenings with him, but he had seen well enough and heard more than plenty. He had always trusted his government, the police, and the news media uncritically. After the events following the funeral—and the fact that the funeral was a closed casket because there was never a body found, or at least not released, which bothered him—he wondered why he used to simply accept what was told him, and why that was no longer good enough.

Now, when he watched the news, he questioned what they said. The news had claimed that protesters had arrived at Franklin Greene's shop to riot. That was not the case at all. Archie knew it and talked about it. Customers brought up the news reports, unaware of Archie's connection. He wouldn't share his connection, but he shared his opinions and newfound distrust. "Why, I don't know if you can trust anything they say anymore. They just want ratings and will say anything to get them. If that's not what's going on, then I'd say someone with the right-sized wallet is telling them what to say on the news!" he'd proclaim.

One day in particular, as his coworkers would later recall, a customer came in looking at a Dodge Brothers limited edition cargo van. He asked questions about its carrying capacity, which is totally normal for a buyer of a one-ton van. Then he asked, "How much steel would fit in it?"

Archie glibly replied, "All you can fit! The GVW of this unit is 8,200 pounds, so it will haul a good deal more than most vans. With the added length, I imagine you could haul poles ten feet long in it!"

The man nodded, "I imagine if I wanted to haul a tesla bomb and get it in somewhere, I could haul a big one in this, couldn't I? Be just like that guy Frank!"

Archie flushed red for an instant but had been in sales long enough to keep his mouth and emotions under control. He simply replied flatly, "That's not funny, sir. People are pretty tense about that sort of thing anymore. It will haul whatever—legal—cargo you would like."

The man doubled down, "Well, I ain't a bomber or a terrorist like some of those protesters anyway. I saw them throwing bottles at the police. They should'a shot 'em all!"

Archie maintained a measure of cool but couldn't be silent. "Sir, I'm going to have to get you another salesman. I was there; no one was protesting. The news is lying to you, and you are a fool. Franklin Greene was a saint, and you can ask anyone in The Bull's Run or Truitt or any of the housings and industrial zones, and they'll tell you the same. Someone murdered him, and there's proof of it. Now," Archie straightened his jacket, "I apologize for my outburst. I'll get you another sales manager. If he gives me the signal, though, and you continue to talk like you are, I'm the owner, and I'll have to ask you to leave." With that, Archie walked off.

As he was walking away, the buyer yelled, "What proof?" to which Archie shot back over his shoulder, "Video, I hear," then muttered under his breath, "same as all of you believe without a second thought."

The man nodded, oddly unsurprised, and left before the next salesperson could be asked to go take the sale.

Archie was unnerved and uneasy when Braegan called later that night to warn him about investigators. Nothing, however, seemed to happen as a result, and within the week, Archie assumed that any storm brewing had already blown over. There was decorating to take in hand and a sale to plan! The lot was all gussied up in the best he could muster. There were orange and yellow 'Harvest Day' banners and treats and snacks to get ordered and set. The fall sale was probably one of his most profitable. The colleges had opened again, and the students who hadn't needed a car all summer—but now did—had grant and scholarship money to spend. Archie spent every day that week helping the other salespeople wash and wax every vehicle and detail the interior.

In addition to simply forgetting about any possible danger, Archie also became bolder and bolder in his discussion of Frank Greene, though he never again mentioned any evidence. Frank was his friend, and he felt he was dishonoring a good man by letting the rumors swirl. Most of the people who came in, though, agreed with him. Instead of happily accepting the agreement, though, he would share his stories of Frank. Customers typically didn't mind, though there were some who seemed uncomfortable and would quietly question the bombing and the shootout. They'd quote news media reports that Archie would quickly refute. He was still a sly salesman, though, and never overstepped so far as to be unable to turn the conversation positive once more and beguile his customer.

The surveillance camera had stopped working and was a late closing in preparation for the "Harvest Day Sales Spectacular!" Archie and his staff had worked so hard to host. The sale was the next day, and everyone was gone but Archie. He often stayed late to double-check the lot's preparedness for a sale. During the check that evening, he noticed the camera was off. It wasn't uncommon for the wires to come loose in the blowing night winds from the river valley and buffeted against the mountainside, sweeping across the city in a gusty and blustery warning of impending winter.

His fiery red hair blew in the strong winds. "Darned wind," he muttered, knowing that was the cause of the late-night repair. It was quiet all around except for the clanging of the flag cables on the pole and the wind whistling through the streets. Traffic was light after dark on his street. He enjoyed the quiet but always thought it was strange how the city would roar to life, then lull for a few hours, then come back for the nightlife. The light pole with the camera was across the lot from the office. He carried the ladder carefully so as not to scratch or ding any of the newly washed and waxed cars.

Archie whistled softly. He'd had to repair this camera before. This time, however, the wires were not loose. They were cut. Sudden, crippling fear hit him. He imagined that this was how nearly all major car lot thefts had begun, and he had taken the bait. Here, late in the dusky evening, too dark to see more than a few feet, but not completely pitch dark, his eyes had trouble adjusting from the horizon to objects on to the ground. His eyesight was poor anyway, and he had wandered out into the lot without a flashlight or lantern.

Exposed, afraid, and vulnerable, Archie stood on the ladder, frozen for what seemed like minutes, waiting. He closed his eyes and listened for the footsteps he was certain were coming. Cars went by on the interstate. Sirens blared across town. He could hear bat wings fluttering as they began their nightly feast on insects as mosquitoes buzzed the streetlights.

Finally, Archie calmed his pounding heart and descended the steps. He wanted to be able to run, and the ladder would not allow it. "The ladder is cheap enough; I doubt anyone will steal it if I leave it out here," he mumbled to himself. He couldn't finish his ledger tonight, not now. Every creaking door or whistling gust of wind carried the threat of attack. He had no way to do a final check of the lot without going out and doing so with his own eyes and his dim flashlight. He went to the parking spaces and looked under his car. It was clear. No one was hiding under the car. He shone the light through the windows on both sides, clear. No one was hiding in his car. He sighed a deep sigh of relief and hit the ignition. The faithful steam power quickly hissed, and he was off for home. He decided to call the security company in the morning to ask for a technician to fix the camera ASAP.

He made his way down through the City Centre, the fastest way to the incorporated zones on the other side at this time of night. The familiar sights of nightclubs with their neon lights and the movie theaters with their lit-up posters helped calm his nerves. Past the upper-middle-class diners and stylish dance halls, he drove. He began to think of the day's sales. He had a love for sales. The banter, the game of working a deal. He didn't cheat or deceive. The buyer came to buy, or they wouldn't be there. He simply tried to help guide them to what they wanted or needed and then maybe convince them to get a few extras. It was an adrenaline rush for him and one of the best paydays of the year!

Archie whistled happily as he pulled into his driveway and parked, then half skipped along the cobblestone walkway to his door. He slid the key into the lock and swung his door open wide, stepping in at the same time. There, filling his living room were odd-looking parts he didn't recognize. Stacked on the floor up to almost eye level were rounded metal tanks with placards on the sides. He recognized the olive drab as military and knew immediately that much of it was an old army surplus of some kind, but could not identify any of the items.

His eyes scanned the room in complete confusion. There, at the open doorway from the living room to the kitchen, his wife and children sat tearfully. They were bruised on their faces, and their hair looked to have been pulled to the point that some had been pulled out by the roots.

"Now then," he heard an oddly familiar voice, "we looked for them videos, and they ain't here. Reckon we could haul all'a this in that van?"

With a loud *thud* in the back of the head, Archie Kilcarney's poor vision went black. Barely conscious, he could still hear. His wife and children screamed and wept. He heard the footsteps of his attackers and the clicking of their cameras as they took pictures. He struggled to regain control of his senses.

"I think he's waking up," said the familiar voice. Archie heard the round being racked into a pistol and knew that the setup had been successful and there was no reason for them to leave him alive. Silently, in those last fractions of seconds, his heart melted, and he felt sorrow for his family. He tried to say, "I'm sorry. My big mouth has gotten us all killed. I'm so sorry." All that came out was a hoarse breath as his eyelids fluttered.

The other man's voice chuckled quietly, "Night, night, fella."

The news called it a successful raid. Thousands of pounds of explosives and nerve gas were seized from a suburban home and held in police lockup. Another conspirator and friend of Franklin Greene had been stopped before they could carry out their plans to attack the Haynes building in The City Centre. There were four fatalities as the other inhabitants, whose names were being withheld at this time, were killed when the terrorist panicked during the raid.

Chapter 17

A Penny for Her Thoughts

Not far from Archie's home, Penelope Hammonds lived her paycheck-to-paycheck life much like Archie. She went to work. She came home. She had her family. The only real differences were that she worked steel and had no children. Everyone who knew Penelope thought she was the most beautiful soul they had ever met. Her heart was bigger than her entire body. Her empathy was flawless, and she was always there for her peers.

Penny was not what most would call a beautiful woman. Her complexion had an oiliness that she could never get cleared up, and that left her with frequent, mild acne even though she was in her thirties like Josh and the rest. She was small and wiry with a muscular physique. Her sinewy muscular build was the only characteristic that might cause a person to take notice. Her looks, neither good nor bad, did not draw attention. She was, by her own definition, average.

What made Penny exceptional was her kindness. She had four dogs that she had picked up as strays and kept. The feline situation in her home was the same because her husband had told her she could only have four pets, and after finding the four dogs all in one day, she told him, "Four dogs aren't balanced without matching cats." He was a tenderhearted man as well, and they soon found that they had four pets each, dogs and cats. In their free time, the two of them volunteered at the library reading stories to children. Penny's favorites were science fiction books, while Gene loved mysteries. However, at the library, they tended to read early reading and children's stories to the younger children. Although they had always wanted children, the two had never been able to have any of their own and so had unofficially adopted the entire neighborhood. Overworked moms and single parents would frequently pay the two to babysit their children for the evening, and the young couple would do it for free.

Gene and Penelope Hammonds lived what many would have called the middle-class American Dream. They had a nice home in a nice neighborhood of the Incorporated Housing District, Soaring Heights. They had a nice little brick home with a nice little white wooden privacy fence and a nice two-car garage where they each had used cars—purchased from her old classmate, Archie Kilcarney, of course.

Frank would often comment whenever he'd stop by that their neighborhood looked exactly as The Run once had. They worked decent, typical blue-collar jobs and made a nice living and hoped to retire someday quite nicely. The death of her former classmate, Franklin Greene, had been a tremendous shock to Penny's life. She knew that Josh, Braegan, and Akira were looking into things and trying to figure out what had really taken place. She knew that Emmett had managed to buy the old shop. She also knew that it didn't matter what they found with the media having already set the narrative. It had been months now. Summer had come and gone, Autumn would soon be passed, and for that entire time, every broadcast had been telling people what a terrorist Frank was. Not only that, but Frank was gone. He had no family, no next of kin. Emmett had bought it all, and that was roughly the end of the matter, no point in disrupting their own lives any more over the ordeal. It was time to grieve and move on.

All the classmates and long-time friends Penny knew had other friends, family, or classmates who had died or been killed in rough neighborhoods, but Frank's death was more brutal in its suddenness and inexplicability. It hurt more. And when they lost people, the media usually misreported the circumstances. Their school had been a lower-income school near the Bull's Run. Death and police involvement and media making a different story of gang violence had always been the case. She still sobbed heavily, on occasion, after work, when she thought of Frank on her drive home.

She also had to laugh a little, though, because she was the only woman in the group who had not been romantically interested in him. In Frank's larger group of acquaintances, not many women were as interested as Melody or Akira. Still, in this closest group, she stood out as the one he could talk to regularly without having to worry about relationships. Frank's sense of humor was both endearing and unpalatable to many women. Penny just thought he was wonderfully eccentric.

Tonight, it seemed, was one such night when thinking of Frank. Sighing deeply, she looked out at a neighborhood boy on their lawn repairing his bicycle. He had the same thoughtful expression on his face that Frank had as he wound the chain around the sprockets and tested the tension. There was no anger at a broken machine like most would have, just piecing the puzzle back together. She looked out the window at the young trespasser whom she had no intention of telling to leave and sipped a glass of cool water. She was lost in remembering that they were all only ten years old, and Franklin Greene had fixed all their bicycles and even tried to modify them so they were improved. A tear slowly rolled down each cheek as she missed that innocence, that fun, and Frank.

So taken in her own memories was Penny that she didn't see that someone had come to her front door until the bell rang. The sound jarred her back to the here and now and made her physically jump in surprise. The boy in the yard didn't seem to notice her or the person at the door. Penny wasn't one to make someone wait at the door. She was embarrassed that she had no tea or snacks for company, but it would have to be OK this time: surprise guests should understand. She looked out the peephole and saw a man walking away down her sidewalk. Had she waited too long? Opening the door to call after him, she noticed a card laid carefully under the edge of her doormat. She looked up to see the man wave backward at her as he continued walking calmly away. The card read, "We believe you are in danger. The police are coming. Know nothing."

Penny was not a skittish woman, but the card was unnerving and so bizarre. She quickly closed the door and looked out the window for the man. She read it again. "We believe you are in danger. The police are coming. Know nothing." She thought out loud, *We who?* Gene wouldn't be home for a couple of hours. She was not a fighter like Akira, and she didn't have guards like Melody. She closed the curtains. Penny was frightened. What could such a strange warning mean? She debated calling the police, but if the police were part of the danger, then she knew she could not.

Penny nervously swept the floors, started another load of laundry, and began scrubbing the kitchen sink. She always chose to work instead of worry, and that's what she did now. It would be dark any minute now. The sun didn't stay up very late in the fall anyway, and with the City Centre's buildings looming like black monoliths between the sunset and the housing, the dark of night would be coming sooner even yet. The balm of physical activity soothed the uneasiness she had felt at first. "Take your mind off of it," she had said as anxiety had begun to creep up on her. Physical activity was how she dealt with stress. This was why she had been so long at the steel mill and was one of the few without a college degree in a shift manager position. She had always thrown herself into work with all her energy. She had sunk herself deep into her work when her parents had passed away in their fifties, both the result of sedentary lives full of television and discontent. Diabetes, for her mother, had caused early liver failure and heart failure for her dad. She worked until the day of the funeral and only had taken that day from work. The rhythm of the machines and the daily routine, along with the hard work and physical exhaustion, was her comfort.

The yard had now become dark and shadowy as the sun began to sink behind the city. The sky, still blue above, seemed to glow in pink and orange striations with the lowering sun. She wondered for the thousandth time if this was how it felt to live at the foot of a mountain. Feeling much more comfortable and calmer with the strange mail drop only a couple of hours in the past, she went outside and began to prune her roses and mulch the cannas that were in their last full flush of bloom before the weather would turn too cold for their liking. A tiny hint of orange was only just peeking from between the gaps in the skyscrapers to the west. She looked up at it and wondered at how the skies changed colors for different weather and different times of day. All around her, the yards looked similar. The flowers may be different, the fences slightly white or natural wood tones, but the brick homes and the small yards and the general layout were all the same. It was comforting to her, in a way. She didn't need to worry about being picked out for a robbery; all the homes were the same. She didn't have to worry about anything upsetting her daily life; every day was a routine.

The dogs and cats were making noise inside. Phineas, her oldest male cat, was likely being cranky with one of the dogs. She rolled her eyes as she replaced a divot of soil where she had just pulled out a weed, stood up, and turned around face to face with a short and obese man in a long coat and shabby-looking hat. He quickly stepped back and adjusted his coat and hat. How awkward he looked, she thought. He popped a cigarette into his mouth and looked uncertain of how to say what he needed. Penny was mindful of the warning she'd received, but surely this pudgy little troll of a man could not pose a threat.

"Hello, sir," she began in cautious but friendly tones.

The detective nodded and took a heavy drag from his cigarette; it smelled of cheap tobacco sweepings and tar. Finally, he fastened his eyes on her. She could see the doubt and uncertainty in them as he began to speak quietly. "Miss, I ain't always done what's right, not even since I been a cop, not e'en since I been a detective." He paused and looked ashamedly at the ground and drew another long inhale from the disgusting smoke. "What I done, though, I always tried to do 'cause I thought it was best in the long run."

Penny didn't know how to answer or what to say at this unusual encounter.

"My name is Don Weltshore. Most in the precinct just call me detective Don. I'm known for getting things done, even if they look impossible. They sent me and my partner, Jeremiah Loving, to Frank's when he got broken into."

Penny drew in a deep breath, not sure what might follow.

"Now, I know you was warned not to talk. I saw the fella drop off the card. See, me and a few other fellers known for being willing to, umm, bend some rules, well we was sent to take care of some squeaky faucets, so to speak."

Penny eyed the man with increasing distrust as he kept talking.

"But I thought we was just gonna scare a few folks with threatening to arrest 'em. Your buddy Archie, and the fella that worked part-time for Frank, Josh I think ..." He looked at Penny as though she would verify.

Penny stood stiff as a post and was careful not to show any reaction.

"There was another, weird name with a B. Anyways, I don't know what took place, but I know they did something pretty awful to Archie tonight. I ain't a cop to be in a gang. Knowing stuff ain't always a crime."

Penny stood in shock. "What happened to Archie?" she asked.

Don shook his head. "I don't know, miss. I don't know what they did 'ner why. I waited on your messenger feller to have time to get to Josh and that B fella. I thought about it while I was watching you work in the house and then in the yard. I have to ask you a couple of questions so's I can turn in notes to my supers. When I leave, though, I'm gonna get a coffee and eat a burger. I reckon it'll take me about an hour to eat and then another half to find those fellers. Now, if I don't report that I am heading to see them in that time, the station will send som'un else. If a good friend was to call them and simply tell them to get the hell outta town for a few days, maybe even a couple 'a weeks … well, that'd be a fine friend, I'd 'magine. Cause you're only on the list cause'd of driving them around and folks thinking they told you somethin'. They're on the question list because they definitely know somethin' that some'un don't want 'em knowin'. Again, this ain't why I'm a cop. I just want to protect my city and my family and the good people what works here. I reckon what I just told you is doing part of that. We clear, Ma'am?"

Penny nodded, dumb with fear, confusion, and worry. Don took a final drag from his cigarette and started to throw it on the yard then looked at Penny and smiled, turned, and threw the cigarette butt into the street.

"Ma'am, do you know anything of any blueprints that was stolen from Franklin Greene's warehouse?"

Penny looked totally perplexed. "No," she answered.

Don nodded and wrote "No" in his notes and circled it. "Ma'am, do you know anything 'bout any stolen traffic camera footage?"

Again, Penny looked baffled. "No, sir. I don't even know how someone could steal that."

Again, Don wrote a clearly circled "No" in his notepad. He nodded, seeming relieved. "Ma'am, I wish you a good night. Tend to your friends, and I wish all you honest working folk in the City the best there be." With a tip of a hat with his right forefinger and another nod, Don Weltshore, the same detective Frank had disliked so strongly, walked off Penelope Hammonds' lawn and disappeared into the shadows of the early evening.

Penny waited until he was out of sight around the corner of her fence, then she ran inside to call Josh. Her husband, Gene, was just pulling in the driveway as the front door swung closed. She really wanted this phone call to be over before he got done unpacking his things. She didn't want him to overhear just in case that might put him in danger as well.

"Hey, it's Josh," Josh answered happily on the other end.

Penny looked out the window at her husband getting his briefcase and whispered, "The card is for real! Run and hide! Get out of town, Josh. I can't say more. Take B with you!" She hung up the phone, took a deep breath and smiled for her husband as he came through the door groaning in exhaustion from a long day.

"Hey baby! I cooked you some chicken!" Life might be crazy, but he didn't have to know.

Chapter 18

Fluffy Robots

The weather in Tokyo was perfect, for Tokyo in the fall. The humidity was higher than the rest of the year, and strong winds gusted daily, making the air seem fresher than the typical haziness of the basin that the city mostly lay within. There was a danger of typhoons this time of year, but Akira wasn't too worried. The airline was always excellent to contact them if there was any danger. Virtually any city excited Davyn. He was rushing from market to market and looking for a gift for his wife and son. Akira was positively giddy. Although she was of mixed racial ethnicity, she looked more Japanese than any other background and so fit right in.

Eagle's Roost was in the heartland of the country, and although the Asian population was higher now than when she was a child, she still received her share of comments: "Wow you're tall for an Asian! I didn't think Asians were built like you are—wow! I thought Asians were all really light-skinned—are you part Mexican? What part of China are you from? Hey, there's a cat. Are you hungry?" She had heard a lot of it. She understood it, mostly. Men found her attractive; being different meant they didn't know how to start a conversation. She always found it amusingly pathetic. Here, though, with only minimal effort, she was just another Japanese girl with a good tan, not a popular trait in this country. She was not the best Japanese speaker as she interacted with shop owners, but she understood and spoke it well enough that the only questions she encountered were about her accent.

Robots wandered here and there, drinking from the public fountains to refill their water reservoir, clicking, hissing, and clattering about the streets. Akira was mesmerized by them. They swept the sidewalks, picked up what little trash there was, watered plants, and even helped the elderly cross the streets. Their artificial intelligence was limited, but they performed a multitude of menial tasks. She had settled into an open-air bar along the sidewalk that served fruit drinks and nectars. She watched with interest as each of the robots strode by. Her odd passengers and all the strain of the last few months seemed so far away as she sat and sipped pineapple juice and watched these robot men. People came and went from the little juice and snack bar. They would nod or bow to her, and she would return the courtesy. She loved the thoughtfulness and kindness in Japan. As part of their programming, the robot men would also bow to people who bowed to them. She was completely taken in by their actions.

So engrossed was Akira in the simple activities and not quite fluid motions of the robots that she did not notice the young man who sat down next to her. She reached for her drink and saw him for the first time with a start. He smiled at the corners of his mouth and spoke in perfect English: "I did not mean to startle you. They are amazing, aren't they? The robot men."

Akira nodded, settling her attention back upon the robot she had been watching.

The young Japanese man continued, "We do not differ from them so greatly. We go about our tasks, we consume fuel, and drink water. We seldom interact in our environment outside what we need to survive."

Akira turned to him, looking at him thoughtfully then asked, "But we have the ability and desire to, at least occasionally, choose not to complete the same tasks and to change our interactions. In that sense, we are not automatons. The aspect of emotions and connections aside, we do have the chance to change ourselves daily."

The man smiled. "*Konnichiwa*, my name is Reo," he said kindly.

"*Konnichiwa*, Reo. My name is Akira; yes, it is typically a boy name."

Reo laughed softly, "Yes, it is, in Japan. In India, it is a very good name for a female. I hope you will forgive my intrusion into your afternoon. I have seen you watching these robots, and for some reason, you seem familiar in my mind. Do you come to Tokyo often?"

"Not often," Akira answered, "but I fly in a couple of times a year. It is one of my favorite spots. Maybe you saw me here."

"Perhaps," Reo considered. "So, if you thought the robots could choose, would you say they are less machine and more human?"

Akira thought for a moment, "They would be more human-like. They would be anthropomorphic machines, but not more human, only more human seeming."

"So, what, Akira-san, makes us more human than our choices or our jobs? Most Americans will talk about their work, but you have not yet said what it is that you do. Work defines the identify of many," Reo said.

"Our souls," Akira replied quietly. "Right and wrong, moral compunction. A robot merely responds to its programming. Even if it has some form of artificial intelligence, it doesn't have a human soul."

Reo nodded. He was ready for this and heard her argument as he replied, "Is our morality not programmed by who raised us?"

Akira looked down and thought a moment. With her head cocked to one side, she stated, "No, not entirely. Even the most morally bankrupt person has some sense of universal right and wrong. It may be warped, but they have it."

"Ah," Reo said, "You do believe that people are genuinely good deep inside."

Akira smiled, laughed slightly. "I guess, I must. When not corrupted by greed or other wrong motivations, I suppose they are."

Reo was smiling broadly as he took a sip of his juice. "What if I told you that I am a terrorist?"

Akira's face went flat. Her thoughts went immediately to Frank. What if this seemingly friendly man actually was a terrorist, now she had been seen with this man as well as connected to Frank? The police might think her to be a suspect of 'terrorism' as well!

Reo laughed sarcastically, "I am not a terrorist. Not in the way that you likely think. I am trying to develop artificial intelligence for use in these robots for home defense. Our government has questioned me three different times about whether I intend to use them as a private army for a rebellion."

Akira laughed out loud, perhaps more than she should have, because of how similar this seemed to what had gone on with Frank.

"Do you know of a Franklin Greene?" Reo asked.

Akira's jaw locked, and she looked him in the eyes, weighing her response.

Reo's eyebrows raised as he tilted his head, "Our news in Tokyo played all his interviews, and they are popular on the Internet today. I see you not only know the name but either feel strongly about what went on or knew him personally. He is an inspiration to me as well as many others in Japan. We do not believe that he was behind any bombing or terrorist action. If he died in a firefight with police, he died a martyr for people's freedom. Our news media speaks of him much differently than your own. Our media says he opposed the government outlawing these power emitting generators because it would give your government too much control and hurt the poor. Defending the poor is always honorable. I don't think Mr. Greene was aware that his city was not the only place attempting laws like that. It is your whole nation, and it has spread to our own and many others. It is said to be about safety, but we all believe it is about money and control. I would not speak so openly, but no one has ever turned so red with anger at mentioning his name. I also thought you looked familiar from the video of his funeral." Reo took a breath as he studied Akira's response. "You did not know the news covered the funeral?"

Akira shook her head, "No."

"I think you are on my side in this debate," Reo said. He was not smiling, but his eyes shone with confidence as he put his drink down again.

Akira stared at him, not knowing exactly what to say. She had no idea there were greater players than her local city involved. She had no idea anyone else had heard of what seemed to be only a local, event. "So, what will you do?" she asked.

Reo raised an eyebrow as he looked straight ahead into the pavement. "Continue. We will continue our work."

Akira shook her head, "I mean, what will you do to keep them from killing you? I … there are those who believe Frank was killed by our city government."

Reo nodded, "I also have thought that. I have some protection in place. My greatest defense, however, is to stay out here where everyone can see me as much as is possible. I do not think I am viewed as enough of a threat for them to take any such measures. Your Franklin did not realize how far his fame had spread. We saw him speaking live at a political rally not even a year ago. We have watched his television interviews before that. We knew that he stirred the hearts of those who would resist government control, and it was obvious that he did not know. Why did he think the television and newspapers kept coming to interview a mechanic? Look at this…" Reo produced a tablet from a satchel beside him, showed her an electronic newspaper, and typed in a date quickly. There was an artist's rendering of Frank in his blue and white striped coveralls, holding a welding torch over his head and *The Expert's Guide to Steam Generators* in his other hand, like the Statue of Liberty.

Akira could not help but laugh loud and hard. "Frank would have hated that!" she exclaimed.

Reo smiled broadly, "It is a good likeness, though? This was in our state paper. Read the caption." It said in Japanese, "Simple Small Town Hero or Political Revolutionary? Franklin Greene's interview stirs the hearts of both opponent and supporter."

Akira asked him, "Is the interview inside?"

Reo answered, "Yes, but the cover is all that is available now. After his accusation and death all the articles thought to possibly stir dissension were blocked."

Akira sighed. "He didn't want to be famous. He didn't want anything except for the government to let people live. If there was to be a power grid extension, some company should do it, not the government. He also didn't think they should make it mandatory or outlaw the older, cheaper to buy, used cars. That's all. He wanted to live and let live."

Reo looked down the street and said, "It was nice meeting you Akira-san. You have someone looking for you."

It was Davyn with an armload of stuffed toy robots and other touristy gifts for his children. "Hey, I just got the buzz message that our passenger is done speaking and will be ready to lift off in about two hours."

Akira looked shocked. "Wow, we were scheduled for a couple of days' layover here."

"I know," said Davyn. "Either they didn't like his speech, or he's already homesick."

Akira looked at Davyn's load of gifts and smirked, "Fluffy toy robots because metal copies of metal copies of men would be too weird?"

Davyn picked one up where it had fallen from his arms as he explained, "Kids can't hug a metal one, and c'mon Cap, these are so cute!"

The two pilots laughed, Akira turned to bow to Reo and then followed Davyn, picking up his stuffed animals as he occasionally dropped them along the way.

Chapter 19

Running Hot

Josh stopped at the open door about to go outside, door knob in one hand, bike helmet in the other. He seldom got a phone call after dark. *I bet it's just a salesperson*, he thought. *What if* popped up in the back of his mind, and he turned back inside and went for the phone? "The card is for real, run and hide, get out of town, Josh. I can't say more. Take B, with you!" It was Penny. He was just going to pick up B and go for a ride anyway. He had hoped a ride at dusk would ease his mind. That didn't seem to be likely now.

"I think I know why they are after us," he muttered under his breath. The news had just shown Archie's house, and they were hauling military-grade explosives and all kinds of things out of it. They said he was stockpiling for some sort of terrorist attack in Frank's name. They had shot him and all his family in the 'raid.' The word burned angrily in his mind. No one who knew Archie would believe the news, but more people in town didn't know him well enough than those who did.

"Bye Penny, thank you," he quietly said as he processed what he needed to do. He looked out the window in deep thought and there saw a small card stuck in the pane. Through the glass, he could read the card hastily written in ink: "You are in danger. Escape. Do not trust or call the police." Josh stared at it for only a moment before throwing the window up, taking the card, and then stuffing it in his pocket.

Josh quickly jogged to his garage where he kept his autocycle and turned on the lights. There on the floor, beside his cycle, were two duffle bags full of drug paraphernalia. He knew he only had a limited time; the evidence had already been planted to be discovered. No doubt the news would report that he was killed in a firefight or some other illegal reaction to being found out as a drug smuggler for terrorists. He quickly unscrewed the license plate from his bike and threw it on the bags. Then he removed the painted fairings, only three screws each. His cycle was now less recognizable.

"Ten minutes, too long. That took too long," he mumbled.

With that, Josh grabbed a backpack, quickly rammed whatever clothes were within reach and ripping up pavement, and sped out of the driveway for Braegan's house. His bank was only a block off the route to B's house, and he'd stop and empty his accounts if they hadn't seized them already. Braegan lived farther out from the City Centre than Josh. He was still in the incorporated zone but almost on the border with Truitt. Josh accelerated hard but tried to mind his speed. The last thing he needed was to be stopped for speeding by police who were on the take. Even the 'honest and good' police would call in his name, and he would be found out. *Then what? Would his life be forfeit because of what he and Braegan knew?*

The streetlights zipped past. "No, no, no! How can this light always turn red when I pull up?! Every single time!" he hissed. He waited as the snail slow cars eased around him turning left from the side street. The light turned green, and he had to breathe deep to keep from jerking the throttle wide open and potentially raising the front tire in a wheelie. "Don't draw attention, Josh," he told himself. Truth be told, he was surprised to find that he was both exhilarated as well as terrified. Down Prospect Avenue to Truth Avenue, right onto Truth. Down Truth to number 7751. "Good, he's home, and the lights are on." Josh pulled into the driveway and pulled off his helmet. He took a deep breath. The neighbors wouldn't even notice him if he didn't act noteworthy. He walked with forced calm to the door. Braegan opened it. Josh could smell the liquor on his breath. "Braegan, we have to go," Josh said in a hoarse whisper.

"Go? Why?" Braegan answered.

"Good," Josh began, "you aren't drunk…"

"No, I just had a shot when I walked in, wha- …"

"We gotta *go*, B! They've killed Archie. They're looking for your videos and the blueprints you took."

"Killed Archie!? *Who* did?

"No time, B! Grab some clothes, that evidence, any money you can, and let's go! Get on it, now!"

Braegan could make enough sense of the situation that even without details he knew it was time to go. "Sweetheart, I know you're gonna be mad at me. Umm, I called this guy a … umm, really unkind thing at the liquor store, and it turns out … um, turns out he's a gang leader from Bull's Run. You should go to your mom's for a while. I have to leave right now. You should hurry. He said he was bringing them to get me as soon as he figured out where I live."

Josh looked at him like he was mad and pantomimed "Why?"

Braegan, having gathered up some clothing and a bottle of something while yelling to his girlfriend now stuffed them in a plastic bag, came to the door, and answered Josh's look with a whisper, "Think she'll believe my story or yours?"

Josh nodded, "Yours. Get your old bike, and let's go."

"The old petrol?"

"No, you still have the old rotary that you laid down, right?" Josh replied.

"Oh, it's kinda beat up, Josh."

"Runs good, right? It's off the records, and no one has seen it in a couple of years," Josh stated.

"Good thinking. And yeah, it runs great. It'll keep up with your bike," Braegan answered.

They had to push an old mattress and some knickknacks out of the way to get to the old bike. Its faded and scratched lime green paint peaked out from the clutter.

"Are you kidding me?! I have to run for my life because you can't keep your stupid mouth shut?! I don't understand why I ..." Braegan's girlfriend could be heard cursing and yelling as she packed things into suitcases.

"She'll be safe now," Braegan winked and smiled as they pushed the bike out. "Whoa, Josh, what happened to your bike? Oh ... disguise. I guess you're going to tell me more of what's going on once we're away?"

"Yes, do you have that footage and print?" Josh asked.

"Oh yeah, "Braegan patted his jacket pocket. "If it's what the stink is about, I am not about to let it go easy."

"Money?" Josh asked again.

"Yeah, I don't keep anything in the bank, so I left some for her, but I got enough for us," Braegan said.

Throwing a leg over his bike, he hit the ignitor, and the old bike hissed and smoked as cobwebs and rats' nests smoldered on top of the reactor housing. "Oh gosh ... that smells disgusting. Let's get in the wind, Josh. I'm going to vomit, that smell ... I don't have much water in here, though. We'll need to find a hydrant as soon as we leave town," Braegan said as he net-strapped a plastic shopping bag onto his passenger seat. The loop handles flapped in the breeze comically as he turned it around in the driveway.

"Fine, we had better make some good time now if that's the case," Josh answered as he threw his leg over his own bike. Mounted on their autocycles, they sped off into the night. The wind whipped at the plastic bag on Braegan's seat as the wind tried to pull his bag out through the netting. The two men under their helmets with the visors down, their leather jackets pulled tight around them, and denim jeans with the cuffs fluttering in the wind could have been any two men from anywhere to an onlooker. They were as unrecognizable and anonymous as could be. When the streetlights illuminated the white plastic of Braegan's shopping bag luggage, Josh just couldn't help but shake his head and laugh inside.

They were in a decidedly unfriendly-looking part of Truitt—where the line between it and The Bull's Run blended together—when Braegan turned on his blinker and exited the four-lane road they were on. Josh followed him down the ramp and off onto a side street. Braegan pulled over in front of a ramshackle house and shut off the cycle's lights. Most of the streetlights in this area did not work. The trees were already losing their leaves, and it was hard to say if it was lessening the light of fall or from not being watered. Several of the houses had pit bulls, mastiffs, or some other large and aggressive seeming dog on a log chain in the yard. Cars were up on blocks in the street, either from having the wheels stolen or from being broken down, who knew which.

Braegan had pulled out his wallet and was writing on a piece of old scrap paper when Josh walked up with his hands uplifted in a gesture of "What are we doing?"

Braegan looked up. "Shh, I was thinking about my little story to my girlfriend. She may not be packed before the police show up. This will be a helpful distraction. Josh looked at the note. It read, "The popo saw me with the stuff and took it. Some dirty cop said he was gon' stash it then come back later for it and shoot the girl if she tried to ID him again. I'm going on the down low. 7751 Truth Street if you want to fight the cops for it. I didn't get in this to fight cops."

"No way that will work, B," Josh complained to him.

"You just watch. I know this dealer. I see him around my block all the time, and he's so smoked out he doesn't know what day it is. He does know that the cops are watching his stuff, though, and he thinks that cops that close to Truitt are usually dirty. He also knows that anyone willing to ID a cop is a friend." He ran up and dropped the note through the mail slot on the door and ran back to the bike.

"Gas on it, Josh, for real!" Braegan barked and leaped onto his bike, speeding away. Josh ran and jumped onto his bike, almost jumping all the way over it and pulling it over on top of himself. Quickly recovering, he too sped away behind Braegan as he heard," "Who's at the door?! You better hope you're gone when I get there!"

Officer Don Weltshore finished his double cheeseburger and chocolate malt; he'd take the French fries with him for later in the night. He was pretty certain this was going to be a long and late night for himself and many in the police force. None of it made much sense to him, but he wasn't going to step out of line too far and put his own family at risk. "Thanks, lady," he said to the waitress as he laid down his tip and left. He walked out the greasy glass doors and took a drink of his coffee, looking around and then up to the sky. It had turned dark, but the moon had not yet risen, and the light pollution from the city made stars impossible to see. He sighed heavily and mumbled, "I don't know who you boys ticked off, but I hope you did leave. I don't want to arrest folks tonight for what I think is innocent."

The radio in Weltshore's unmarked sedan announced loudly, making him jump, "Units dispatched to 7751 Truth, please advise your ETA."

Don grunted displeasure. "Waited too long. They sent someone else." He opened the door to get in. "City Centre, unit 52 we are en route, ETA 1 minute." His expression showed his surprise. *They ain't messing around*, he thought. *It's at least twenty minutes from the station to that part o' town. I wonder if they sent anyone to that other place yet for the first boy, Joshua whatshisname.* "Car 12 on scene at 41 Hope Lane. The anonymous tip was right. There is a great big bag here full of contra. Umm, there is an autocycle license plate here laying on top of the bag of stuff you said was reported." Don smiled when he heard that report. He knew what had happened. *Good for you, fella. Backslang it and stay out 'til things smooth out.*

He was not pleased at all at the thought that someone had planted evidence. He knew the local gangs and even the supposed bands of Nuko-Steam activists. This young man was not in them; he was a good man who volunteered and helped folks. "I think I'm going to see if evidence is missing a bag full of some dope and contraband. They can take care of this from here, tonight," he said to himself.

The radio said, "Car 27 reporting, we just saw a pair of bikes with no plates heading out of Truitt and just about to enter The Run. I think these might be your guys."

Dispatch quickly replied, "Affirmative, be advised, suspects are to be considered armed and dangerous. Repeat, suspects are armed and dangerous."

"Bull...!" Don exclaimed. "I hope those boys can ride them cycles!" He ate a fry even though he had meant to save them. "Nothing I can do," he murmured. He started the car and backed out into the lot. Turning on his headlights, he sucked a bit of beef out of his teeth thoughtfully. "Still, checking evidence lockup won't hurt."

Braegan was all but out of water when he and Josh pulled into the service station. The station had distilled water at the pumps so there wouldn't be any calcium or black sulphur buildup in a bike's boiler. Braegan wanted to save money this time, however, and pulled to the free water hose around the back. They were not quite to The Bull's Run yet, and the alley was dark. He was glad he was not by himself. He and Josh both filled their tanks as full as they could and sloshed a little over. "What do you think, Josh? Ready to let the cat out of the bag?" Braegan asked.

"Not yet, B. We're not out of town yet. I figured we would go to my aunt's old rental place between here and Astin. It's empty right now, and she won't mind. Plus, since she's only an aunt by marriage and her husband passed years ago, no one knows she's family" he snorted sarcastically, adding, "Not even any of our friends."

Braegan looked him over seriously. "You think one of our friends is doing this?"

"No. But I think one of our friends may not know what to keep silent and what to let slip. We need to get going again before someone sees us." Joshua slid back onto his stripped-down cycle and Braegan onto his, and into the night they went.

The night was becoming quite nice. The air was cool with autumn encroaching but not cold. The wind was breezy but not gusty. The sky, as you got farther from The City Centre, began to let stars peek through the glare of city lights. Josh started to relax and enjoy the ride. The Bull's Run lay ahead, and the highway would narrow to a two-lane. The sky would be even less inhibited by city lighting. There would be fewer people out, even though it was not even nine o'clock at night yet.

"It's actually kind of nice out," Josh thought out loud inside his helmet. "If we weren't being driven from Eagle's Roost like criminals, this would be a fun ride. At least we got out without any real drama." They would not be going through The Bull's Run for more than a mile. The main road that led out of Truitt and past The Run—and past Frank's shop and later his house—only went into the edge of The Run and then separated the two districts as sort of a dividing line. It was here at the merge warning signs, hardly needed out here where the city had abandoned its residents, that the police car slid onto the road behind them and began a pursuit with its lights and sirens blaring.

Josh angrily shook his head. "I had to say something like that." He yelled a curse word into his face shield as he rolled the throttle on his cycle wide open.

Braegan looked at him and winked. This was just his sort of fun time. He loved to antagonize the police.

Josh was too busy hunkering into an aggressive riding stance to pay Braegan much heed. He gave him a slight nod as the two bikes groaned under acceleration that left the police car desperately trying to keep up and mumbled, "I hope you can ride the way you say you can. I hope I can too."

Down through the bottleneck of four lanes to two, the pair of sports bikes rocketed. The radial-style engines, popular for their torque and rhythmic exhaust note, now roared. They were inside The Bull Run district, and any moment now the road would turn sharply east and become straight. Behind them, the police car could not keep pace and was quickly falling behind. Now they were at the corner; Josh and Braegan leaned hard into the corner, slowing only slightly. There were sparks from Braegan's footpegs as they made light contact with the pavement. Josh knew that Braegan's face had a huge grin of enjoyment on it at that moment.

Up ahead the road stretched out like a long ribbon. They would run that ribbon past Frank's, over the couple of hills between here and the old chip, and seal two lanes that they would take to his Aunt Florence's. The city lights cast their glow into the sky behind him. The lights from scattered homes that were unabandoned in The Run and Truitt twinkled like lost stars. Josh was tense but hopeful given the limited police response thus far. They had gotten out quickly, so perhaps the police were unaware of their escape.

Something caught Josh's eye far ahead where the road sloped up as it went past the shop. He closed his eyes for a split second in frustration. Frank's shop was still locked down … by police. There were at least a half dozen patrol cars near it, and they had quickly mobilized a roadblock. It was still far ahead, but they couldn't get around it without winding through the circular pattern of the 'old road' that Frank would typically use to come and go into town. That would be hard riding. The corners were sharp, and there were a lot of them. The roads were often cobblestone and could cause your bike to hop. With all of this—and in order to get out of town rather than back into it—they'd have to cut through the dead center of The Run, head north toward Truman Forest, and then cut down the little, ancient, and poorly maintained county service road at the city limits.

As if that wasn't bad enough, the path over the ridge that did not take them past Frank's house, where there would doubtless be more police, was a dirt road. High speeds on a dirt road didn't sound like a good thing to him. Braegan had slowed down slightly so Josh could come alongside. He had seen it too, a roadblock, now less than a mile up the road. The officer behind them was gaining ground quickly. A decision must be made. Josh released his grip on the throttle to point at the blockade. "We'll run it!" he screamed into the roaring wind of their speed.

Braegan pointed into The Run. There was no time for consideration. Braegan leaned hard left, and into the circle maze of The Bull's Run and old town he went. Josh gritted his teeth, yelled another expletive into his helmet, and leaned hard to leave behind Braegan. The cobblestone was such a sudden change that both Josh and Braegan wobbled when they ran into it. "No, no, no, no ... stay with me, girl!" Josh said to his bike. "I have to say, Braegan, so far you definitely can ride."

"Holy ..." Braegan yelled in fright into his helmet. "What was I thinking?! That cobblestone about got me!" Braegan was a skilled rider, but now the rhythm of the cobblestone that he and Frank had enjoyed on their afternoon rides around his shop was accelerated with his advanced speed and sounded more like a stoplight rumble strip. "A chainsaw! The road sounds like a chainsaw ... what are we doing, anyway?!" Braegan felt behind himself as something slapped him on the back. It was the plastic straps of his shopping bag. "Stupid, this whole night is just stupid!"

There was a loud screech of tires behind him, and he looked in his mirror to see the police car slide off into a yard as it tried to make the turn off the main road. He smirked in pleasure. The bikes leaned this way and that, navigating the sharp turns in The Run. Hard into a corner over the cobbles, both bikes skipped sideways more than once. It was hard, dangerous riding, but desperate people do desperate things. They were desperate to escape. The high-speed pursuit cars from in town were on their way, and he could see their lights. *The helicopters, too,* he imagined. *If they get the chase copters out, we ain't getting away,* Braegan thought. They had already been fortunate that the news zeppelins were on the other side of town covering a college football game, or the police would have commandeered their cameras with live coverage on television as well.

The two bikers screamed down the old two-lane roads in The Run disregarding stop signs and skittering around corners. The smell of scorched steam flowed out of the two bikes and made a perfume that both riders knew and loved. Braegan drank in the moonlight, the aromas, the adrenaline, and the excitement from the chase. He wanted to commit it all to memory, but there were really only two things on his mind now: escaping and riding. "First let's slow down so these folks aren't calling the police and giving them updates," he mumbled to himself. The police were coming but had lost visual contact and only knew mostly where the fugitives were. He eased off the throttle, and Joshua nearly ran up his tailpipe. Braegan laughed to himself: *He's keyed up even more than I am. We can't go the direction we need to until we aren't going to be followed. Where do outcasts go to hide? … Truman. We need to look like we are going to Truman Forest.* They followed the road out and through The Bull's Run. The *dadump dadump dadump* of the tires repeated at near legal speeds now until Braegan stopped.

Josh pulled up beside him and slipped off his helmet, unwittingly sitting in the same spot Franklin Greene had just a few months ago. "We need to go North," Braegan said, "Throw them off." Josh stared, "You think it's better to get mugged and murdered by a bunch of … outlaws?"

"Josh, *we* are outlaws," Braegan stated matter of factly.

Josh's face was stunned, and he replied only, "Oh."

"We need to go that direction because they expect outlaws to go there," Braegan continued. "I don't want to actually go to the Forest, but we need to look like we are until we have some other plan or until they give up following us. They can't know where we really go."

"That makes sense," Josh admitted. It was roughly the same plan he had been entertaining, but it was good to hear someone else confirm it. He shook his head. "How will we go there, then come back out, without them seeing? They are going to start looking in the woods. This won't be the first time they raided Truman."

"I know," said Braegan. "I mean, I don't know. We're not in real danger of being found out if they don't scramble helicopters. The sirens from the pursuit cars are getting closer though, and they'll be harder to outrun on dirt roads. Let's go. We'll have to make it up as we go. Think you can ride without your lights?"

Josh looked around for a moment. The moon was coming up, and although it wasn't full, the sky was clear, and the light was adequate to see the ditches and any large hazards. He looked up the northern road and back to Braegan, "I don't know. I think so."

"It'll be just like we used to do trying to impress girls," Braegan said with a smile.

Josh laughed for the first time that night, and with their lights turned off, they rode northwest as fast as they could go.

The pursuit cars screamed down the roads of The Bull's Run. Josh and Braegan were barely far enough away from where they had turned north to not be noticed, and they pulled into an abandoned home's driveway to hide behind the hedges and watch. "There's our chance, Josh," Braegan said. "Look, they are going house to house. If these on the end here didn't see which way we went, and they don't come this way, maybe we can hide the bikes in this old carport or out back of the house long enough that they pass by, and we can start off for your aunt's place with them after."

Josh nodded quietly, "A lot of luck, but maybe." Loud yelling and gunshots echoed from several blocks away. Josh and Braegan looked at each other anxiously. "It feels wrong to be happy to hear that," Josh said.

Braegan smirked again, "Not at all. We didn't do that, and the cops being here might help the situation, plus ... they may be distracted." Tires squealed, and more gunfire erupted amid yelling and a loud bang that could have only been an auto collision. More tires squealed, and they heard a vehicle speed away. "They can't afford to not think that's us," Braegan observed. "Look, now. They're all taking off after whatever went on there. This is our window of opportunity. Hey, remember—lights off, and let's go as fast as we can. Maybe we'll actually survive this for you to tell me why I am running for my life, even though I can guess."

Down the road headed south along the edge of The Run and the few small houses outside the city limits they went. These were large farm plots that had been split up into five-acre yards with trailer houses. People with a couple of cows or a horse or two that farmed them for a hobby lived here. Many of the houses still had lights on as the two friends sped past in the dark. They could only manage about twenty-five miles per hour in the shimmery but dim moonlight. Every time Josh saw a window with curtains open, he feared to see faces looking out, marking their progress to call the police. Thankfully, the hypnotic flickering of television glowed in every home. No one looked from the windows. No one saw the two falsely accused terrorists slipping away in the night.

The road made sudden and strange doglegs around old farmsteads and had a surprising number of big humps that made the bikes jump. The landings, even though only an instant later, were treacherous on the crooked, loose gravel road. It took an eternity, it seemed, to finally be on the dirt road. Braegan stopped under an old oak tree on the roadside.

"No, Braegan, we can't stop yet—unless it's some sort of emergency," Josh said.

"I forgot to throw out my phone," Braegan explained. "I had no idea what sort of thing was going on, and still don't entirely, but now that I know the police are going to be searching, I thought I had better shut it off and throw it in this water trough or some such. Anyway, you know you can't get reception in The Run or even in much of the city because of teslators, right?"

"Yeah," Josh answered. "Do we really have time…?" he began.

"Shhh, so I just got the voicemail from my girlfriend. She's super ticked because some cop showed up and started talking about selling dope for terrorists, and then this big scary drug dealer showed up. Well, listen."

Braegan held the phone up for Josh to listen to the message and hit play: "So I don't know what you been doing, you worthless pile of …" she listed a very unbecoming list of names. "But I'm glad you warned me because I am in the car and those two are arguing and, oh my gosh! He hit the cop! He hit him! I'm outta here! If you ever get yourself straight, call me, but don't you even send me a letter until you get all this bullcrap figured out!"

Josh was laughing, trying to stay quiet, with tears rolling down his cheeks. "OK, Braegan, that was worth the stop. Let's get going."

Braegan threw the phone into the water trough that was under the oak tree. It smelled like a hog pen, so he imagined it would be destroyed and ground into pieces long before anyone could track it. His girlfriend was safe. He and his best friend had escaped. He mounted his cycle again. "Yeah, kind of a sucky day. But … we're still riding."

Chapter 20

The Silver Cloud vs The Angry Cloud

When Davyn and Akira arrived at the tethering dock, her passengers were already on board. Marcus looked uncomfortable and saluted as he explained: "I couldn't keep them from boarding, Ma'am. They demanded to get on. The main fare claimed he had never felt more insulted, was embarrassed by what happened in town, and would not take no for an answer. His security stiff-armed me and pushed past to load."

Akira's jaw was solid. She hated it when passengers let something foolish that they had done dictate their treatment of the flight staff. She turned to Marcus and tried to soften her expression despite the fiery spark in her eyes. She returned his salute and said, "It's OK, Marcus. This is not the first time we've had rude passengers. You informed the kitchen so they could serve the passengers and get them calmed?"

"Of course, Ma'am, thank you." He relaxed as they all climbed the stairs.

Davyn looked around as he climbed with them and stated, "I suppose it's just as well. The most recent tropical depression has been upgraded and could head this way. It's a good time to get flying, honestly."

Akira didn't want to talk about the weather just now. She knew she could not confront her passengers and that there was little to do about their behavior. She looked around as they climbed; it did look like storms might be brewing in the distance.

Marcus interrupted her thoughts: "Captain, here are the logs to sign. We have all the passengers and cargo on board," he said.

"Cargo?" she replied.

"Yes, Ma'am. I assumed you knew. Corporate and our passengers worked out some cargo crates. They're heavy, too. It only says, 'Appliances' on the shipping tags."

"How odd. This trip could not get stranger," Akira mumbled. "Did you get it all strapped in and secured for flight?"

"Yes, Ma'am. Rather, the engineering crew on the ground did. I walked the hold and inspected it. The crates are strapped in. They must be refrigerators from the height of the boxes, but there are no markings, and I couldn't tell for certain."

Akira nodded disinterestedly. *The Silver Cloud* was a large ship by most standards. It would likely have been referred to as a cruiser, being significantly larger than a frigate class in the Navy. It was not uncommon to end up hauling freight in whatever storage was left when the passenger load and supplies for the flights were not enough to meet the maximum weight it could safely carry. The uncommon factor, however, was that she typically knew well in advance about any further loading of her ship beyond passengers.

Akira reviewed the paperwork; everything was stamped with Jet Air's corporate seal. "I guess it's all in order, and we're freight hauling home," she said as she signed. Her conversation with Reo had her mind on home and on what she would do in just over a week from now when they touched down, and she had a few days to chase down any evidence. The seclusion this trip had brought from the situation was a welcome break, but it had also allowed her to decide to pursue her investigation further rationally. If what Reo had said about Frank unwittingly becoming a symbol of resistance was true, then there would have been even greater motivation for foul play by people in power. She didn't want to believe it. She believed in the country she had fought for but also knew what the people in charge could do when they were misinformed or felt threatened.

"Captain Logan?" Davyn was asking.

"Hmm, yes?" she replied.

"We need your authorizations for power up and liftoff, Ma'am," Davyn stated.

Akira looked at the gauges and Marcus, who gave her a thumbs up. "All systems 'Go,' Captain," he stated.

"Very well, sir," she pushed the radio button and spoke: "Tower, with your clearance, release the tethers." Turning to Marcus, she said, "Engineering, fill the ballonets. We have a light tailwind currently, so we will leave thrust at zero until we get her in the right direction. Easy does it on the rudder, Captain Morris. Don't swing around too quickly. It'll come around fast with that five mph wind at our rear."

"Aye, Captain," Davyn replied with his hand on the steering controls. He smiled at her reminders. Some, with his experience, might have felt insulted by her directives. He understood that she was going over everything in her mind. Captain Logan didn't leave any box unchecked on the takeoff checklist.

"Tethers away, Madam Captain. Have a good flight. Watch that storm on the horizon. Tower out," came the announcement from the landing tower.

"Affirmative, Tower. Thank you. We have it on the radar and are getting updates over the printer," Akira replied.

Davyn kept the ship's tail in the wind until they cleared the tower—no small task. Any deviation from the wind or the rudder angle meant that the entire ship began to slide this way or that quickly. Once they had lifted past the tower, he eased into the rudder, and the ship made a smooth rotation of 180 degrees to face the wind.

"Nicely done, sir." He smiled as Akira praised him.

"Chief Engineer Homan," she called to Marcus.

He snapped to attention in his seat as was protocol when formally addressed. "Yes, Captain!"

"Easy, Marcus," Akira chuckled. "Set thrust for 75 percent, and let's head home."

Marcus smiled warmly. This team of officers had made plenty of trips, and he had already done what she commanded. Waiting on her to say it was a mere formality. They often knew what each other would say before they had said it.

"Aye, Captain," he replied, smiling.

The crackle of the atmosphere around the engines instantly boiling as the reactor heat was turned on sizzled in the air for a moment, and then the low whistle of the air began. The three of them listened silently to the comforting sounds that had been a major part of their lives for so long. Akira suddenly frowned, looked at her two commanding officers, and said, "I guess I need to go see why Mr. Walker is upset and see if we can comp him a meal or something to make him happier."

Davyn groaned. "Why? If he was so embarrassed and pissy, why not let him have time to sulk like a wet cat?"

Akira laughed. "Wouldn't that be nice? Part of it, though. We must be ambassadors for the company!" She said in a singsong voice, quoting the training videos. Marcus tapped a gauge on his instrument cluster," I think I need to stay here and ... um, watch this. The air temperature outside is temperate, so..."

"It's OK, Marcus," Akira interrupted, "Not your job. It's the flight chief's job, and since I am the high-ranking Captain, that's me on this trip—you're welcome, Davyn. With you being a Captain as well, I could have delegated."

"Oh no, Captain Logan, you are the right one for the job, and seniority is important at Jet Air!" he jibed.

"Set your course north to hit the short route trade winds. That way, maybe we can pass by above this storm without having to take the scenic route across Europe like we did coming over," she directed Davyn.

"Aye, Madam Captain!" Davyn saluted with a grin. "Going east both ways!"

Akira pushed his head from the back into his salute, making him hit himself as she walked past him toward the passenger cabin. He chuckled as she left the room, looking over to Marcus, who wore a thin smile. Marcus was more serious than Davyn despite still occasionally enjoying a good joke. The control cabin banter often left him smiling but seldom engaging. A typhoon was building if the radar and his experience could be trusted. They would need to get north of it soon if Akira hoped to skirt it to the north and fly past it rather than running west. Heading east across Europe was the suggested route if a central U.S. storm blew into Eagle's Roost. It did not require calling; it required no authorization. It was simply a protocol that was already spelled out in the handbook.

Similarly, heading west from Tokyo was the expected route in case of a typhoon. Jet Air should verify Akira's decision to go east toward the storm. Davyn would let Ms. Logan do that later. Up into the trade winds—as long as the storm was not too large—should be safe enough, particularly with the speeds the wind would carry them. In a jet, a typhoon was dangerous and frightening. Turbulence could cause injuries and mechanical trouble. Lightning could cause electrical difficulties. Rapidly changing humidity could cause the heaters to either overheat or cool suddenly. All those same problems happened in an airship but were compounded by more than simply the size multiplier of the two. An airship is many times the physical size of a jet, causing it to be that much more likely to have adverse wind buffeting or attract lightning. Still, it was also much less aerodynamic, adding difficulty in navigating storms. Not to mention that an airship might be easily blown off course in a storm where a jet could more easily pass through or above it. Some military airships had methods for achieving high altitudes; they mostly tended to be much more massive if they carried any sizable payload. All airships, however, relied on buoyancy for their lift. This meant that even these higher-flying dirigibles had a ceiling. When faced with the high-altitude turbulence of a typhoon, that ceiling seemed frighteningly low.

Marcus eyed the gauges and the radar for a moment. "Captain, do you think we should call in our route to traffic so they can advise on the storm and whether that's our best direction?" he queried.

Davyn leaned forward from his reclined position and looked at the weather radar. He pursed his lips for a moment, then shrugged, "Protocol is to head east if there is no typhoon. There isn't one yet, so we're just following protocol. I think it'll be fine. If the storm takes a northern route, grows, and speeds up, then we could be in for some excitement, but that's an awful lot of things to happen to cause us headaches."

"Aye, sir," Marcus replied, still looking at the radar," I've seldom seen it happen, just … thinking."

"Well, there ya go, Master Holman! You've been in the commercial flight business longer than I have. If you haven't seen it happen by now, it probably won't happen!" Davyn stated glibly. He pulled his cap back down over his forehead and leaned back comfortably. He could hear Akira's voice muffled through the ship as she spoke with the passengers. Her tone was calming even to him. He tilted his cap out of his eyes and turned his head toward Marcus. "What's your take on the Captain, Marcus? Does she seem different lately? You've known her longer than I have."

Marcus replied flatly," It wouldn't be my business if she did."

"Oh, come on, she's a fantastic woman. I don't mean that from a romantic sort of viewpoint, mind you, but she is always making jokes, and even though she doesn't just 'chat' a lot when she does, it's always right when you need it. This trip and last, she's been more reserved and broodier, at least until takeoff. I mean, she was a little more herself then, don't ya think?" Davyn pushed.

Marcus looked up at him from under his brows, "Again, if that's true, it's not my business. If she is less cheerful than normal, you should be careful she doesn't catch you talking about her. She's kept up with all her hand-to-hand and reservist training all these years, and if she decided to beat us both for talking about her, all we could do was take it, and I hope she lets off before we break."

"Oh, she wouldn't beat us. She doesn't even like to fight. She's got a gentle soul. That's why she didn't like the military. As much as she loves to fly, she'd have never left if she didn't have a problem with possibly hurting innocents," Davyn responded dismissively. He asked again, "So what's your take? She's a friend to both of us, and I think something is up."

Marcus sighed. "Look, you know who she was always calling or writing letters to on long flights, don't you?"

"No. I assumed it was family."

"It was Frank Greene. She wouldn't ever say so, but I am pretty sure she was closer to him than anyone else in her life, and, well, you know what has happened," Marcus finally confessed.

"Oh wow," Davyn quietly exclaimed. "No wonder, then. I wonder if she knew?"

"Knew what? That he was a terrorist? I don't think anyone knew. I don't know if I believe it completely, and there are many, many more that don't believe it all. That would likely include the Captain. It's probably best we don't talk about it anymore," Marcus warned.

Akira opened the door to the cabin, "Talk about what?" She asked.

"That storm brewing to the south," Davyn quickly interjected.

"Oh, is it something to worry about? When we disembarked, it was just a depression," Akira said.

Marcus looked knowingly at Davyn and informed Akira, "It is a tropical storm now, a strong one."

"Well, I guess we must keep moving," she commented. "You wouldn't believe it, but I walked back there, and they were all laughing and playing cards. I apologized for their drama in Tokyo, and Peter Walker was just like, 'Hey, no problem, probably just a cultural misunderstanding.' His guards even spoke to me a little and asked if I had fun on the ground and if I had eaten at this one restaurant … I haven't ever looked off the beaten path. The security lead's name is Sean Drimmell. Seems nice enough for former spec ops."

"Special Operations for who?" Davyn asked.

"I didn't want to get into it. I just told them we would comp them a meal, which means it is complimentary, and they said they knew the term. I felt silly for explaining it, and we all laughed. Weird change of attitude from what you described, Marcus."

Marcus had a mild look of surprise. "Yes, indeed. Maybe they needed to push and yell to feel like we would take their desire to leave early more seriously. Definitely a surprise!"

Akira walked over to Marcus and looked at the radar. Davyn's asking about her emotional well-being had him thinking of how sad he was for her and how she must feel about Frank, regardless of how much of the media hype she believed. *You deserve better than that*, he thought silently as she peered at the gauge cluster.

Akira reached forward and put her finger in the eye of the storm. "Right there, that's what we need to watch. It's not very developed yet. If it becomes more defined, we must watch right there. Let's hit full forward power, Mr. Holman. I'd feel a little better if we get some distance between us and that thing's possible paths."

"Yes, Ma'am," he answered, pushing the throttle levers forward to the red line. There was an overload setting past this where the engine heat would give a few more knots of speed. It was dangerous, however, and could melt the venturis. This was for high-moisture air and for the direst need for power. It always seemed to be an odd thing to include on an airship. The three to five knots you would gain wouldn't get you out of any situation much faster, and the chance of accidentally overheating the engines should outweigh that little benefit. The newer airships didn't have this feature, and Marcus considered it a holdover from when flying was more a seat-of-your-pants thing than it was now.

The sun was setting to their left, and the lights of Tokyo were lighting up below them. She picked up the microphone and addressed the passengers: "To our left is a beautiful sunset. The old saying, 'Red sky at night—sailor's delight,' comes to mind. As we sail our airship north, you may occasionally look to the south and east and see clouds being pushed ahead of Tropical Storm Muroto. Below, you may see Tokyo lighting up. The city will not be visible for long as we are traveling at 85 knots due north. Dinner service will be at your convenience starting at 7 p.m."

Akira turned to her other officers and smiled. "Looks like we are underway. Smooth skies and smooth wine, to quote my old Commanding Officer," she said as she settled into her Captain's seat.

"How long have I been asleep in the seat?" Akira wondered as she woke up to another slight nudge from the ship caused by a gust of wind. It had happened far more quickly than anticipated. Muroto had grown suddenly and had headed much more north than could have been anticipated. To make matters worse, they had to slow down to a snail's pace due to a partial failure of an engine temperature gauge while engineering had repaired it. They had barely maintained measurable airspeed the entire day with only one engine operating. This was all that the fast-moving storm had needed. It was heading north and slightly east. It had built from a tropical storm to a category three typhoon in only a few days and then rapidly shot north. Although nowhere near them, the winds and weather created ahead of such a storm began to buffet the large ship. Akira had been minding the gauges and the radar but had fallen asleep after the stressful day as things finally had begun to calm. Marcus and Davyn had been resting in quarters as she managed the helm. Akira wiped her eyes and looked around the cabin.

Marcus was at his post, silently watching the radar. He looked at her and smiled, "You weren't out for long. I got my mandatory time and was able to sleep. It was smooth skies. It's not now, and it doesn't appear it will be."

"Wonderful," she replied, her voice rich with sarcasm.

Marcus shook his head and looked worriedly at her: "We aren't going to get around it entirely, Captain. Assuming we can maintain our current speed, we will not be in the worst of it, but we're going to pass through the outer arms of the pinwheel. It's going fast, and it's big. We need to double our maximum speed to clear it entirely on our current path. We just cannot."

"Call traffic. Let them know our situation. Maybe they can advise a new route," Akira ordered.

"The long-distance radio seems to be out, and the storm has cellular transmissions down at enough towers that I haven't been able to get through to anyone," Marcus replied.

Akira picked up the radio, adjusted some dials, looked at the lights, and tapped on the top," Marcus, we need to be able to advise them of our position, if nothing else. See if you can fix this. When did it quit?"

"I don't know. It's been really quiet, but they don't usually contact us often over the Sea of Japan," Marcus reported.

Akira nodded in agreement. She pointed to the radio and told him, "We need that fixed, Marcus. I'm going to address the passengers in person. What time is it?"

"It's 10 p.m."

"Well, I'll let them sleep if they are not in the gaming room like this group usually is at this time," Akira said. Then she added, looking at the radar balefully, "I hope they are asleep."

Akira walked the short corridor from the bridge to the passenger cabin and looked up to the slightly raised stage, the gaming room. She sighed heavily as she saw all four of the security, the two secretaries, and Mr. Walker all playing cards. Akira mumbled, "Of course, they're not sleeping. Luck has not been with me this trip, so why would it be now?" She walked up the four steps to the game platform and watched momentarily as they played pinochle. She watched only one hand before commenting, "That's not a card game I expected. I haven't seen Pinochle since I was a kid."

Sean Drimmell had just won the hand and laughingly replied, "I don't think any of these have ever seen it! What can we do for you, Captain? Or have you just come to observe?"

"No, I wish that was the case. Due to the earlier engine trouble, we will pass through the outer rings of a cyclone or typhoon. Muroto has grown rapidly and is a straight shooter. As such, it has caught up to us. I have flown through storms before, and it will be bumpy, but if you wear your seatbelts when I direct or stay in your bunks as needed, we'll all make it safely through," she explained.

Sean raised an eyebrow, "You've flown through storms this size before? I have ridden through them on dirigibles and blimps of different kinds. I wouldn't classify it as something enjoyable. This old rigid body will be better than a non-rigid, though."

Akira nodded, "Yes, we're on the best ship for it." She shook her head, "No, I wouldn't call it fun. With any luck, it will only amount to a little turbulent wind, and we'll be home free." The others nodded as they returned to their game and drinks. She walked away and thought, *With any luck … We definitely could do with some luck.*

The rough skies bounced and jostled the big airship relentlessly. The sheer size of an airship meant that the turbulence involved fewer sudden jerks and movements but was more of a heavy, hard shove that covered much distance and caused you to lean and sway with the feeling of the stomach-upsetting motions of a roller coaster. The lightning crackled around the ship, and Akira had the engineering crew check the fire extinguisher systems for the gas envelope every hour on rotation. The passengers who reportedly had been so rushed and agitated at loading were calm and reserved as they sat belted into their large, luxurious seats. The billiard balls were all secured into the pockets, and virtually anything that could move was strapped or fastened in some way.

Davyn was a basket of nerves. Though he remained professional and had his head about him, it was clear that this was not something he had done before nor wished to do. Marcus was busy with the engineering crew, minding gauges, watching radar, and monitoring the engine room.

Only Akira and the passengers remained eerily calm. She would regularly walk back to the passenger deck to ensure their safety and return looking puzzled. "I just don't get it, Davyn. Either they are so petrified they cannot react, or they have flown in bad conditions so often that this doesn't worry them," she had already said more than a few times.

Davyn just looked at her from his copilot station and snorted, "I don't know how they can be calm, nor you and I don't know how you can stand and walk about while this ship is bucking and churning like a child's balloon in a windstorm! I tried to get up a minute ago, and I think when I stood, the ship's floor rose more than I did! It put me right back in my seat!"

Marcus was motioning to Akira as he stared at the radar. As he waved his hand to her, she walked over to the gauge cluster he was minding and looked at the green glow of too many illuminated objects representing clouds. He pointed to a spot toward the bottom: "Do you see it?" he asked.

"Blazes, Marcus, of course, I see it," she whispered, exasperated and fearful. "I …" she began with a choke in her throat, "I suppose the odds of outrunning that are next to none with this horrid headwind we are already fighting." Her voice was weak, and her face pale.

Marcus nodded slowly.

Looking back at Davyn and around the cabin at her seat where her dog, Captain, would be sitting if she had her choice, then at the passenger door, Akira pondered her words carefully.

"Captain?" Davyn queried as he adjusted the rudder slightly.

"Tornado, Captain Morris," she stated matter of factly.

Davyn's eyes widened. It was not uncommon for a typhoon or hurricane to stir up tornadoes as their sheer winds encountered land masses. It was not good news, however. He opened his mouth to respond but could not and shook his head.

Nodding her agreement and straightening her back, Akira pitched slightly to the left and was in the air momentarily as a strong gust of wind shoved the ship down and to the right. She was quick on her feet but still had been tossed a good distance across the cabin. She looked defiant and angry as she regained her wide-stanced footing and turned to Marcus. "Chief," she commanded, "wide open throttle. Put it in the red. There is enough water in this air to keep things cool and maybe give us a little boost that we will need. Captain, adjust the heading; turn her 17 degrees north. There is a very slight chance that we might hit a bit of a break in the storm fronts and get around that tornado. I will tell the passengers what's happening."

Davyn and Marcus echoed, "Aye!" and set themselves to task.

As Akira walked the short corridor, she sarcastically announced in a mumble to make-believe passengers: "Welcome to Jet Air, ladies and gentlemen! I am your Captain, Akira Logan. I'm going to make a couple of bad decisions and probably get us all killed in a massive storm." She walked into the passenger cabin to see the passengers standing in a circle, feet wide, arms on hips, or pointing at Sean Drimmel's tablet computer. It was not what she had expected, and her puzzlement obviously showed on her face as she walked up to them. The ship pitched and rolled as the wind they had been nosed into was now striking the starboard side with a solid push as the gusting continued.

Sean looked up as she approached and lifted his tablet to address her, "Miss Logan!" he called cheerfully, then stumbled a little to the side as the ship rolled again, "Come here, and I'll show you what we're doing. Akira walked up slowly, watching her footing as the ship's floor constantly moved. On Sean's tablet, there was a picture of the large crates of appliances being loaded into *The Silver Cloud* with a conveyor ramp truck. Armed personnel she had never seen stood all around in camouflage in the photo. A rough draft news flash read, "Former Air Force Hero Killed in Foiled Terrorist Smuggling Act." She looked up from the tablet to Sean, who was smiling a smug smile with no warmth. "You're famous for being clever and resourceful as a soldier, Captain Logan," he began. "I was surprised how well you played along with our plan." His face was twisted into a smug and hateful smile as he continued. Her face showed no emotion as she stared back into his. Sean chuckled ever so slightly at her, "Don't be all that surprised! You surely didn't think people would just sit by while you uncovered that Frank was killed to shut him up?" He laughed now. With that, Peter Walker, who was standing next to Akira, thrust a lightning-fast, hard uppercut to her chin and knocked her unconscious.

Akira had no real concept of how long she was unconscious. It was likely only a few moments, she surmised, as the small strike force, for that, was what she perceived them to be, were all still in the passenger cabin laying out the plan to take control of the ship and bring about its destruction. Sean's tablet was stuck to the small dining table and was beeping with the sounds of a weather radar. Akira moved her hands a little and felt the zip tie bite into her wrist. "Stupid," she thought," I didn't even think about any situational awareness at all. I walked around blind." They had made it tight. She was wise enough not to wiggle around and attract attention. Fighting to free herself was pointless until she could snap her arms and break the tie without drawing everyone's immediate attention. The ship took a massive buck and jumped with a hard roll to starboard. Even with their wide stances and training, it was impossible to stay standing when the floor moved from where it had just been under them. Akira slid across the floor and banged hard across the bulkhead to the crew cabin. She quickly twisted her arms in a jerk and managed only to scratch her arms at the wrists. She put pressure against the tie again, then pushed hard in a scissor-like motion. The zip tie bit into her wrists and hands. *Pop*! It snapped in two.

The hijacking passengers were beginning to regain their footing. There was little time to act without assuring certain failures in a bleak situation. Faintly, among all the other grunts, creaking furniture, and noises of the ship, she heard the crew door open just down its little corridor from her. Davyn or Marcus had decided to see what was taking her so long and if things were OK. The ship bucked, and a solid thump followed by an "Oomph" came from the corridor. It was Davyn coming to check. One of the "secretaries" had fallen again. The other was holding on to an armrest of a leather reclining seat. All the would-be hijackers were disoriented and looking around for their plans, notes, or gear.

Even though *The Silver Cloud* used a hydrogen blend that was less volatile than elemental hydrogen, it was still only a chemically bonded hydrogen and could be ignited with extreme heat. She knew she would not have to face gunfire. Using firearms to hijack this ship would have been suicidal and foolish. Not only might the heat from the barrel ignite something when the hot air blasted out, but the friction heat from the projectile could easily cause enough spark or enough raw heat to ignite the hydrogen itself, not to mention that poking holes in a balloon you're riding is generally irresponsible.

Akira was bruised. Her entire right side had smashed hard against the bulkhead. The emotions and stress of piloting through this storm had her exhausted, but the time was now if she was to save any of her crew. Akira planted both feet and pushed off hard. It was three long steps across the wooden floor, and she caught the guard she had heard called Allen with an elbow thrust to his temple. He crumpled to the ground unconscious.

Drimmell had noticed motion in his peripheral vision and was barking orders at his team as he pulled himself into a more upright position with the seat back in the row before him. Akira grabbed the left armrest of the seat she was next to and then whirlwind kicked the secretary who had managed to stay standing moments earlier. The secretary pulled out a long, slender knife hidden in a letter opener case clipped to her jacket pocket and swiped at Akira's legs as she dodged and blocked.

Davyn had stumbled through the door into the melee now, and even though he was having difficulty with the turbulence, he was a well-trained fighter. Sean Drimmell had backed away from the two pilots and was pointing for his henchmen to attack Akira and Davyn. Davyn reached into his armpit and retrieved a small, jointed object. He snapped it, and it extended into a baton.

As Akira was taking up a fighting stance against the knife-wielding secretary and brass-knuckled guard approaching her, she had a moment of impressed surprise. *Davyn flies armed?* she thought to herself. Davyn squared off against Peter Walker, another guard, and the other secretary, who was regaining her feet and turning to him.

Sean Drimmell had put his tablet back in its case and was shouting commands as he appeared to be splitting the direction difference between the defending pilots. With a quick motion forward and a whip, Davyn caught the not-entirely-recovered secretary squarely in the back of her head just above her neck, sending her reeling and disabled. He overextended himself with his motion, and the black-dressed guard took advantage and pummeled his ribcage.

Walker unfolded a large knife from his pants pocket and sidestepped the brawlers, trying to get behind Davyn. Davyn was wise to the movement, and despite the multiple rib punches ducked his shoulder into his current attacker and upswept the baton into Walker's groin with a hearty thud. Having exposed himself again, he was rewarded with two firmly placed right hooks into the back of his head. He stumbled and joined the temporarily incapacitated Walker on the slick wooden floor. Feet and arms squeaked on the polished wood like a basketball court. The ship bucked straight up, and only Akira and her female assailant were left standing as they alone had a handhold on the chair backs. Attention focused on each other, each smiled menacingly as all the men in the room fell over or under seats. Akira thrust one, two, and three calculated punches at the other fighter. Each of the lightning-fast attacks were blocked with the back of the other's arms. *Slash, jab, slash, thrust* from the hijacker, which Akira deftly dodged. It was critical that she end this fight quickly, and she knew it. These were trained fighters, and although she was trained as well, these were younger, trained specifically to kill, and she was outnumbered.

Akira took her pilot's jacket off slowly, keeping an eye on her opponent as the attacker edged to the starboard to move to the same row of seats as Akira. She spun it into a quick twist of cloth as the hijacking woman moved parallel to her. The hijacker thrust with her knife and Akira barely slid to her right in time to not be cut in the chest. The thrust nicked her left shoulder as she wrapped the jacket rope around the attacker's arm and twisted it, spinning her around. With the weapon arm trapped and the assailant off balance, Akira torqued her entire body around onto the woman's back and shoved her into the floor face first. The knife pierced the hijacker's shoulder and the impact on the floor dazed her. Akira quickly pulled the knife from her hand and with bitter anger dispatched her.

A hard kick to her posterior drove her face down onto the floor as she attempted to rise. It was Sean Drimmell. He had not gotten close enough to grab her but just close enough to kick. His last guard, not counting the one fighting Davyn, had gotten to his feet with Drimmell's help, and both were now moved into position against Akira.

She yelled to Davyn, "Morris! Get up! Get in the cabin and call security!"

Davyn was pushing himself up into a pushup position at the moment and nodded affirmation.

"Don't worry about it, friend," Drimmell chided, "we gassed the quarters. It's just the flight crew left for last."

Davyn was still rising with the other guard almost at his shoulder. The guard grabbed and pinched the nerves in Davyn's wrist to disarm the baton, which Davyn released painfully. This time it was not he who had overextended but the guard. He pushed off the floor hard and twisted his body to stab at the guard's eyes with his fingertips digging in. He scooped the guard's eye out of its socket and stood, leaning against the bulkhead wall as the guard screamed in anguish. Davyn looked nauseous in his victory.

Walker, who had been about to rise from the floor when the ship's turbulence had bounced him down onto his chin, was rising once more, and Davyn planted a hard field goal kick to his chin adding one impact to the last and with a crunch breaking his jaw and knocking him unconscious.

The ship, at that instant, bounced hard straight to port. With Davyn's foot held high in the air with the follow-through of that kick, he was flung across the room and into the starboard wall, stunning him.

All three of the remaining fighters tumbled out of the seat rows and onto the slick wooden floor. The hijackers were still in 'costume,' dressed as security for a businessman. Their black jackets were flung open for movement and their glasses long since discarded, but their dressy shoes and slacks were less than ideal for fighting on a highly mobile, heavily polished, wooden floor. Akira had broken the uniform code when the weather had turned sour and put on her athletic shoes. Experience had taught her well that being able to stand meant more than dress codes. Although she was still in the black slacks of her uniform, the rubber soles of her shoes were made for basketball courts. The two men slipped and struggled to get to their feet.

Akira stood up and eased herself to the railing of the gaming room platform. She pulled on the railing, slid it through to the gyro-stabilized billiards table, and unsnapped a cue stick. The two hijackers walked toward her, slowly, maintaining their balance on the slick and rocking floor. Sean reached down and picked up Davyn's baton. "Leo, you take the right; I'll slip up here to the left. Ms. Logan, if you'll just lay face first so we can string you up, it'll go a lot easier."

Akira twisted the long stick in her hands in anticipation, "Come and find out why I'm famous," she growled to Drimmell. Leo vaulted the stairs with one hand on the railing and drove a hard right hook toward Akira that she batted away easily and parried with a *thwack-thump-whack* to his groin-leg-head. Though her attacks were quick, having to absorb his powerful swing took a lot of the power from them. His attack was not entirely intended to damage but to distract. Sean had jumped through the railing and was upon her with a stinging *shwack*! to her neck and shoulder that she was unsure, at the time, didn't break her collarbone. She brought her to stick backward hard into his solar plexus, and he sucked in hard to get his air.

Leo grunted as he swung his brass-knuckled fists jab-uppercut-left cross, right cross, Akira parried each one, but his force, speed, and intensity pushed her backward. She leaned far backward as he swung a wild left hook—stepping too far into it reaching for her. She jumped at her opening and blasted him with a flurry of blows from her makeshift staff. She delivered such a storm of staff blows upon him that the smaller end of the cue finally broke off. Leo was no amateur and had blocked or partially dodged many, soaking up most of the force on the meatier parts of his arms, legs, and back, always keeping his head and vital areas protected. When the staff broke, however, pride rose, and he dropped his guard slightly to gloat. Akira thrust the end of the cue with all her might into his ribs and heard multiple reports of snaps as his ribs caved and broke. He wasn't dead—might not even be finished fighting—but for a moment he was too busy to fight back, and she needed that break from him.

Sean had regained his wind and was in a fury. He whipped the back of her shoulders, causing her to drop the cue. She rolled out of the way with lightning reflexes, and Sean—already swinging hard—hit his henchman as he fell. The blow to the already stumbling fighter fell across the back of his skull, and there was a loud *crack* as the metal and fiber of the baton hit full force.

Drimmell yelled a curse as he jumped forward to avoid a leg sweep from under the billiard table. Akira slid out onto the same side as Drimmell, the two sizing each other up, and taking a moment to catch their wind. Fights don't tend to last very long, in general, especially intense fights. Their endurance was running low. Akira was serious and boiling with rage, but her exhaustion was beginning to show. Her shoulders slumped forward from weariness and pain, her face, though red, was also white around the temples and her mouth where she was turning pale with the exertion.

Sean was roughly ten years younger and still training actively; he had a great deal of fight left in him, and both of them knew these things. "You're tough, for sure," he said, "but it's tougher being old and tired, isn't it?" he taunted.

Akira just sort of half nodded as she breathed heavily. She couldn't think of a witty comeback, and she didn't have the spare breath to say it if she had. All Drimmell had to do now was to defend against her attacks and outlast her. He could wear her down now until she could not defend herself. Davyn could be heard rising to his feet. Akira's back was to him, but Sean could see him standing from the corner of his eye. Her breathing was still fast and heavy. She was almost finished, exhausted. Sean knew that Davyn would be no challenge without her, but the two of them would outmatch him easily.

She smirked tiredly, "Seems," she took another breath, "pressure might be," breathe in deeply, "back on," she said. He leaped forward with a wreckless swing meant to off-balance her and a follow-up swipe with the baton. Akira had anticipated his attack. She dodged the punch and rolled onto the billiards table grabbing the 13 ball as she rolled and drove it hard into Drimmell's forehead. He stumbled and fell with one leg sliding out under the railing and the rest of him on the platform. Akira jumped down from the table, unsnapping another cue from its rack on the side as she went. He was badly stunned but not unconscious. He swung clumsily from the ground with the baton, attempting to trip Akira as she set her feet from the table onto the platform. Still, Akira had closed the distance, picking up the cue stick on the way and drove the stick's chalked tip through his eye until all her weight and forward motion had stopped. Drimmell lay twitching in death spasms as she stood.

"Davyn, are you OK? She asked as she stared at Drimmell's corpse. Her voice was raspy, exhausted, and emotionally drained.

She moved to Leo as he was struggling to regain his air and stand. She kicked him with all her force in his broken ribs evoking a deep gasp for air and a loud moan.

"Yeah, I think. I mean, Aye Captain." Davyn was shocked. The stories he had heard of her were now much more believable, and the cold and stony look of her face, as she stared at Drimmell lying dying, would haunt him for years.

"I don't think those formalities matter much now," she said. "These were sent to kill me, not so much any of the rest of you. Toss me Walker's knife."

Davyn nodded blankly, "Drimmell was down, Captain. ... Shouldn't we have tied him up or given him over to the law somewhere?"

"He would have been a danger for the rest of our lives if that's even very long. We can't leave survivors. I don't know what we'll do, but whatever it is, we don't need anyone giving away the news we survived before we have a plan to deal with that."

Akira took a zip tie from Sean Drimmell's corpse and tied Leo's hands behind him and around his belt so he wouldn't be able to snap free as she had.

"Tie the survivors so we can deal with them in a moment. Marcus needs to know what has happened."

Akira tied the unconscious women as Davyn fixed ties on Walker. Akira walked toward the control cabin, "Captain Morris." She beckoned with a head nod. Davyn followed silently.

Marcus was minding the controls and keeping an eye on the gauges simultaneously. While he could fly the ship, he was not a pilot, and his lack of skill had been largely responsible for the worst of the turbulent ride. He was quite aware of how things had to have been riding in the passenger cabin during his piloting and when he heard the door to the flight deck swung open, he nervously quipped,

"Hope all of you aren't too shaken up!" Then he stopped, staring in horror at the pair of Captains, "Oh my word," he barely whispered.

"We were briefly hijacked, Marcus," Akira told him. "Davyn did wonderfully, and the two of us defeated the hijackers. All the rest of the ship's crew is dead. The 'appliances' are really robots or were made to look like that anyway. We've been framed as terrorists— mostly I have been—and you two were collateral damage in taking me down. Take us north, Davyn. Straight north out of this storm, then turn back west."

"Captain, that's the opposite…"

"Yes, that's a long way home and the opposite of the direction we went when leaving Tokyo. I don't know what to do, and I need time. I fear that without contact from the assassins, they will send fighter jets to shoot us down as terrorists anyway."

Marcus spoke up, "Assassins? Fighter jets? You think this was a military operation and not just a hired hit?"

"Oh absolutely, Marcus. Mr. Drimmell told me as much. It was because I was looking into Frank Greene's death. I need more proof for my own sake, but I am quite certain. That's who they would send to stop a terror attack, isn't it? Now I not only put you all into danger by trying to fly back the short route to keep investigating, but you might be in danger from the, well … whoever is pulling the strings. I need some time to think. I need some rest to think. Where are we with that tornado, Marcus?"

"It went southeast. You gambled right turning north. It's still going to be very rough riding for a while, but we should be in smoother skies soon."

Akira began to walk to the corridor, sighed heavily, turned to Marcus, and said darkly, "Don't come back here for a while," her voice was thick and heavy, threatening in a way neither of the other two had heard from her. "Davyn, we need to make sure no one can report our survival."

Davyn nodded grimly and began to rise.

Akira raised a hand. "No, you pilot us north until we're nearly out of the storm like I said earlier, but get us below the radar as soon as it's safe to do it. Then you can turn us west, get this ship lost to all the plans that anyone made."

Akira walked into the passenger cabin. Bodies lay all about, some moaned and some would never make a sound again. Her very first victim was lying on his side barely what anyone would call conscious. She walked over to a table, and picked up a notepad and pen, as the airship continued to buck, this time with the added vertigo-inducing motion of turning sharply nearly the opposite direction. She walked over to the gasping soldier and laid the pad and pen in front of him. "Tell me who ordered this, just a name," she commanded. As she spoke, she made eye contact with the other survivors. Her eyes were dark and her face menacing and cold. She knew Peter wouldn't be able to talk. The so-called secretary had regained consciousness but was foggy-headed, and she could tell by looking at her that she would have to torture her to get any information out of her, and that wasn't ever something Akira was comfortable with. Killing must sometimes be done, but tormenting people and making them suffer was not something she could allow. The times she had been forced to conduct interrogations of that nature still haunted her sleep, and she wanted no more of it. No, she wasn't going to torture anyone. She pulled the gasping guard upright and leaned him against a seat making sure he was secure enough to not fall over again. The ship bucked hard, and its skin groaned and creaked around the airframe. The less she had to ask of her hostages, the clearer and more honest the information would be.

He shook his head, still gasping, "You won't," he scribbled. She looked into his eyes and said, "I promise you. I won't take you back, but I will give you medical attention for your head. It'll only get worse, and you could die."

He wrote, "Don't know."

Disgusted and frustrated, Akira walked over to a table and picked up another pen, this one shiny and brass. She knelt to him and said, "I keep promises. One more thing, and I'll get you some help. Who ordered these robots, and who ordered me dead?"

He scribbled, "No robots MT. Don't know."

Akira's fury rose as she began, staring straight into his eyes, "I will kill you. If you …" There in his eyes she could see sincerity, maybe even apology. He didn't know. She nodded in understanding. She had been the uninformed soldier many times. While it did little to calm her rage, it made it clear that anger with this man was misplaced. "What was your evac?" she questioned him.

He shook his head and shrugged a little, "Drim" he scribbled down. Drimmel was the only contact these men had.

"Drimmel did all the reporting, all the contacting. Who was your second in case something happened?" With his eyes, the man motioned to Peter Walker. What if they both died or were not able to continue? The man patted his chest pocket on his shirt. Akira reached in and found a tracking device. She looked at it for markings or instructions on what else to do. There were none. Nothing else in his pocket, only a small tracking device such as a person would hide in a valuable luggage bag.

"That's it?" she asked. "You were to continue the scuttle then sit and wait until someone found you by using these? They would have never found you with just this! You'd have died in the water waiting … and that was the plan for you from the start." The soldier nodded. Akira looked at him with a twinge of pity then rose and walked to the bulkhead and retrieved the medkit. Lifting his head, she bandaged his head and gave him painkillers. She put a seat cushion under his head. She spoke to him as she worked. "In my military years, I would have killed you already. You killed my crew, you nearly killed me, and you probably are working for whoever killed my best (a sudden lump in her throat stopped her), my best friend."

His eyes stayed on her face as she worked.

"I don't know if I am getting soft, or if I just understand that we do what we're told and believe it's best when sometimes it is not."

Still, he watched with no response at all.

"Drimmel was wrong about our lifeboats on this ship." The soldier's expression changed slightly but not such that she could tell what he thought. "I know that he had to have intended to use the emergency boats to survive crashing my ship," she continued. "But they are not the inflatable type with the buoyancy balloons that a lot of newer ships have. Ours are the oldest still allowed by the FAA, and it is why I wondered how he intended to survive scuttling the ship. You see," she had finished bandaging him and stood up, leaning against the seat by her, propping an arm on the body of the 'secretary' who had attacked her. She was surprised the lady was still breathing, although shallow. The other woman sat against the bulkhead of the flight deck in a daze. "It's under that gaming platform. There are a dozen small gondolas, or pods, I guess, that detach and drop out of the bottom of the ship like bombs, then large freight parachutes open, and they theoretically fall safely to earth. They each hold about five people if you pack in fairly tight. So, I think I am going to drop you on an island to give us time to figure out what to do. If you live, great. If you don't, well that's OK too. Any family?"

He shook his head to say no.

Akira nodded and began going from body to body with the slender knife she had used earlier and slit every throat. Only Walker made any noise, sort of a low moan as the air ran out of him. She laughed a quiet snort at the sound, not knowing whether he had been alive or dead—and not caring. The last one was the secretary against the bulkhead who sobbed as Akira approached. Akira looked at her for just a moment then told her before completing her task, "I wish you could know how much I hate this, but if I don't and you're any soldier at all, you'll bring us nothing but death, and danger later."

Akira walked back into the flight deck to surprised looks from Marcus and Davyn. "I was lying to myself about being able to take a break. I also lied to you about no survivors. I was able to question one a little, and I don't know what to do with him now."

Davyn and Marcus both looked quizzically at her but dared not voice their concerns or questions.

Akira sighed and said, "It's harsh to have had to kill so many. The survivors could rat us out easily. There are a lot of questions and bad decisions. I don't know all the answers. I just try to do what seems best at the time."

Davyn started to speak then stopped. Taking a breath, he said, "You're in charge, Captain. I trust your decisions."

Marcus echoed his thoughts, "It's OK, Captain. Decisions must be made then the consequences lived with later. Let's get this ship somewhere safer, and we'll deal with the other things as they come."

"Aye," echoed Akira and Davyn. The tornado avoided, the hurricane being dealt with, the assassins defeated, and the danger was at least temporarily much less. Akira walked back into the passenger cabin. The soldier had managed to sit up in a seat, blood still dripping from his head onto his shirt.

Akira began to casually converse with him: "You know, I totally get following orders. I hope you don't think that I'm cruel for, finishing ... everyone. I had the same in mind for you, but you had some information I wanted. I hoped you did, anyway." She moved over by him and picked up a bottle of water that was rolling around on the floor. Looking at him she asked, "Are you thirsty? I can't imagine you wouldn't be."

He nodded, and she leaned forward over the back of the seat in front of him. With a slashing motion made clumsy through injury and exhaustion, he attempted one final time, to complete his assignment with a knife he had found on the floor. Akira easily grabbed his wrist to block the attack and shook her head. She had a saddened expression, disappointed. Taking the letter opener knife from him she slid it across his neck. She kept eye contact with him as he stared in understanding back at her until he had a couple of spasms, and the light left his eyes.

Akira walked slowly back to the cockpit. Disappointment, frustration, sadness, and anger wearied her. She opened the door as another gust of wind tossed the dirigible. She leaned against the door frame. "Davyn, Marcus, you have the controls. We no longer have a survivor. I'm going to my quarters after all. Once we are safely out of the storm, let me know. Oh, vent all quarters to the outside atmosphere. If any staff is alive, I want them to maybe survive this."

Davyn and Marcus both saluted wearily as the ship was buffeted once more by the strong winds. The constant push of the winds made them have to continually correct course as they were blown around like a child's balloon on a windy day. Akira did not notice their salutes nor even the bouncing and jostling of the ship. Exhaustion washed over her. She had thought, in passing, that the government was somehow involved in all the events she and her friends had endured. She was simply too tired to process all her thoughts right now. It was time for a break.

Akira's tired mind and body melted into the bed, and though her mind couldn't relax, her fatigue took over and through the flow of tears, she was asleep in moments. The design of the airship's berths allowed for the rough skies, but from time to time the ship was still tossed so hard that she bumped hard against the ornately decorated brass bed rails and awakened briefly to mutter a curse at the storm then sighed, "Least we're still flying."

Finally, the flight smoothed, and she slipped into a deeper sleep and then disturbed dreams.

Chapter 21

Lost Hope

Penny woke up groggy and cranky, an unusual feeling for her. She had not slept well since the day the detective had interviewed her about Frank and warned her about her friends. She frequently saw police patrols idling through the neighborhood when, before, it had been an uncommon sight. It had only been two weeks since that night. Akira was out on a long aerial cruise. Josh and Braegan could not risk making calls from anywhere that could be located. She had gotten one call from a gas station phone just a couple of days after the two best friends had fled. She had picked up and was told only, "We're safe." There was a click and the dial tone. She believed it was Josh, but it could have been Braegan. She couldn't be certain it wasn't entirely coincidental as it was so short as to be hard to tell who was on the other end.

Archie's murder hung centrally in her thoughts day in and out as she went about her work schedule and daily life. Every day when coworkers asked what she had been doing outside of work, even though it was just normal small talk, she bristled and tossed about in her mind how she would answer. Were these people going to report her? Was she being surveilled? Her husband noticed the change in her, and although she had told him about the detective, she hadn't told him how afraid she was every day. Right now, all that was available was running the rat race as she had been and waiting to see if Emmett, Akira, or Melody contacted her with some new information. She kept her opinions to herself now, but she had hope that they would find the evidence needed to prove Frank innocent and begin unraveling the web of lies and cover-ups that surrounded the whole mess.

The call from Emmett didn't come. The weeks passed by. She wondered how Akira was handling being gone while wanting to investigate some new idea or evidence she had hinted at. She should be on the way home by now. Being a war hero, veteran, woman, and respected pilot gave Akira some shielding from the same kinds of attacks the other friends had to be concerned about. If they came after her, it would be too obvious and dangerous.

"Dear," her husband Gene said, interrupting her thoughts.

Penny turned her head toward him, slowly coming out of her thoughtful silence. She smiled at him, "Yes?"

"What's the matter tonight, Penny?"

"I'm just in my thoughts."

"About Frank and Archie?"

"More about Akira and the detective who spoke to me a couple of weeks ago."

"Let's talk it out. You've been so distant and, well ... different."

Penny sighed deeply. "OK, I was warned to be careful and also to get my friends out of the City and hidden."

Gene nodded in acknowledgment as he had heard this part.

"So, I did, everyone but Akira. I couldn't get in touch with her as she had already left for Tokyo. I was just thinking about how I hoped her experience with the military would help shield her a bit and keep her safer than the rest of us."

Gene nodded and sat quietly for a moment or two. He smiled weakly at her and put his hand on hers, "I'm sure it does. It would be a public and embarrassing thing for a well-known person like her to suddenly be harmed."

It was getting late, and it was dark outside. Penny and Gene sat quietly, comforted with each other's presence. The television was off, the radio off, and only the ticking of their old-fashioned countertop clock disrupted the silence. *Ticktock, ticktock ...* then another rhythmic sound, footsteps falling almost in time with the clock. Penny heard them just as the knock on the door thundered through the silence. Gene jumped, startled, and she sprang to her feet. Normally, Gene would have answered the door, as he valued being a gentleman and the man of the house, but Penny was already walking to it and waving him with the back of her hand. Though the knock had seemed loud in the silence, it was not aggressive or angry, not pounding on the door, just a knock. *Thump, thump.*

Penny opened the door as Detective Loving was bringing his knuckles down for the third rap on the door. Jeremiah Loving stood there with a blank look on his face. Penny stared at him expectantly for a moment, then raised an eyebrow and queried, "Yes?"

Loving shifted uneasily. "Ma'am, my partner, Don, wanted me to come tell you that you don't need to be frightened about the news. He wouldn't say anything more than that, and it doesn't make sense. Does it to you?"

Penny shook her head, "No."

Jeremiah nodded, "Well, Miss, I am assuming he means about the two fellas that fled the city. In that case, that's all I was told. He said to call the police station and leave this message if you had any questions." Loving handed her a sealed envelope, nodded his head, and shrugged—then turned and walked to his car.

Penny found a sloppily written message in the envelope: "Use this to get in touch. I have the roast on for tonight." She laughed at how ludicrous the code was.

Hearing the conversation and her sarcastic laugh, her husband asked, "What is it, dear?"

She looked up from the letter and told him, "I think we had better turn on the news."

Penelope and Gene Hammond watched in horror and surprise as the news reported exactly what Drimmel had shown Akira. The reporter gave the fabricated story of terrorism and robot smuggling to rebels while stock footage of an airship crash, sold to the public as *The Silver Cloud's* wreckage, ran in a loop on the screen. There was wind, there was rain, and there were the burning remains of an airship. The reporter spoke of the heroism of a small strike force that had scuttled the ship in hurricane winds, unable to escape themselves, sacrificing their lives for our safety. Along with Akira's face, the faces of the crew—innocent fatalities unaware of her evil intent—were displayed on rare occasions. The faces of the 'heroes' were on-screen even less.

Penny began to cry silently, sob, and weep. Lifelong friends of hers had been killed, and she didn't know why—only that it was for knowing or saying something that the government didn't want to know or say, and she couldn't even tell her husband all her suspicions.

Gene tried to comfort her, sitting with his arm around her as she wept. Eventually, she rose and went to the kitchen, with tears still running down her cheeks and wetting the front of her T-shirt. Even sobbing, she looked like a portrait of "Rosie the Riveter." Penny poured a glass of cold water and sat down as she calmed down. The detective had said not to be afraid.

She looked at her husband. "Business as usual," she said, snorting a little sour snort, "That's all I can do, and you, too."

Gene was slowly nodding his head.

She stated again, "Day in and out, we do what good we can, business as usual." She drank from her glass. "They weren't too afraid of making a public spectacle."

He nodded and tried to think of a retort, a comforting word, a comment. But there was, after all, nothing really to be said.

Chapter 22

The Cloud in a Fog

Turning back north with the typhoon turned out to be a decision with questionable wisdom. All the passengers were dead, all the support crew dead, the two pilots and the engineer exhausted, and *The Silver Cloud* had been tossed and buffeted about like never before. The lines retaining shape and rigidity of the envelope inside creaked and moaned. The resistance cables, springs, and slack adjusters pinged as lines were unstressed and then suddenly snapped to their max.

Davyn and Marcus fought *The Cloud* as she rolled and pitched, sometimes seeming she would roll completely onto her side. This was a ship built when ships were built tough, but no ship was ever intended for this sort of abuse—and not so many years after its christening, either. There was no chatter, no banter. Akira had passed out from exertion in her bloody and tattered uniform, and the two men fought the ship to deliver it entirely from the chaos of Muroto.

Occasionally, Marcus would let out a sigh as a pressure gauge came back into 'normal' readings. When he threw a lever that still responded perfectly, he would gently pat it in appreciation. Davyn would give a nervous laugh or a snort or a whistle incidentally as he tried to fight the rudder or ease the stabilizers against the gusting wind. The typhoon was falling slowly behind them, but since they had turned north, it had turned slightly north-northeast as if it wanted to hold onto its toy balloon just a little longer and toss it about the sky.

The sky lit up blue with lightning so often that it seemed unusual when it returned to the darkness of the storm. The brass accents around the flight deck flashed brilliantly as they reflected the storm's fury. They glistened happily in the dark as though this were a leisure flight above an Independence Day display. The massive storm stirred up other tornados, and the radar screen looked like someone had spilled green paint on it, leaving only small patches where there was anything like calm skies. Sweat beaded on Davyn's forehead, and he fought and wrestled the ship valiantly, but they were off course. They had been blown farther out to sea than anyone had wanted. They were effectively lost with their radio down and their gauges all surely damaged or untrustworthy. Akira came back to the flight deck looking unrested but calmer. She looked around through the windows as the sky showed glimmers of stars to the north and black, roiling clouds over them and to the south.

Davyn tried a clumsy salute. Marcus, standing and holding tightly to the brass rail by the engineering station, gave a stern nod as he tapped on a gauge for the ballonet pressure. He tapped several times, then gave a sidelong look at Akira that she pretended not to see. She walked with a little stiffness to the Captain's seat and plopped into it. She peered to the north, just to the left of the center of their direction of travel, despite Davyn's constant corrections. Turning in her chair to Davyn, she gave a little salute.

"Captain Morris, good job, sir."

"No, Captain, we're off course. I don't know … I don't know where."

"Under the conditions, we are still flying, and that's well done, both of you. If we were not already reported dead and certainly wanted by either the government or some part of it, I'd recommend you both for promotions," she smiled wryly. Turning her seat forward again, she said, "I'll take control again, sir. Once we have a horizon that is not simply ocean, I will want a set of maps so we can find out where we are. Perhaps Drimmell's computer is working, and we can use it to find out without tipping anyone off. I don't know, for now, though, you're exhausted. Take a break."

Davyn nodded and laid back in his seat, too tired to even get up. Akira took the controls and pushed steady on the rudder, easing the throttle on the starboard engines up and the port engines down. Marcus cleared his throat and stared at his panel. Having been on many flights together, Akira knew a few of his unspoken cues and asked, "Yes, Marcus, everything OK? Or, rather, everything functional?"

"Yes, Captain, mostly. The engines are fine. I'm getting some disturbing readings from tension gauges, though. I'd send my crew to check them if," he choked up a bit. His crew had been his alone for many years, and the fact that they were all dead, having been gassed in their chambers by a mercenary unit, was difficult to take. Marcus was no combat pilot and had never served in anything but a civilian post. Death and killing were unfamiliar to him in the line of duty. Finding his composure again, he continued: "They are old mechanical gauges, so just the severe temperature changes of this storm could have made them read incorrectly. It's probably fine," his voice trailed off.

Akira knew it probably was not fine. This antique ship, overbuilt and sturdy to a fault, had been overstressed and pushed beyond its limit for many, many hours. Akira threw the throttles wide open and laughed, "Let's get farther ahead of this storm, then! If the engines are fine and nothing else is, let us use what we have that works!" Akira settled back into her chair with a disgusted look on her face. The skies had returned to a much smoother flight as they got farther from the storm, but the skies were not yet clear, and the occasional wind gust still tugged at *The Silver Cloud* with force. Akira might feign casualness for the crew, whether they believed it or not, but she knew they were caught in a no-win situation. All she could hope for was to bring them over land before they were forced down either by mechanical failures or by the fact that they simply could not allow anyone to see them on a radar screen and ping their identification.

Marcus looked up, startled, and then back at the gauges as he monitored the inner workings of The Silver Cloud, which was pushing out and away from the massive typhoon punishing Asia's eastern coast. First, one warning light glowed orange, then another, then another: tension line pressures at max, gas pressure at maximum allowed, coolant at minimum—sloshed out in the bouncing and jostling of the ship as quickly as it could be collected.

Akira turned in her seat and looked at Chief Engineer Marcus Homan. He stood, turning knobs and pushing slides ever so slightly, his face illuminated in splotches of orange and eerie green of the gauges and radar. He said nothing. He respected her command and knew that she would not risk them or the ship more than needed. He knew that the situation was dire and that, with no political or military background, he had no idea what to do. What he did know was how to tweak and coax every last ounce of life from a ship that was older than anyone flying her.

Akira saw his determination as he stood staunchly, defying the natural forces that would try to stop his ship. She wanted to remember this image of him. She thought silently about how he was a good man, but his life had forever changed because of her. She felt no self-pity, nor in fact guilt—just a pang of sadness for Marcus. What could she do to help him once they were safe if they were ever safe? His life in Eagle's Roost was over forever; he was a good man and didn't deserve that.

The sun was beginning to shine through under the typhoon's cloud mass. Not only that, Akira mentally noted, but the skies were beginning to smooth out. They were out! Truly out of the clouds that were the storm. She smiled ever so slightly, afraid to sigh in relief but pleased that she could back the throttles down and lower altitude to bring some of the ship's systems back into operating range. The line tension gauge was now bright red, and although Marcus hadn't said anything, Akira knew it might be too late to bring them back into a safe range.

Davyn, who had been leaning with his head against the cabin wall in an exhausted sleep, came to with a jerk and a hand on his weapon. The baton returned to his side. Akira smiled in understanding and saluted him. He returned her salute and looked out the windows in the growing dark orange light of the sky.

"Captain," he said to Akira.

"Go ahead, Davyn."

"Is that a shoreline to the port side?" he asked.

Akira looked hard, and following his finger, her smirk grew into a wide smile. "It is, Davyn. We're near land once more. Engineer Homan, sir!"

"Yes, Captain," Marcus choked out past the lump in his throat from the relief that he was trying to hide.

"Prepare to land for emergency repairs, sir. It's OK to be relieved. God knows I am!" she said as she steered the big, old ship toward land and felt her own eyes becoming a bit more moist than normal. The ship groaned and creaked. One tension line warning light went dark as the needle jerked, then went to zero as the line snapped. Marcus closed his eyes and silently wished for them to make it to shore. He wasn't sure they would. Akira saw his silent prayer, even though he was not a religious man. She, likewise, did not hold the same faith that she had admired in both Frank and Emmett. Tonight, though, she closed her eyes and whispered under the noise of the engines and the groaning of the ship, "God, I don't know what to say, and I don't deserve anything. Please let us make it to shore and land this thing. For these men who don't deserve to die out in the water, please."

Chapter 23

A Discordant Melody

Melody fidgeted with her hair, twirling it in tight curls around her fingers. It was an involuntary action she did when deep in thought. She lounged on her giant, plush couch in her apartment. It was the first time in a good long while that she had been able to simply relax. The events of the year had all piled up, and she hadn't had time to process them. She drank a small drink from her wine glasses. "Oh, Frank," she thought out loud. Her mind went through the dozens of memories of her old friend. "I sent searchers to find your body before the funeral. You were the only man that ever let me get away. I can't say I loved you, but I can't say I didn't, either. I certainly respected you. Wow! The way you could immediately draw a crowd in. That's the power of conviction, sir. I wish I could say I had that sort of conviction. I wish I could say I had that kind of conviction about much of anything," She muttered to herself in the dim light with her shades pulled closed against the sun low on the horizon.

"Archie," she sighed and softly shook her head as she continued to talk through her thoughts, "I know the news has it wrong. The police, too. I wish I could clear your name. I don't know what's happening around here, really. I know Joshua and Braegan think they know—Akira, too. They're all a bunch of jobbernowls. Oh, I guess that's not fair. They're all too smart for their own good, honestly. The FBI, CIA, and Homeland Defense all told me that Braegan had some sort of blueprint plans or something for tanks and silly whatnot. Of course, there were plans like that in a World War 2 era car factory! It's beyond my ability to do anything about it when those agencies are involved. I hope that's not what happened to Archie."

Melody took another heavy drink from her glass, glided smoothly to the windows, and opened the curtains a crack. "The sunset in The City Centre is so beautiful," she admired. Melody meandered about the apartment with its expensive paintings on the walls and looked briefly at each one. *It's funny how life goes*, she thought to herself. *I was poor compared to now, but I wouldn't compromise on success.* She finished her glass and then spoke into its empty bottom: "Now, all I do is compromise, make 'deals.' I miss things being simpler. I miss being at odds with Akira over who is prettiest or smartest and with Penny over who is toughest. I wouldn't trade it, though. I'm Melody Maine. I made me. That person never existed before I created Melody Maine. I made her a powerhouse model, a household name, then I made that person into a political figure, and now I am making that political figure powerful internationally."

Her hand was clenched around the wine glass. The news reported that Akira and *The Silver Cloud* crashed off the coast of Asia from her bedroom television. Melody stopped for only a moment to sadly shake her head. "It would be me if I had not been up here or in the Capitol building the whole time. They'd think I knew something more than I do and would be wanting me to tell them, in return for political favors, deals with the devil himself," she intoned.

She stared at the floor for a moment, "The news people probably think I am a friend to all these terrorists, and I must be one, too. Well, then there's Emmett. No one questions him. I wonder how he has managed all of this. I don't know why he would ever want that dirty old garage of Frank's, but I guess it held some sentimentality. It's amazing to me that Emmett got rich being a big old softy like he is," she contemplated as she walked back to the window.

Melody looked down to the street where a few people were returning home as it got dark. On the sidewalk of her apartment building stood a strangely dressed man. His head scanned this way and that slowly as if memorizing something about the building. He was in clothes that did not fit in The City Centre and looked to have slept in them. She picked up the phone to call the front desk. Just as she was about to report the suspicious figure, he turned and strode away. She watched him walk, and something struck her as odd about his stride. She went about her normal nighttime routine. She was saddened by the things that had befallen her friends, but there was little she could do. She didn't even know where Josh and Braegan were but hoped they were well and safe. Penny was as solid as the steel that she worked; that was comforting to Melody.

She lay in bed, partly asleep and partly awake, "I bet they all think I'm insulated in my high tower and that they hate me," she mumbled in her state of lessened consciousness. "Frank's dead, the best man I ever met. Josh and Braegan disappeared, maybe dead. Akira crashed and died on another continent. Penny may be in danger. Archie's dead, and his whole family. Emmett hasn't spoken to me since the funeral. Even Meriwether hasn't been bootlicking around like normal. I bet they all think I am heartless and don't even care since I am still pushing forward with work. How can I not, though? People need power, and my feelings don't change what those poor folks," she yawned, "need."

Finally, Melody was asleep and dreamed of the man in front of her building. In her dream her mind she said, "I thought you were killed?" Melody woke up in a sweat. She couldn't remember what she had dreamed of but couldn't go back to sleep. "I guess it's naptime pills," she sighed and went back to bed.

On the outskirts of The City Centre, where the largest of mansions saw the sunset and the tops of the forest's trees over a large, concrete security fence, Emmett had a visitor. The study was lit dimly, and the old grandfather clock ticked away once more. Emmett sat in his large leather chair with a quizzical look on his face. He had his fingers in enough of the local and state activities to hear rumors and whispers. This puzzle, though, had left him with very few pieces to work with, and the ones he had found didn't seem to fit. He had cogitated and considered every aspect of the evidence before him. He had not started with the preconception that Frank was assassinated, as Akira had. He was certain that the media story was not truthful from the very beginning but that the government had put a hit on Frank was too far-fetched at first. Then, more and more didn't align with what did make sense. This realization had caused him to call that meeting at Frank's by that wonderful ornamental tree. Who built that, anyway? Did Frank and his grandfather? His thoughts were drifting, and he couldn't allow that. Emmett had known that even a secret meeting would likely put things in motion. He had moved a knight or a bishop; Akira and the others were too important to him and this whole debacle to be considered pawns. It seemed the other player had countered with their queen. The most powerful piece on the board must be in play to have left so much destruction in its wake. But he had yet to determine who the other players, or players, were. Did they know that he was the 'other player' from their own standpoint, or were they merely seeing the game through, following the path before them?

Akira, Josh, and Braegan had done well cleaning and sorting out the mess at the shop. The goods they had reserved for storage had all been delivered quietly, and no one seemed to have discovered what went where. He had moved everything twice after its arrival. He had mixed everything in with storage unit buyouts that he already had and had inventoried every piece, then sent it all out to other, more secure, locations. He did not know what game was being played but knew the stakes were high. He knew that for a fact before his old friend, Archie, had been framed and murdered. Terrorists, *psshht!* he snorted under his breath as he thought of it. This drew a nervous little cough from the guest in his office. Archie had never sold weapons of any kind.

Now, with Braegan and Josh in hiding and Akira presumed dead at sea under cover of a typhoon and framed for smuggling contraband to supply terrorists, he could no longer stand to wait. He must move the pawns he knew of in order to maybe put whomever in check. He had called his guest in to interrogate him. Although only in the vaguest of terms, his name had been the only one above that of the simple street officers that continually arose in the scuttlebutt of the town. Things were much, much, larger than only Eagle's Roost. Emmett had heard breathless rumors from people he knew at the state level, and even his few federal contacts had asked about the happenings in his hometown. It consumed him. What had been a mild curiosity just months before when he commissioned his friends to help was now was an obsession—*the worst kind of obsession,* he thought. It was the sort of obsession that he could not risk discussing with anyone and could not ask for help from anyone. So, it ate into his soul and devoured his thoughts.

He would interrupt his own endless musings on the matter by accusing himself, "I'm only so preoccupied because I feel guilty for their deaths," he'd say. Then he'd return to his turning it all over in his mind. What could be going on that would cause anyone at the federal government to care about a rural electricity bill or a steam engine mechanic, a 'do-gooder' garage inventor?

Emmett was brought back to the moment by the creaking of the old leather-bound wooden Victorian chair. Realizing he had been lost in thought for many minutes, he looked up and said, "I apologize. You and I know certain things that many do not. For instance, we know that certain individuals with which I have been known to associate have been made to appear as criminals. We also both know that Captain Logan's flight recorder was manually disabled—not crashed and left on—off the coast of a line of tiny islands in the Pacific Ocean. There is a lot on my mind. I am hoping that you have a few of the answers to questions I have not, as yet, asked anyone."

With an unsteady hand, Meriwether Lewis wiped his glasses on his pocket cloth and nervously cleared his throat, dabbing at his forehead with a handkerchief.